THE CASE OF THE DOTTY DOWAGER

THE CASE OF THE DOTTY DOWAGER

Cathy Ace

Severn House Large Print
London & New York

This first large print edition published 2015
in Great Britain and the USA by
SEVERN HOUSE PUBLISHERS LTD of
19 Cedar Road, Sutton, Surrey, England, SM2 5DA.
First world regular print edition published 2015 by
Severn House Publishers Ltd., London and New York.

British Library Cataloguing in Publication Data

Ace, Cathy, 1960- author.
　The case of the dotty dowager. – (The WISE Enquiries
　Agency mysteries)
　1. Women private investigators–Fiction. 2. Wales–
　Fiction. 3. Detective and mystery stories. 4. Large type
　books.
　I. Title II. Series
　813.6-dc23

ISBN-13: 9780727872920

Severn House Publishers support the Forest Stewardship Council™
[FSC™], the leading international forest certification organisation. All
our titles that are printed on FSC certified paper carry the FSC logo.

Typeset by Palimpsest Book Production Ltd.,
Falkirk, Stirlingshire, Scotland.
Printed and bound in Great Britain by
T J International, Padstow, Cornwall.

For my family in Wales, with love and thanks

ACKNOWLEDGEMENTS

My thanks to my mother and late father for encouraging my inquisitiveness and for teaching me what it means to work hard and stick at it, and to Mum and Sue for being my first, and very patient, readers.

To the entire team at Severn House Publishers for allowing the Women of the WISE Enquiries Agency to live in these pages, and to Priya Doraswamy for bringing them to their attention in the first place. To every formatter, printer, distributor, reviewer, blogger, librarian and bookseller who has helped you, dear reader, to find this book. And thanks to you for sharing your most important resource, your time, with me and my creations.

Finally, I would like to thank my husband; without his love, patience, support and encouragement I wouldn't be writing at all.

ONE

Henry Devereaux Twyst, eighteenth Duke of Chellingworth, was terribly worried about his mother. He wondered if the Dowager Duchess had finally lost her grip on reality and gone completely batty. Given the way his father had acted for the last decade of his life, he supposed she'd done rather well to make it to almost eighty with her faculties pretty much intact. But now?

For a few months he'd been catching snippets from the staff at Chellingworth Hall which alluded to her mental capacity. He'd even overheard, '. . . a few sandwiches short of a picnic . . .' being muttered on several occasions. But now he feared the worst; this might be the beginning of the end. If it was, it would be a dreadful pity. A brilliant woman in her time, everyone agreed that Althea, Dowager Duchess of Chellingworth, was all but the human equivalent of the Jack Russell dogs she'd bred and doted upon for decades; compact, strong, full of energy, and never one to let go of a cause or an argument.

But, Henry reasoned, for her to telephone him from the Dower House in the middle of the night claiming she'd found a corpse on the floor of her dining room – well, it beggared belief.

Henry hadn't phoned the police, for obvious reasons; he didn't want his failing mother to be

1

gossiped about in the village. Having no doubt she'd imagined the whole thing, he felt he'd acted quite correctly by urging her to go back to her bedroom, shut her door and push a chair against the handle, or something like it. In that moment he cursed the fact that there had never seemed to be a requirement for locks on the bedroom doors; he'd always assumed they'd merely serve to hinder servants from gaining entry. He'd promised to rush right over, and she'd assured him that McFli would keep her safe. Henry had to agree that, despite the fact that her one remaining canine companion was almost a dozen years old, he could probably manage to keep his mistress safe – *from a non-existent corpse*. Henry hadn't even alerted any of the staff at the hall. No one other than he himself needed to become aware of his mother's diminishing capacity to differentiate between reality and imaginings.

Clutching an old torch, Henry tramped across the bottom pasture toward the lower copse, and thence to the Dower House itself. All the vehicles had been shut away for the night, and he didn't want to wake anyone with the noise he'd make if he revved up an engine. Besides, he hated driving himself.

The night was black. Clouds obscured the moon completely, but Henry's eyes adjusted as he walked. He had silent conversations with himself as his wellington boots made tracks upon the wet, yielding grass.

He was certain he'd find his mother tucked safely into her bed, completely unaware she'd woken him and sent him into a panic. When he'd

2

asked her on the telephone why she was poking about in her dining room at such an ungodly hour, she'd retorted that McFli had woken her, she'd heard a noise and had gone to investigate.

What was she thinking? was what he'd wanted to ask. *Why hadn't she woken her staff?* was what he'd ended up saying instead. *Why should she?* she'd replied huffily and hung up.

As he walked determinedly into the copse, along paths he'd known for a lifetime, Henry Twyst kept telling himself that everything would all be all right when he got there. He just had to keep the whole thing quiet and no one would be any the wiser.

It was the middle of September, almost the end of the Open Season. That was how they referred to it at Chellingworth Hall. The six months of the year when the masses traipsed through the venerable pile which Henry, like so many generations of his gilded ancestors before him, called home. He hated the whole process of opening the doors of Chellingworth Hall to the public, but it had to be done. The upkeep of the hall was exorbitantly high and it was an obvious way to make some money. At least the Twysts hadn't descended to the point where they had to accept PGs. Paying Guests marked the low point for any family. It smacked of putting oneself on display in the same way animals were paraded about at a circus, performing tricks that amazed the viewing crowds – like using the correct cutlery. The Twysts, not the animals. Henry would have none of it. He'd accepted the necessary influx of public visitors for limited hours each day, but had not gone as far as allowing overnight guests, nor catered events like weddings.

His mother also hated the daily invasion. She hid inside the Dower House, an architectural delight that had been built in 1669 to provide a home for all the Chellingworth dowagers since that time, as bulging family cars and garish coaches crunched along the sweeping pea-gravel drive toward the hall. Althea Twyst had even been known to close all the curtains on many a perfectly beautiful August day just in order to be absolutely sure that no wayward members of the public would have the opportunity to attempt to peer into her sanctuary.

Henry cursed aloud as he stumbled on a protruding root. He wasn't cursing the root, but the countless feet which were widening the natural pathways as day-trippers jostled through his once peaceful and idyllic woodlands. He played the beam of light from his torch onto the ground and steered himself toward safer footing. The night was fresh, almost sharp, and there was a promise of autumn in the atmosphere. The earliest of the leaves to drop from their branches rustled beneath his tread, even though they were damp. Light showers had stopped after tea time. At least they'd cleared the unseasonable humidity of the morning, thought Henry. Beginning to pant a little, he noticed that, for the first time since the spring, his breath looked like little puffs of steam in the cool night air.

As he emerged from the ragged fringes of the

copse, Henry could see the dark shape of the Dower House glowering down on him from the higher ground ahead. Some architectural scholars claimed the building was a square version of Wren's famous circular Sheldonian Theatre in Oxford. He'd never been clear about how, exactly, one building was related to the other. He saw them with the eye of an artist, albeit a frustrated one. He'd never grappled with the concept of the bones beneath the flesh and skin of a building. Granted, the edifices were certainly similar in terms of their honey-colored stone, upon which the evening sun would always linger, and their style of decoration, which he'd always thought of as elegant rather than showy. But, beyond this general impression, Henry was unsure about other similarities. As far as he could tell, the breed known as architects had their very own language and used it in the presence of others as a way to exclude the uninitiated from any possible comprehension of their conversations.

At the thought of architects, Henry's shoulders sagged. He'd met so many of them in the decade since his father's death. They each had their opinions about how he should schedule the constant upkeep and renovation of the hall, but none of them seemed to agree with each other. It had dawned upon Henry in short order that owning a Grade I listed home meant one was simply a guardian of a building for posterity. Something that had never occurred to him during his father's lifetime, when Chellingworth Hall had merely been his home. Since the day his father had died, and Henry became the eighteenth duke, it had become an all-consuming responsibility. Sometimes Henry thought he'd simply like to pack a small duffel bag and slip away somewhere. Somewhere he could indulge in his love of art. Where he could paint his watercolors and dream of beautiful trees, enjoying nature in all its glories. Somewhere where there weren't dozens of people all working at different tasks in his home every day, as well as hundreds of complete strangers shuffling through it *oh*-ing and *ah*-ing at every little thing for months on end.

But he knew that was unrealistic. He had a job for life. He was the Duke of Chellingworth and Chellingworth Hall, set in the glorious Welsh county of Powys, was his to nurture, repair and run – as far as possible – as a paying business. It would be his legacy to his son. Should he ever manage to find himself a wife to bear one.

As this, his greatest shortcoming, flitted through his mind, Henry almost stopped walking. His mother never tired of reminding him that, at fifty-five years of age, he was fast running out of time in which to procreate. He felt the weight of this other responsibility more personally, because he had always promised himself he would marry for love. But, to date, that particular emotion was still alien to him.

Pressing on in anger and frustration, the walk up the steep incline to the Dower House took it out of Henry, and his breath began to resemble the output of a steam engine. While his mother might have been likened to a small, active dog, he admitted to himself that he was probably more akin to a less frantic creature. Not a sloth – he wasn't that inactive – but he was certainly not a nippy little terrier. Maybe a koala? He smiled as he pictured the rotund little creatures with their comical features, which he supposed were not very unlike his own, and he recalled something about their liking for eucalyptus leaves, which meant they were usually half-sozzled – a state with which he was far from unfamiliar. He found that a few brandies after dinner took the edge off his worries about balance sheets and creditors during the evening and allowed him to sleep more soundly at night. Which was why he was especially cross at being hailed from the comfort of his bed at such an hour.

Just as Henry arrived at the Dower House, the light of the half-moon pierced the ragged-edged clouds above him. A light showed in what he knew was the window of his mother's bedroom. So she really was awake, after all. He wondered if she'd woken Jennifer yet. If she had, he was sure that whatever emergency might have occurred would be halfway to a peaceful solution. Jennifer was a very competent young woman. Somewhat plain, but competent.

He couldn't help but smile to himself as he recalled how Jennifer Newbury insisted upon being referred to as Lady Althea's 'aide'. A lady's aide, rather than a lady's maid. He understood why, in the twenty-first century, a professional woman in her thirties would prefer one title over the other, but it amused him to hear his mother frequently refer to her as a 'maid', only to have Jennifer equally frequently – and always politely

– reply with, 'You mean *aide*, ma'am,' to which his mother's invariable response was, 'Do I?'

It was like a little battle his mother always enjoyed. He wondered why Jennifer bothered to participate. Maybe she thought she'd eventually win, one day. She clearly didn't know his mother very well. But she'd only been in residence for six months or so. They usually lasted about a year, he recalled with a sigh. It was a shame. Jennifer was an efficient young woman, and he had begun to believe that her presence was helping his mother. Maybe he'd been too optimistic. Too hopeful.

Henry pulled a set of keys from his pocket and let himself into the Dower House. As he pushed open the front door the beeping of the alarm began and he punched his code numbers into the panel which glowed in the entryway. He sighed with relief. His mother had imagined it all. The front door had been locked and the alarm was in working order. It was all a wild goose chase. He supposed that was better than there being an actual dead body on the premises. But the implications regarding his mother's mental acuity depressed him.

Flicking the switch that illuminated the chandeliers in the portrait-bedecked hallway, his first thought was to make his way upstairs to check in on his mother. He didn't call out to announce his arrival. Jennifer, Cook and Ian would have heard the beeping of the alarm upon his entry, and know there was someone about. He expected their imminent arrival. They'd all want to find out what was going on at such an hour. Knowing

8

he'd need to be able to answer their inevitable questions, he walked directly to the dining room. Moments later, with chandeliers flooding the oak-paneling and brocade drapery with light, it was clear to Henry that the room was devoid of any human presence, dead or alive. Relief and sadness washed over him in equal measure. *Poor Mother.*

No one having arrived to welcome him, or seek out a possible intruder, Henry climbed the sweeping staircase toward his mother's room with a weariness borne of dread. He was deeply concerned about her state of mind. Knocking loudly on her door – *where was everybody?* – he waited for a reply.

'Come,' called his mother's voice. He was heartened to hear that she sounded quite like her usual self.

Striding into the room, he found his mother wrapped in an embroidered blue silk dressing gown that swamped her small frame. He could recall a time when it had fitted her well; *had she diminished that much?* Her hair was bound up in a vibrant purple scarf of some sort which trailed down her back. She was sitting on the edge of her bed looking quite alert, brandishing a brass poker above her head, and gripping McFli's squirming body, which Henry suspected was the only reason he hadn't already been attacked by the eager little creature.

Henry was struck by her incongruous, poker-wielding figure sitting in a room where flocks of painted birds flew through exotic branches upon the walls and cabbage roses bloomed on every piece of upholstery.

9

'Mother, what on earth is going on?' He knew the right tone to adopt was one of supportiveness, but he couldn't help but sound cross. Henry was immediately annoyed with himself. He tempered his voice as he continued, 'I don't think you need the poker, Mother. Everything's quite all right. I have been into the dining room and there was no sign of a dead body at all. I think maybe you dreamed it. Come along now. Let's get you back into bed.'

Henry thought he'd handled himself, and the situation, quite well.

Althea, Dowager Duchess of Chellingworth, stood with as much dignity as her billowing attire allowed. She retained her grip on the fire-iron as she did so. 'Thank you for coming, Henry. You say you've been into the dining room?'

Henry nodded. 'Yes, Mother.'

'And you say there is no one there? No one dead, that is?'

Henry nodded again. 'That is correct, Mother. No one dead, nor alive. No one at all.'

His mother sighed. 'So where's he gone, then? The dead cannot simply walk away. If he's not there any longer, someone must have removed him.'

Henry's mind whirred. He wasn't sure about the extent to which he should mollify his mother by subscribing to her delusions. He wished he had been possessed of the foresight to know that this day would surely come, and to have taken professional advice ahead of time.

'Would you like me to show you, Mother? We could go and look together. I could help you down the stairs.'

10

His mother looked wounded, then indignant. 'Why on earth would I require assistance to walk down to the dining room? I've never needed it before. Henry dear, I am neither infirm, nor gaga. Though if, as you say, the body has been moved, then I think we should telephone the police, post-haste. There might be an intruder still on the premises. Hence the poker.' She settled her small shoulders and raised the implement higher above her head. 'Once I saw the boy, I picked up this potential weapon from the hearth in the dining room and telephoned you. I considered pushing a chair against my door, but they're all far too heavy for me to move.'

Henry panicked. 'I don't think we need to bother the police, Mother. The alarm was in working order upon my arrival, the front door was secured and, as you know, every window and door in the Dower House is connected to the alarm system. No one could have come in, or out, of the house without it sounding. I assume it hasn't?'

His mother shook her head. Her small, wrinkled face puckered with a mixture of puzzlement and defiance.

'Did you alert Jennifer or Ian to the situation?' asked Henry. He thought it a reasonable question, though if her answer were yes, the next question would be: where were they?

'Of course not,' replied his mother in a no-nonsense tone. 'Why would I want to get the staff involved with a murder?'

Henry stiffened. 'A murder? You didn't mention murder.' His concern for his mother heightened.

Althea made her way past her son to the door. 'Oh, for goodness' sake, Henry, if a young man is lying on the floor of my dining room with a nasty head wound, what on earth could be the reason for it other than murder? You can be very dim, on occasion.' She swept out into the corridor and toward the head of the staircase before Henry could catch up with her.

'Mother, I don't think . . .'

'Exactly, Henry. Quite often you don't. So let's just do, rather than think.' She released her wriggling charge and said firmly, 'McFli, stay.' The little dog sat upright, wagging his tail, then showed he would try his best to obey his mistress's command by laying down and resting his head on his front paws.

Henry was pleased to see that his mother was steady on her feet, and that she made her way down the stairs with ease. Always a fit, active woman – she'd ridden a variety of horses over the years, every day, until well into her seventies – he'd noticed that her movements had, of late, become a little slower. But she was extremely sprightly for her age and, at that moment, her agility was all but putting Henry to shame, as he cantered awkwardly to keep up with her.

Once downstairs in the entry hall, Henry's mother stopped and listened, indicating that her son should do the same. He did. He heard nothing. Which was very curious, because he'd expected the staff to be up and about by now.

Henry managed to get ahead of his mother so that he entered the dining room first. Somewhat rattled by her certainty, he checked again to ensure that the room was unoccupied, then announced, 'See? No one. Nothing. No dead bodies. No intruders.'

His mother entered the room in the oddest of manners. Henry noticed she was walking on tiptoe, the poker raised, ready to strike, her whole body alert and her head swiveling to take in the entire room. Eventually she was satisfied and relaxed. She lowered and rubbed the arm with which she had been holding the poker.

'Have you searched all the other rooms?' she asked abruptly.

Henry heard himself tut before he replied, 'No, Mother, I haven't. You told me there was a corpse in this room. I didn't think to check the entire Dower House because I didn't envisage the place being overrun by the walking dead.'

'I suppose he might not have been dead at all. Just stunned, you know, like the blue parrot, in the Monty Python sketch,' said his mother quietly. She brightened. 'That must be it. Oh, I say, thank goodness for that. He must have regained consciousness and left.'

Henry bit his lip, trying to prevent himself from over-reacting to his mother's inappropriate levity, then spoke, 'I don't think that can have happened, Mother. As I have already said, the front door was locked and the alarm was set.'

'I don't care what you say, Henry, I know what I saw. I saw a young boy wearing one of those hooded jackets that everyone, regardless of age or sex, seems to favor these days, even in the height of summer it seems. He was flat on the floor in front of the fireplace. On the Aubusson rug, off to one side. Look for blood there, Henry. I hope he didn't bleed on it.'

Henry did as he was asked. 'There's no blood, Mother,' he said as gently as he could.

'Good,' replied his mother. 'I wouldn't want it ruined. And, by the way, where the devil is everyone? I decided not to involve them initially, but what are they all thinking, not coming down to find out what's going on with us rattling about the place at this time of night?'

Henry knew his mother had made a very good point, and noted she hadn't made it unkindly, but in a very puzzled tone. Other than his concern about her mental state, he was feeling more than a little uneasy about the lack of attention that his arrival, and the wanderings of himself and his mother, had brought.

'Why don't you stay here, Mother, and I'll go to Ian's room to find out what's up?'

'Very good, Henry. I might be quite happy to use the stairs when necessary, but I don't need to march up and down them all night just to prove my capabilities. Not at my age. You're youthful enough to get up to the top floor in a few minutes. Young Ian's in Old Ian's room, of course. It seemed appropriate that his son should have it after him. You know the one?'

Henry nodded as he turned to leave. 'There really isn't any need to refer to him as *Young* Ian any more, Mother; his father's been dead almost five years now. I think we can simply call him Ian.'

'He'll always be Young Ian to me,' responded his mother firmly as he left the room. Leaving

14

her alone in her own dining room, Henry was quite happy she was perfectly safe; there couldn't possibly be any intruders in the house – dead, or alive.

By the time he reached the top floor, Henry was out of breath. Again. For a brief moment he wondered if, maybe, he should cut back to one cigar each evening. He took a few deep breaths before knocking on Ian's door. He waited patiently for a moment, then less so. He knocked again, this time as hard as he could.

Eventually he set aside his good manners and shouted, 'Ian? Are you there?' There was no response. Finally, Henry turned the doorknob. The door creaked loudly as he pushed it open. The room was dark. No moonlight peeped in at the curtained window. Henry felt along the wall and switched on the overhead light. In the middle of the sparsely furnished room, Ian Cottesloe was fast asleep in his bed, flat on his back, snoring quietly each time he exhaled.

Throwing caution, and all his breeding, to the wind, Henry crossed the room and shook Ian by the shoulder. All Ian did was turn onto his side and snuggle himself beneath his blankets.

Henry couldn't believe it. *What on earth . . .?* He shook Ian quite violently. The man finally rolled onto his back again and peeled open his eyes, groaning.

Henry watched as the factotum rubbed his face and eyes with his large, calloused hands. Finally propping himself up on his elbows, Ian peered at Henry as though a mile or more lay between them.

A sudden realization of what was happening showed on the ruddy face, and Ian Cottesloe tried to leap out of his bed, only to trip and fall onto Henry. Both men hit the floor, Henry making first contact with his backside. Rarely had Henry been so grateful for the fact that his rear end was rather well padded.

'I'm terribly sorry, Your Grace,' spluttered Ian as he helped the duke to his feet. 'Are you quite all right?'

Henry assured Ian that he was, indeed, all right. He also noted the look of terror on the younger man's face.

'Is something the matter, Your Grace?' asked Ian. He was clearly very confused that he'd awoken to find the duke in his bedroom, in the dead of the night.

'Rather,' replied Henry. 'The dowager and I have made some very considerable noise about the place during the past twenty minutes or so, to which you have not responded. How on earth could you have managed to sleep so soundly? I thought you were supposed to be looking after Her Grace.' Henry sounded more annoyed than he had meant to; there were lengthy connections between the Twysts and the Cottesloes which meant a great deal to him.

Although Ian Cottesloe was just twenty-seven years of age, he was the grandson of the original Cottesloe who'd come to Chellingworth Hall as a gardener after World War I, long before Henry's time. This Ian was a strapping young man with hands that spoke of rugged toil, and a complexion which indicated that most of his work took place outdoors. Henry always felt dwarfed by his six-foot frame and intimidated by Ian's broad shoulders and muscular arms. In the confines of the small room, Henry was more than usually aware of his bulk, and drew back, unsure of how to conduct himself in such unusual circumstances.

Ian rubbed his head. 'I'm terribly sorry, Your Grace. I don't know what happened, honest I don't. I felt so tired after dinner that I came to bed early. I haven't heard a thing. I feel a bit groggy, if I'm honest. Maybe I'm coming down with something?' He didn't sound convinced. 'Is Miss Jennifer about? Or Cook? I mean . . . I'm sorry, Your Grace. If you just give me a moment I'll pull on some clothes and be with you as quick as I can.'

'Neither of them has appeared either,' replied Henry sulkily. 'I'll thank you to rouse them both, as the dowager will need attending to. I'll see you in the dining room in a moment,' he added. He withdrew while the young man dressed and made his way back downstairs to his mother.

Upon re-entering the dining room, Henry was alarmed to realize that the dowager was no longer there. 'Mother?' he called as loudly as he could. 'Where are you, Mother?'

'Don't shout inside the home, Henry, it's terribly bad form. Besides, there's no need. I'm right here.' Henry knew his face must have betrayed his apprehension as his mother marched in from the main hall. She was still grasping the brass poker, though he noted that her headgear was askew, and she was looking a little flushed.

17

'Where have you been, Mother? I asked you to stay in the dining room.'

The dowager spoke defiantly, 'I've looked all about this floor and there's no one else here. Young Ian, Cook and Jennifer can search the rest of the house. But I'm quite convinced he's been taken away. I've been thinking about it, Henry, and I am more certain than ever that he was, in fact, dead. I realize I only saw him for a moment or two, but the expression on his face was not that of a man who has lost consciousness. It was that of a human being for whom life no longer exists. I am one hundred percent sure that he had, indeed, shuffled off this mortal coil.' Althea twinkled wickedly as she used a comedic voice for this last sentiment.

'Mother!' scolded Henry. 'There's a time and a place for Monty Python references and I do not believe that this is either.'

Henry had never understood his mother's love for, and fascination with, the entire canon of those Monty Python chaps. He didn't think they were even slightly amusing. Whenever he dared to mention this fact, his mother would tell him he'd been given a sense of humor bypass immediately after she'd given birth to him, which always resulted in Henry choosing to leave the room, the conversation at an end.

When all three members of the staff had arrived, each claiming to have been in a very deep sleep, Henry admitted to himself that he felt very uneasy about the whole affair.

The dowager explained again, clearly and slowly, exactly what she had seen in the dining room. Henry noted that his mother's staff managed to contain their amazement quite well, and tea was requested prior to a search being conducted. Henry sat for a whole hour with his mother and McFli, who'd been summoned from the dowager's bedroom with a piercing whistle, and had arrived bearing an expression of excitement and delight at being reunited with her. During that time, Jennifer Newbury and Ian Cottesloe made a thorough search of the ground floor and the two floors above it. Cook checked every cubbyhole, pantry and walk-in cupboard of her domain below stairs.

Finally it was agreed that every door and window in the building was secure, and there wasn't a single sign that there'd been an intruder. All three staff members agreed they had slept unusually soundly, and had not heard anything at all, not even McFli's barking. As he heard his name being mentioned, McFli nuzzled harder against the dowager's ankles, licking her sleepily.

By three o'clock in the morning, Henry Twyst was flagging. He decided to stay in a guest room for the night, unable to summon the strength to walk back to the hall, and not wanting to leave his mother unattended. His mind was made up; he would seek professional advice about his mother's likely condition as soon as he could find someone discreet and reliable.

With the staff all returned to their beds, Henry and his mother were finally alone again, outside her room. The dowager grabbed her son's arm with surprising strength and said quietly. 'I know you think I'm imagining things, Henry, but I saw what I saw. And if I didn't' – she pulled something from the pocket of her capacious robe – 'then where did I get this?' She handed Henry a hat, knitted from black wool with a dirty blue bobble on the top.

Henry took the hat from his mother and examined it. 'Where *did* you get it?' he asked, somewhat apprehensive about what she might answer.

'It was on the floor beside the dead man,' she replied triumphantly.

Henry's whole body sagged. But this time it wasn't because he feared that his mother was becoming senile, it was because he'd realized there was blood on his fingers. Blood that had come from the bobble.

He knew immediately that he wasn't going to get any more sleep that night.

TWO

Annie Parker sprayed almost half a can of heavily scented air freshener into the toilet cubicle and around the washbasin area.

'I know you've been hanging out of the window smoking in there, I can smell it from here,' called a cross voice from the open-plan office beyond. 'It's not fair, Annie. I'm four months pregnant. You promised you'd stop doing that when I told you about the baby. You're over fifty now, and even though I get it that you use cigarettes as some sort of mark of rebelliousness, it's high time you gave it up. Your mum's not stupid, Annie, it'll dawn on her one day that you didn't give up ten years ago, like you told her.'

Annie entered the office somewhat sheepishly, pulled the door to the lavatory shut tight behind her, and smiled at her friend and colleague across the large, neatly ordered room. 'Sorry, Car. I left the window open, doll. It'll be safe for you to go in there in a mo. I 'spect the smell of primroses will make you want to chuck though.' Annie's broad cockney accent always made Carol feel warm and safe. She had no idea why. It just did.

Carol Hill's gentle eyes peered out from beneath her naturally curly, dirty-blonde hair and over her large, round spectacles, which sat comfortably on her happy, round face. She tried to sound stern as she said, 'I am not a motor vehicle, Annie. My name is Car*ol*. It's just one extra syllable. Can't you *ever* make that much more effort to say my entire name?' It was a request she'd made on countless previous occasions and, as was always the case, Annie Parker responded with an impish grin and a wink.

'Sorry, doll, it's just me way. You know what I'm like.'

Carol couldn't help but return her good-natured friend's smile. 'Yes, I do indeed, and I'm not your "doll" either . . . though I'll let you off with that one, because I know you use it on everybody.'

'Right you are,' quipped Annie, 'except, of course, you're my little blue-eyed, pink-cheeked, Welsh pregnant-doll, not my glamorous, posh

21

Irish tottie-doll, who's Chrissy, or my prim, neat, Scottish bossy-doll, who's Mave. What would you call me if I was your doll, Car? *Carol*,' added Annie, stifling a chuckle. She answered her own question with: 'Tall, black, big-bummed English clumsy-doll I 'spect.' Annie busied herself untying the laces on the battered old trainers she wore for her bus and tube journey from Wandsworth Common to the offices of the WISE Enquiries Agency just off Sloane Street every morning.

Annie had always been extremely quick on the uptake, so it had only taken one disastrously misplaced step at the top of the escalator down to the platform in the Sloane Square tube station to convince her it was more sensible to travel in squidgy sports shoes than wear any sort of heels for her commute. She squirmed on her ergonomically-designed chair – she was a martyr to her back, as she liked to mention whenever the opportunity arose – and seemed, to Carol, to be no more than a mass of gangly arms and legs wrestling with uncooperative footwear for several moments.

Carol smiled at Annie's efforts. As usual, she found it difficult to be cross for very long with a person who frequently described herself as being 'as curvaceous as a stick insect, with a big St Lucian bum' and had a generous soul, if a sharp tongue. She chose to ignore Annie's frequent, loudly-whispered cursing. Instead, Carol Hill checked emails at her desk. She tutted as she did so.

Carol was worried. The company wasn't making enough profit to keep it going for much longer and, with the lease on their office space due to be renegotiated very soon, they'd have to do some fancy financial footwork to make the bank happy about allowing them to make a commitment to anything bigger than a shoebox – in the Outer Hebrides. If they didn't get some cases with big fees soon, all four of them would have to have a Very Serious Conversation about how they would progress their business endeavors. If at all.

Before Carol could mention her concerns to Annie, Mavis MacDonald bustled into the office. At sixty-two years of age and a shade over five feet tall, she was as trim, spare and energetic as many people twenty years her junior. Hooking her short, neatly bobbed, gray hair behind her ears as she entered, both Annie and Carol knew what she'd say before she even removed her coat.

'Och, I need a cuppa,' were, as ever, Mavis's first words. Her accent was as gentle as the rolling hills of the southwest of Scotland where she'd been born and raised. A long career as an army nurse, traveling the world, meant she'd polished it for clarity but could always sharpen it when needed.

'There's one in the pot, doll,' said Annie looking up. She glowed with perspiration. Despite the deepness of her skin tone, she still managed to look a little pink in the face.

'Fresh?' asked Mavis, carefully removing her coat.

'No, stewed, just the way you like it,' grinned Annie, wiping away the sweat her exertions with her shoes had produced.

Mavis didn't look amused. 'Ach, away with your sauce,' she chided in her version of a comedic Scottish accent. 'All I ask is for a decent cup of tea to be ready when I get here. It's no' that much to expect.' She carefully placed her sensible all-purpose outer garment on a hanger, then hung the hanger on a hook on the wall. Happy that she'd done a good job, Mavis made her way to the little area where the tea and coffee-making supplies resided. 'I expect I'll have to do it myself. As per usual.'

'You know I'm fibbing,' said Annie Parker, finally slipping her feet into a pair of leather ballet flats. 'I made it five minutes ago. It'll be just right. Go on, pour yourself one, and you can do one for me and one for Car – I mean *Carol* – too. Ta, doll.'

Mavis MacDonald gave Annie Parker a mock-withering glance, as she replaced a carton of milk in the small refrigerator. 'Doll, indeed! Any sign of our Honorable Miss yet?'

Annie grinned wickedly as she accepted a steaming mug from Mavis. 'Oh, come off it, Mave. You know our bit of posh won't be here on time. I bet the Bentley wouldn't start, or the chauffeur never showed. Summat like that, I 'spect.'

Mavis shook her head as she sipped her steaming tea. 'Och, now, that's unfair, Annie, and you know it. While I get to Sloane Square thanks to the number nineteen bus from Finsbury Park, you take the bus and the tube from Wandsworth and Carol nips around the Circle Line from Paddington, that poor wee girl Christine has to

24

drive herself all the way over the bridge from Battersea to get here, then fight for a parking place when she arrives.' She winked over her tea at Annie. 'That said, I swear the number of cars with residents' permits in this mews is growing every day. I don't know where they all live, given how wee those mews houses are.'

'She could get the number nineteen bus like you do, Mave,' sulked Annie. 'It's not too far for her to walk to get it at Battersea Bridge Road. She chooses to drive and you know it.'

'Aye, and we have the use of her car because of that, when we need it,' replied Mavis tartly. 'When do you start your driving lessons, by the way?'

Annie wriggled uncomfortably in her seat. All three of her colleagues were pressing her to learn to drive. She was the only one who couldn't. She'd never needed to when she'd worked in the City. The trouble was, she knew they had a point. You couldn't always get public transport if you wanted to get from A to B to C quickly to follow up on a lead. Especially outside her comfort zone of her beloved London.

'Sorry I'm late,' called Christine Wilson-Smythe as she lurched into the office. 'I couldn't find anywhere to park. Any chance of a cuppa, or has Mavis drunk it all? Could somebody pour me one while I pop to the loo? Can't wait . . .' She pushed open the swing door in the corner of the room. 'Poo – you been in here smoking, Annie?' Christine called before the door swung closed.

'Told you,' said Carol from behind her screen. She didn't notice Annie poking out her tongue as she poured the dregs from the teapot into a mug and plopped it onto a coaster beside the one small sofa in the room, ready for Christine's reappearance.

Settling herself back at her desk, as Mavis did the same at hers, Annie Parker said, 'Anything new come in, Carol? Like the payment of the reward for me finding all that money from the off license robbery?'

Carol Hill shook her head. 'Not yet. And Mrs Monkton is refusing to pay the fee we charged for finding her cat, too. She said she couldn't possibly owe us anything because all you did was find the cat downstairs in her own home.'

Annie gave her full attention to Carol. 'The Case of Mrs Monkton's Missing Moggie? I told you she'd never cough up, didn't I? When I turned up at her front door the first thing she said was that she hadn't expected me to be black. I gave her my usual big grin, and told her not to worry because I'm cockney through and through, even though me mum and dad are a lovely, exotic blend of Caribe and African from St Lucia, but she looked at me like I had the plague. Bitter old . . . so and so. Deaf as a post, she was, too. No wonder she couldn't hear her poor cat screaming its head off inside her tumble dryer. It took me two minutes to find the creature. Scratched me something rotten it did, when I tried to pull it out. 'Course, I have to admit it was a bit of luck that thieving lot had chosen her tumble dryer to hide the cash. The cat hadn't made too much of a mess of most of it. Gawd knows where her nephew is now, but I bet they find him. She had shedloads of photos of him all over the place. Kept telling the coppers what a good boy he was. They knew different, of course. Imagine that; hiding all that money in his old auntie's house, and her being none the wiser.'

'Serendipity,' said Christine as she emerged from the loo and grabbed her mug of milky tea.

'Serendipity my backside,' said Annie. 'I've got a nose for finding things, and you know it. An instinct. I've read every private eye book they've ever printed. I know how to follow a lead, and how to put two and two together. Besides, I've got me Security Industry Authority License like the rest of you.'

'Girls, stop bickering. Nattering over a cuppa is all well and good, but I think we should have a Serious Chat,' announced Mavis, drawing eyebrows raised in apprehension from her three colleagues. They all knew that when Mavis MacDonald said they need a 'Serious Chat' most of the time she was going to tell them off about something.

'What have I done now?' whined Annie. She knew from experience that she was usually the one to blame for *something*. Quite often, for everything.

Mavis smiled warmly at Annie. 'Och, it's not you, this time, my dear. It's all of us, myself included.'

Bottoms wriggled uncomfortably on office chairs and a sofa as their owners wondered what was about to be said.

Mavis hooked her hair back behind her ears as she began, 'I don't know what the books are telling you, Carol, but I suspect it's nothing good. Am I right?'

Carol nodded. 'Cash flow's almost stagnant and we're paying ourselves out of a rapidly diminishing pool of money. In fact, we haven't had a really substantial amount in since we rescued your cousin Harry Wraysbury from his kidnappers, Christine. We all need to take some money each month, just to keep our heads above water, but, pretty soon, there won't be any left to take. With the lease needing to be renewed on this place, or the prospect of finding ourselves something much cheaper somewhere else in London, or even outside London, we need to do something that brings in some cash, and soon.'

Despite the fact that Carol's delightfully lilting Welsh accent usually made most of the things she said sound like an enjoyable song, they all knew how bleak the picture was that she was painting.

'My redundancy money from my last job's almost gone,' said Annie Parker heavily. 'I know I haven't been pulling my weight since I was injured, but I do my best. Really I do, Mave.'

Mavis nodded. 'I know you do, my dear, and we all wanted to make sure you had recuperated fully before you came back to work.'

'Injured in the line of duty,' added Carol. 'Not like me. I'm stuck behind this desk for the foreseeable because I managed to get pregnant.' Carol's miserable expression brought a chorus from all three women. Mavis won the right to speak.

'Carol, we were all very well aware of your

deep desire to become a mother. That's why you left that stressful job in the City and joined us, after all. So let's not beat about the bush, let's admit that you're our anchor when it comes to gathering information, and that, somehow, we'll manage to work out some way to allow you to continue to be a valued member of our team. If we decide that we're going to keep on being the women of the WISE Enquiries Agency, that is.'

Christine Wilson-Smythe held up her hand, requesting that she be allowed to speak. Mavis nodded to give her consent. Being the oldest of the group she'd become their organizer by default.

'I think I have a case for us,' said Christine bluntly. Three surprised faces turned toward her. Expressions melted into anticipation.

'Tell us,' said Mavis. 'And no flourishes.'

Christine nodded. 'I got a phone call from someone I sort of know last night—'

'Oh Gawd,' interrupted Annie, 'and what sort of posh are they then, eh? Not another one like your cousin's lot?'

Christine looked wounded. 'Henry Twyst is the Duke of Chellingworth. I've known him since childhood. He's quite a bit older than me, so I can't recall why I know him. I remember being at Chellingworth Hall when I was young, when I was quite small in fact, that's all. In any case, he telephoned me last night and asked for my help, then swore me to secrecy. He said he'd heard about what I was doing – what *we* are doing – through Lord Wraysbury, you know, my uncle, and he needs someone like me – some *people like us* – to help him.'

Annie, Mavis and Carol looked at each other, puzzled.

'Come along now, Christine, dear,' said Mavis, 'you're a very intelligent girl. Surely you can work out a way to tell us more than that without breaking a confidence?'

Christine sipped from her mug, made a face that showed she wasn't going to drink any more tea, carefully placed her mug on a coaster, and stood. Smoothing down the fine periwinkle cashmere sweater that elegantly showed off her young, slim, yet curvaceous, figure to perfection, she smiled. 'I can't. He made me promise. But what I can tell you is that it involves his mother, who I recall as ancient even when I was very young.'

Mavis's still-even features crinkled wisely as she replied, 'You're *still* very young, girl, not having reached thirty yet, but I know what you mean. So how do we find out more? And, possibly more importantly, will we be well-paid for our efforts?' Mavis was always quite happy to cut to the chase when it came to matters concerning money. She half-believed that the issue would never occur to the young, beautiful, bright and gifted heiress; she knew that Carol would always be too polite to ask, and she didn't feel it wise to leave such matters to Annie, who had been known to suffer from acute foot-in-mouth-itis on many an occasion.

Christine nodded. 'Father says he's land-rich, but possibly cash-poor. Henry's had to open up Chellingworth Hall to the public for the last few years. He's not at all happy about it, of course, which, obviously, one understands.'

Annie sighed deeply as she shook her head. 'I can't imagine anyone wanting to come near my two-bedroomed ex-council flat in Wandsworth, and it amazes me that you don't understand that.'

Mavis shot a warning glance toward Annie, who tried to skulk in her seat. Unfortunately, her specially-designed chair wouldn't allow for that, so she remained bolt upright, looking like an uncomfortable meerkat. Scratching its nose.

Carol raised her hand and got the all-clear. 'Does this mean a field trip?' she asked hesitantly. 'You see, I have a meeting this evening at the clinic that I can't miss. You know, a get-together for all the first-timers. David's meeting me there. We have to bond before the birth.'

'Managed to bond all right before it without classes, didn't you?' responded Annie wickedly, making Carol blush.

'Annie,' said Mavis sharply.

Annie took her first verbal warning like a trooper. 'Well,' she said, trying to toss her hair, which, being not much more than a half an inch of curls covering her head, was too short to allow for any effect at all.

Mavis straightened her shoulders. 'Are we expected to visit this Chellingworth Hall, Christine? And if so, when, for how long, and where is it?'

Christine nodded. 'That was the gist of it. He's invited me – *us* – to stay for a few days and look into something for him.'

Annie tutted. Loudly. Christine glared at her and continued. 'Chellingworth is in Powys. Just over the border in Wales. Nice place. Not too far off the beaten track, so pretty easy to get to, really. Near Anwen-by-Wye. Pretty village, I hear. On his land, of course.'

'Of course,' said Annie recklessly.

Mavis stood. Annie cowered, as much as she was able.

'When?' said Mavis bluntly

Christine lowered her voice. 'Well, he sounded rather desperate, so I said I could be there tomorrow.'

'But today's Friday,' said Annie, too cross to care what Mavis might think. 'Some of us might have plans for the weekend, you know.'

Christine replied sharply, 'Oh, come off it, Annie, you never have plans for the weekend. All you do is turn on the TV and drink wine.'

Annie folded her arms grumpily over her baggy navy sweater. 'Do not,' she sulked. 'Besides, how do you know what I do at the weekend?'

'Because it's the same story every Monday morning,' replied Christine blackly. 'Met your mum at Marks and Sparks, had coffee, did the shopping, went home, watched TV, opened a bottle of wine, fell asleep on the sofa. Sunday? Repeat, sans shopping trip. Same thing every week.'

Annie nibbled the inside of her cheek and said nothing. Her chin puckered.

'Now girls, no squabbling, thank you,' said Mavis. She turned to Christine and said, 'I'll come back to the money then. Did you discuss our fees with this Henry Twyst?'

Christine nodded. 'I told him what we would charge for all four of us to work for him for three days, and he agreed. Full fee. And, of course, expenses. Not that there'll be much more than the petrol, because he'll put us up for the weekend as guests.'

Annie brightened a little. She spoke just before her hand shot upwards. 'I'm in,' she said with a grin. 'I'll go home tonight, find the poshest clothes I've got and get here as quick as I can in the morning.'

Christine began to pick the skin beside her nails, something all of them knew to be a sign that she was nervous, or worried about something.

'You're not telling us everything, are you, dear?' Mavis said.

Christine took a sip from the mug filled with what she clearly thought was a disgusting brew, then nodded. 'There's some question about the possible involvement of people from the village in the . . . incident. So I agreed with Henry that it would be good if we could use a two- or even three-pronged attack. I rather thought that Carol could be point, here in the office, or at her home on Saturday and Sunday if she'd prefer, because she just needs computer access to be able to help. I thought that I would stay at the hall with Henry, and see what's what there. My cover can be that I'm a girl from his past he's invited to stay, so that's easy, because I am, and he has. Mavis, you're so wonderful with the elderly. All those years when you were the matron at the Battersea Barracks mean you're the ideal person to stay at the Dower House, with Henry's mother. She's almost eighty, and he fears she might be . . . um, failing a little. You could be some sort of nurse-type person from her past, how about that?'

Mavis nodded. 'I think I'd need to work on that cover story just a little for it to work,' she smiled. 'I suppose we don't want anyone other than the duke and the dowager to know we're there to investigate . . . something?'

Christine nodded. 'Yes, Henry and his mother, Althea, will both be in on it, but just them. We have to keep it to ourselves. There's always the possibility that someone on the staff is . . . involved. The trouble is, everyone in the village will know we are both guests of the Twysts, even if they don't know we're carrying out enquiries, so that means that no one from the area would talk to either of us about anything useful. Which is why I thought it would be a good idea if Annie were to stay in the village itself. They have rooms at a pub there, Henry said. He'd pay, of course. If Annie were to work the case from that angle, it might help.'

All eyes turned to Annie, and everyone waited for her to explode, which she did.

'So Car gets to stay home 'cos she's a computer whiz and she's up the duff. Mave gets the old bird 'cos she's a nurse and knows how to handle the ones who've gone barking mad. Chrissy gets to stay at the big house 'cos she's the posh one who can speak five languages and knows which fork is which. And me? Being born within the sound of Bow Bells, I'm the one who gets to stay in some rundown old fleapit of a village pub and mix with the peasants. I've got that right, innit?' She strengthened her cockney accent to help make her point. 'I'll stick out like a sore flamin' thumb in a Welsh village, me. Probably the only non-white person they've ever seen.'

'Och, for heaven's sake, Annie, stop it,' warned Mavis. 'We're all very well aware that you prefer to remain within the confines of your beloved London, but we have to take cases wherever they present themselves. I have every expectation that Welsh villages are much more cosmopolitan than you think.' She didn't sound very convinced, or convincing. 'Now, be a good girl, Annie, and heave that chip off your shoulder awhile. We all know you think the world doesn't exist past the M25. It sounds like a very good plan to me,' said Mavis with finality. 'Carol, you can begin by working out the logistics, our detailed cover stories, and getting together a background briefing on the family.'

'I've already started,' said Carol from behind her computer screen. 'I've pulled up the location of Chellingworth Hall, and I can tell you that from here to there it'll take about four hours to reach a place called Talgarth, which is where I suggest you overnight tonight. That means you can all arrive by various means of transport at your target locations without appearing to be together. Luckily for you lot I know the trip from London to Wales pretty well, which means I'll come up with a route for you that avoids the M4 from before the M32 interchange – it's always a nightmare there – and you can probably get to Talgarth quicker by getting off the M4 sooner, rather than later. You should go through Gloucester. Annie, I'll check out buses from Talgarth to

Anwen-by-Wye for tomorrow. How do you fancy being Annie Parker, retired City worker, trying her hand at some Welsh rambling?'

'Ramblin'? Me?' Annie sounded alarmed. 'I don't so much as own a pair of socks I could go flamin' ramblin' in, let alone the whole kit and caboodle. What do you lot propose I wear while I'm flinging myself through Welsh thickets? Me Marks and Sparks jeans?'

Mavis replied smoothly, 'I think they'd be ideal for a Londoner trying out the Welsh countryside for a change. Have you got anything you could walk in other than the shoes you wear to commute?'

Annie sucked her bottom lip thoughtfully. 'Not really. These, pumps, flip flops, sandals and those boots I never wear any more. But maybe Eustelle's got some. Being me mum, it's her fault I've got such giant plates. Dad's feet are normal size, for a man. Her and me? We've got flippers. She might have something that'll fit me. I'll ring her when I'm on the bus going home and maybe she can drop them over to my flat.'

'Maybe you could phone her now, Annie?' asked Carol. 'In the meantime, while you lot all go about your business getting ready to go, I'll hang on here, get my jobs done, and I'll also draw up the contracts. Does the duke have an email address, Christine?' Christine nodded. 'And can I phone him directly to talk about what communications are in place there?'

Christine looked apprehensive. 'I don't know Henry terribly well, but he doesn't strike me as the type to have Chellingworth Hall sorted with

Wi-Fi, Carol. How about I check that first, then we can go from there?' Carol nodded in reply as she began to tap away at her keyboard.

Mavis stood as she announced, 'We'll all get ourselves sorted out and meet back here by' – she looked at her watch, which was pinned to her chest, a hangover from her nursing days – 'two o'clock. On the dot. We should all be able to manage that. I'm assuming you'll drive us to Talgarth in your Range Rover, Christine?'

Christine nodded. 'Absolutely. But I don't need to leave, so I can help Carol. I brought a weekend bag with me.' She blushed as she spoke. 'I was quite sure you'd all agree once I explained things.'

Annie sighed, kicked off her flats, and began to pull on her trainers.

'I'll look it all up, search it all out, and make sure you have printed maps,' volunteered Carol, 'just in case your GPS doesn't know where it's going, Christine,' she added. Every member of the team knew that the heiress, for all her Mensa brilliance, wasn't very good at making sense of, or following, the instructions given to her by her car's system. 'Can you give me any insights as to how I can direct my research into the family, and maybe elsewhere, now, Christine? In other words, would you please tell us what it is we're all going to be investigating?' Carol asked, sounding almost patient.

Christine nodded. 'Now that I know we're going to do it, I can tell you all I know. It happened a week last Wednesday. The Dowager Duchess claimed to have heard an intruder, got

37

out of bed to investigate and telephoned her son to say she'd found a dead man lying on the floor of her dining room.'

Mavis looked puzzled. 'I rather think that's something for the police to be looking into, Christine. I hope you said as much to your friend. Why on earth would we become involved in such a case?'

Christine nodded eagerly. 'I said the same thing. But the problem is that, when Henry got to the Dower House, there *was* no body. Just a bobble hat with some blood on it.'

Silence.

Carol cleared her throat. 'All right then, so we're investigating a non-existent dead body seen by an almost-octogenarian, and a bloodied bobble hat of uncertain origin. Is that right?'

Christine nodded timidly. 'Yes, it doesn't sound like anything really, I know, but poor old Henry sounded very worried about it all – even though it's not much to go on. That's one of the main reasons I wanted you to spend some time with his mother, Mavis. I know you'll be a good judge of how batty the old bird might be.'

Mavis straightened her back. 'I'm not sure I admire your choice of terminology, my dear, but I understand the point you're making. Though, if there's an item of clothing with blood on it involved, then that does give one pause for thought. Have there been any previous concerns in the family that the dowager might be exhibiting signs of dementia?' asked Mavis. 'Are we sure she saw something real?'

'Possibly, and no,' replied Christine. 'Henry's

worried about his mother, which, as I expressed rather poorly, is where I thought we could use your expertise, Mavis. But, of course, the bobble hat has him very concerned too. He's shown it to the local police, who have told him, politely, that there's nothing much they can do. Nothing was missing, you see. The whole place was locked up, the alarm was working at the time, and it didn't sound at all. Henry did mention that his mother is convinced that her staff were all drugged and that, because she didn't eat the stew they all shared that night, she was the only one awake to hear the noises she claims disturbed her. The local constabulary have rather poo-pooed that idea. However, at Henry's insistence, they have agreed to conduct some tests on some items of the food they took away. No news on that front yet. Reading between the lines, I'd say that we're dealing with a couple of local policemen who have said they'll do something to pacify the local gentry, but without giving it much priority. Henry is concerned and confused. And I really do think we can help him by looking into every aspect of the situation for him. The bobble hat, the mother's health, the reasons why anyone would have been inside the Dower House without having stolen anything, and, of course, how they might have gained entry to, and exited from, the Dower House without having tripped the alarm.'

Carol peered over her spectacles and her screen, and observed, 'Well, we certainly need the money, and I think you're right that we could do something concrete, Christine. We do have the right skills, between us, to maybe help this man.'

'I agree,' said Mavis, 'and you all know I wouldn't say so if I didn't think we could help at all. We each have a role to play. So, if no one has anything else for now, off we all go,' she concluded. And they did.

THREE

Alex Bright would never live up to his name. Everyone knew it, and most people told him so. A theoretical father, a mother who inhaled alcohol as though it were oxygen, and a stammer that never left him – no matter how often the kids on the estate tried to kick it out of him – all meant he learned, very early in life, how to become invisible. Especially when anyone from the social services bothered to try to find out why he wasn't at school.

He supposed his father must have been black. Or at least not white, because his mother was, but he wasn't. His skin was just light enough to make him an outcast from the non-white gangs in Brixton, and not nearly white enough to save him from the beatings of the anti-blacks. He reckoned invisible was good. So he practiced it. Alex hunted out all the places to hide in the daylight, and knew where not to hide after dark. He knew how to get from Max Roach Park to Brixton Water Lane without anyone being any the wiser. By the time he hit fourteen, most people either didn't know, or didn't care, that he existed.

He made money by delivering packages, a trade which benefitted from his talent for moving within crowds unnoticed. He never asked what he was carrying. He felt that not knowing was easier. Though, deep down, his soul was aware that what he was doing was probably not only illegal, but possibly very, very bad.

Not much of a talker, and never one to use his real name, because the letter 'A' was especially difficult for him to pronounce, he was known as 'Issy'. It was the noise he'd made when a very large man of Jamaican origin had asked him his name, just before he'd told him where to take the bag he stuffed into the boy's hands.

By seventeen, 'Issy' had somehow managed to gain a reputation as a tough, silent, reliable type. The scars he bore from youthful beatings were interpreted as the marks of battles from which he'd walked away the winner. His silence lent him an air of mystery. His invisibility was legend. It was universally known, among a certain type, that if you needed an impossible delivery made, with no questions asked, Issy was the one you put the word out for. He'd come to you, he'd do the job, he'd take his money. He was expensive, but the best.

As the years passed, Issy almost forgot he'd ever been Alex Bright at all. He was just Issy. He lived a solitary life, filling his hours sitting, unnoticed, in cafes or pubs, where he'd be sure to learn who was who, who did what, and what was going on right across south and southwest London. His patch. By his early twenties he had more money than he really knew what to do with, so he started spending it on the things that had fascinated him, but had been beyond his non-existent means, as a child. Little models with intricate moving parts. Other than these few indulgences, he stashed his money in his small bedroom in his mother's old flat. She was long gone, but no one asked any questions so long as he kept paying the rent. So he did. He kept his head down, learned what he could, including how to read properly, and set about filling in all the holes left by the school teachers he'd rarely met. It turned out that he was very good at retaining the information he read, and he consumed knowledge of all sorts, from many sources, like a man who would die for the lack of it.

When the recession came, Issy was ready to assume his original identity. He set up a few companies that allowed him to buy houses and flats that people were desperate to sell. He employed men thrown out of work to spruce them up, then rented them out to deserving families. It was a cash business, which he could manage at arms' length. His companies employed people he'd come to know over the years. He hired plumbers, jobbing builders, painters and decorators who didn't know him, but whom he had observed as the ones who didn't brag in the pub about how they'd inflated a price for a job they were doing. Those for whom doing a good turn was something about which they didn't boast, but he'd heard about their thoughtful deeds from those who had benefitted. He was careful. Very careful. He paid a fair day's money for a fair day's work and, when it came to setting rents, he never ripped anyone off. That wasn't his style. He always reckoned that if only he'd had a better start, he wouldn't have ended up being a starving, scared kid, as good as living on the street.

He saw himself as a philanthropist. Ten years earlier he hadn't even known the word existed, let alone what it meant.

The day he turned forty, he'd opened a bottle of Dom Perignon champagne and drunk it all himself. He had no friends. Acquaintances, yes, but no one close enough to really know him. Not one. No one called him Issy anymore; he was, once again – or maybe for the first time – Alexander Bright. He'd left Brixton far behind and owned an elegant, minimalist penthouse apartment on Shad Thames, overlooking Tower Bridge. The people he mingled with every day as he drank coffee and raced through the crossword in *The Times* hardly noticed him. His ability to be invisible had not deserted him, though his stammer had. A substantial investment in speech therapy and elocution lessons had resulted in the surprising discovery that he was possessed of a very pleasant speaking voice, which his tutor had described as 'warm and engaging'.

Those to whom he spoke were never quite sure of his origins. His *café au lait* skin tone, the faint scars close to his hairline, his made-to-measure clothing and shoes, the throaty sports car, his ambiguous accent – everything about him was pleasant, though unremarkable. He blended in. He never belonged to any cliques. He was not so handsome that men found him a threat, but his ability to listen – thoughtfully it seemed

– made him popular with women, who interpreted his silence as sensitivity. He was invited to parties, gallery openings, concerts and soirees. Most people knew him as a friend of a friend. He was referred to as a man possessed of wide-ranging tastes and knowledge, with a particular penchant for art, architecture, fine foods and wines, and music.

His real-estate empire, plus the companies he owned which renovated, decorated, managed and rented out property, kept the money rolling in very nicely. He'd begun by choosing tenants personally, selecting those who were trying hard to make ends meet, but who needed a break. They were the people who looked after their homes, were proud of them, and made sure they looked as attractive as possible. Over a period of years, it became clear that areas with 'Marion Rental Properties' – he'd named the company for his late mother – were much more desirable than other rental ghettos. Tenants who took a pride in their homes were 'rewarded' with frequent and timely mainte-nance and upgrades. Those who didn't look after the flats or houses appropriately were found to have been moved on quickly and quietly. Marion Rental Properties thrived. The organization was praised as a social blessing, and even became a model espoused by politi-cians who knew nothing about the set-up's origins. Alexander Bright was very wealthy, but quite anonymous. If anyone went so far, in a social setting, as to ask him what line he was in, he would reply vaguely, using phrases that hinted at property in some way. But few asked. His demeanor didn't encourage inquisitiveness.

Eventually, Alexander decided to indulge the love and knowledge of art and antiquities he'd developed over the years by buying up a struggling business which dealt in their import and export. With a heritage that stretched back to the eighteenth century, the family-run business, Coggins & Sons, had been just about to sink without trace. Alexander was seen by many as something of a hero, rescuing a British gem from the rising tides of multinational conglomerates. He viewed his purchase as a way to be able to come into close contact with beautiful objects on a daily basis, and he became a frequent visitor to the shop and warehouse close to Chelsea Harbour, where he enjoyed nothing more than to examine all the wonderful items that ebbed and flowed through the respected trader's doors.

One day, Alexander found a curious, rather than beautiful, object that had been discarded in a drawer in the office where the last member of the Coggins family – the one who'd been remiss in failing to produce either a son or even a daughter to carry on the business – battled with invoices and bills of lading.

Peering at the bizarre find, Alexander pondered what he held.

'Don't know how you can bring yourself to touch them,' said Bill Coggins as his be-capped head popped through the door.

Alexander looked up, smiling ruefully. 'It is estimated that almost fifty thousand men died in less than twelve hours at the Battle of Waterloo. Battlefield scavengers worked through the night to pick the corpses clean of anything of value. The teeth of the dead were taken, leading to a massive influx of a rare commodity into Britain at a time when false dentures were needed by many, but could be afforded by few. These "Waterloo Teeth", as they became known, were the most sophisticated dentures ever to become available to the middle classes. Real human teeth set into hippopotamus bone with metal pins. I've been fascinated by dentures since I was . . .' He paused, recalling how his mother would put her false teeth into a glass of vodka overnight, thereby providing herself each morning with a clean set of dentures and her first drink of the day. 'Since I was a small boy.' He turned the set of six bottom incisors in his hand. 'A work of art indeed.'

'Well, if dentures is your thing, you'll want to visit Chellingworth Hall, in Wales. A few dukes ago there was one that was mad about them, and they say they've got the best collection in the world. Not that I know much about it. We've never had a lot of them come through here. Specialized market, I'd say. Know him, do you? The duke?'

Alexander gave the matter some thought. He didn't know the Duke of Chellingworth, but he was pretty sure he knew someone who did, and he'd love to see that collection.

'Mind if I keep these?' he asked casually, rather than answering the man's question.

Bill Coggins laughed. 'If you want them, sir,

you have 'em. You own the stock, you know. They're yours to do with as you please.'

Alexander replaced the tissue that had wrapped the dentures and popped them into his jacket pocket. The bulge rather spoiled the line, but he'd take them home and find an appropriate place to display them.

As he slid into the leather-upholstered seat of his Aston Martin, he checked the contacts list on his phone. He knew just the man. He'd propose drinks at the American Bar at the Savoy at seven p.m. He didn't think he'd be refused.

FOUR

By two fourteen p.m. Christine, Mavis and Annie were inching around Sloane Square in the comfort of Christine's vehicle. Annie stopped grumbling about how the Friday afternoon rush out of London seemed to begin at ten a.m., just in time to let out a scream as an apple core flew in through the window of the Range Rover and smacked her in the face.

'Flamin' 'eck!' she exclaimed. 'Ain't got nowhere else to put it?' she shouted out of the window at a surprised young man on a bicycle who almost swerved in front of a Mini Cooper that was wriggling through the knots of traffic surrounding them.

'Just close your window, Annie,' suggested Mavis.

'I shouldn't have to,' retorted Annie sharply. 'People shouldn't go throwing things like that about. Could cause a nasty accident. We should have left earlier. Where the 'eck is everybody going at this time of day? I've never been able to understand why people feel the need to flock out of London at the weekend. I've always been able to live my life quite happily without ever venturing too far afield. Except on proper holidays, you know, like to Cyprus, or the Red Sea.'

'Oh, come on, Annie,' said Christine. 'We got away as soon as we could. We'll all just have to exercise some patience. It might take us longer than we'd hoped to get out onto the M4, but we *will* get there, and we *will* get to Talgarth tonight. At some point. Now please let me concentrate for a while?'

Annie settled into silent grumbling mode, Mavis looked calmly at the chaos about her, and Christine cursed quietly as she nudged onto Symons Street, heading for Draycott Avenue.

The women of the WISE Enquiries Agency had first crossed paths when Christine Wilson-Smythe's grandfather had met an untimely end while residing at the world-famous Battersea Barracks for retired servicemen. Between the four of them, they had, rather unexpectedly, managed to solve a tragic serial killing spree. At the time, all the women had been gainfully employed in their chosen careers. Shortly after they'd met, Annie Parker was made redundant from her job as a receptionist at a firm of insurance and re-insurance brokers in the City, Carol Hill had been advised by her doctor to avoid the stress of her work as a computer whizz for a global re-insurance giant if she wanted a better chance to conceive, Christine Wilson-Smythe had decided she'd had enough of the people she worked with at Lloyd's of London, and Mavis MacDonald had taken advantage of a retirement package offered to her by the Army, and had stepped down from her role as Matron of the Battersea Barracks.

Having agreed to work together, they'd plumped for the name WISE because Carol was Welsh, Christine was Irish, Mavis was Scottish, and Annie, for all her Caribbean heritage, was English. Annie had tried to get the others to agree to call themselves WISE Detectives, but she'd been voted down; her three partners wanted to be thought of as 'enquirers' rather than 'detectives', so she'd had to agree. However, Annie being Annie, she'd never agreed to shut up about her opinion, so she persisted in voicing her love of all things gumshoe and hardboiled, much to the chagrin of Carol who, to all intents and purposes, would do absolutely anything to avoid a confrontation of any sort in life.

Qualifications, trade association memberships, letterheads, business cards and discreet advertisements had all been arranged by Carol and Christine who, between them, had the best business heads of the group. They were still a few months away from their One Year Anniversary, and they all knew they preferred their new lives to their old ones, but couldn't live on air. Even Christine, whose father, Annie always claimed, had more money than God, wanted to make her own way in the world, so needed income to prove a point, if nothing else. But times were tough. They all knew it. Missing pets, wayward husbands and wives, minor fraud or pilferage, and being employed as mystery shoppers to check up on customer service levels, couldn't support four households.

As Christine finally managed to drive at more than twelve miles an hour along the Cromwell Road she said, 'As soon as we're out past Brentford and on the M4, can you phone Carol at the office and put her on speakerphone so she can talk to us all, Mavis?'

'Och, aye,' replied Mavis unthinkingly. 'But we need to talk *about* her before we talk *to* her,' she added seriously. 'We have to decide what we're going to do when she has the baby. We three know very well that she's the glue holding us all together. It's also obvious, especially on occasions like this, how much we rely upon her expertise at excavating the information we need to be able to do what we do when we're in the field. We three only have ourselves to worry about. With a bairn on the way, she's mentioned to me that she and David are trying to find somewhere bigger to live than that tiny flat they've got over in Paddington. And I understand why. You cannae swing a kilt in the place, let alone raise a child. She's much more worried about our finances, and their income levels, than she's letting on about. It's clear she loves what she does with us, and for us, but I think she'll reach a point where she'll have to put us second and her family first. So, what can we do to make sure we don't lose her?'

The silence that met Mavis's questions told her, more clearly than any words could, that neither Christine nor Annie wanted to discuss the future of the WISE Enquiries Agency at all.

'You two can't go sticking your heads in the sand and hoping it'll all turn out all right in the end,' admonished Mavis. 'It won't. Not if we don't plan for it. Head in the sand? Rear end in the air. A very vulnerable position. We must discuss our options and come up with a plan of action. Even if that is to dissolve the business and all move on in some other way. There. I've said my piece.'

Christine hooted her horn at a motorist who didn't deserve it. Annie chewed the inside of her cheek.

'Girls?' prompted Mavis.

'I don't want to think about it now. I'm driving,' replied Christine, obviously delighted that she had a half-decent excuse to avoid the conversation.

'Well, you can listen, at least,' replied Mavis tartly. 'Annie, speak up. Do you have an opinion? I know you usually do.'

Annie sighed. 'I don't want to think about it, but you're right, Mave, we have to be practical.'

Mavis MacDonald tutted twice, quickly and quietly. Annie knew why.

'Sorry, Mavis,' Annie added sulkily, then she clenched her jaw, stretched her neck and tossed her head. 'Right-o then. I'll come clean. I don't want to think about it because it's even bigger than just the work thing for me. I've known Car

51

for a long time, and we've done a lot of personal stuff together. We were proper mates. Of course things changed when she married David and they bought that place near Paddington, and I got it that it made life easier for her so she could get the train to see her family in south Wales a bit easier. But she seems to go an awful lot. Especially now.'

'It's to be expected, dear,' said Mavis patiently. 'A girl likes to spend time with her mother when she's expecting. She wants to ask questions about what it is she really can expect, what it's like to be a mother – if you see what I mean.' Mavis turned to peer at Annie, who skulked in the back seat like a rebellious child.

'Yeah. Right. Wha'ever,' replied Annie, flirting with her second formal warning of the day. 'So, as I was trying to say, in a moment of friendly openness, I expected things to change when Car moved over to be nearer Paddington, but we got back on track with each other after a while. But with her being preggers, you know, not drinking and all that, well it's put a bit of a dent in my social life. And it'll be even worse when she's had it. The baby. So it's not just that I'll miss her 'cos of work – I already miss her in my life.' Annie folded her arms and returned to full-sulk mode as she added, 'Thoughtful enough an opinion for you, Mavis?' Annie's mouth became a thin, determined line.

As Mavis looked around at Annie again, she smiled. She also saw the expression on Christine's face. Grim. 'Och, you're a big softie, Annie, and we all love you for it. No matter how gruff your

52

exterior, we're all privileged to see beyond the hard coating to the soft center. And I know you're right. If she left us, you'd probably miss her most of all, because you're true friends and have been for a lot of years. But she's moving onto a different chapter of her life, and we mustn't make her feel as though she's letting anyone down by fulfilling her dreams of motherhood.'

'I didn't mean that,' cried Annie plaintively. 'I just – I just miss her a lot, already. I don't want to think of a time when I won't be at least working with her. I'd miss her too much then.'

Mavis faced front again. 'We all would, dear. As I said, she's exceptionally good at what she does, and I believe we've only really ever required her to use a tiny percentage of her skills. Which is good for her, because she's less stressed. But, if we are going to carry on being able to have her work with us, then we need to work out how we'll do it. Carol could be largely home-based and still be our information gatherer and disseminator, and keep the books and other administration details in good order. Let's all acknowledge that neither of you two are any good at that side of things, and I might be good at organizing people, but I have no real ability when it comes to online research, and so forth.'

Both Christine and Annie muttered to the effect that they both understood technology and could use it, but they couldn't make it do the amazing things Carol seemed to be able to manage.

Mavis's practical voice continued, 'So, maybe we should all think about working from our respective homes, and meeting for cases in the field only. That way we could do away with the need to carry the cost of having an office at all. We're all used to using technology to keep in touch at least. I realize it's an unusual idea, but maybe we should consider it, because then any money we make could go into our pockets, not into a landlord's.'

Annie sounded glum. 'Yeah, maybe you've got a point, Mavis. It would save a lot of travelling into an office every day, and I don't know how much longer I can go on like this. I know I bought my flat dirt cheap, and I haven't got a mortgage or nothing, but I do have bills to pay, and I think I can do that for another couple of months without much income from WISE. If this duke pays up on time I might get another couple of months out of that, but it's doing my head in, not knowing if I'll be able to pay what I owe down the road.'

'I know what you mean,' chimed in Christine.

'Oh, come off it, Chrissy, doll,' snorted Annie. 'You're a wonderful, beautiful, bright girl, and I love you like a kid sister. But don't try to tell me you've got the slightest idea what it's like to worry about paying bills for electricity, water, gas and the like. You don't pay those bills. You live in a house your father owns, with everything paid for you, and a free car to boot. It's not the same at all. I know you want him to see you can make a go of this, especially since you packed in the career he'd always wanted for you. But to say you understand what it feels like to live hand-to-mouth is not fair to us that has to do it.'

Christine literally bit her lip, then said, 'Sorry Annie. I didn't mean to insult you. But I do have my own issues to deal with too, you know.' She sounded hurt.

'We all do,' added Mavis.

'Yes,' mused Annie, 'we all do. How's your mum doing, by the way, Mave?'

Mavis defiantly pushed forward her chin. '"As well as can be expected" is an overused phrase in the world of healthcare, but in the case of my mother it's both accurate and as informative as possible without my listing a whole raft of medical terminology which will mean nothing to you. Her mind has recovered somewhat since her stroke, but her speech and mobility have not. Duncan, you know, my eldest, visited her last week. I'm sorry to say she didn't know him at all at first, then she was convinced he was my father. It was very upsetting for everyone. Though he did tell me that he had a good look around the home she's in, and is still impressed with the cleanliness and general attitude of the staff there.'

'Gordon Bennett, Mave, I dunno what I'd do if Eustelle was like that. Breaks my heart to think about it,' said Annie.

Mavis replied stoically, 'If the time comes when your mother needs constant care and attention, of the type you cannot give yourself, you'll find somewhere she can live with as much dignity as possible. That's what all we daughters, and sons, do. We have little choice. At least you won't be leaving her with strangers despite decades of nursing experience that you had believed would, one day, prove to be at least a wee bit useful.'

'Don't feel guilty, Mave,' said Annie gently, reaching forward and touching her colleague on the shoulder. 'You know she needs more help and care than even you can give her. And you said her room's lovely, so it's better she's there, in Dumfries, near where she's always lived.'

Mavis nodded. 'I know you're right, my dear, but I'm afraid it doesn't help.'

As the Range Rover began to fly along the M4, past rows of glass-clad office blocks, Christine said, 'A good time to phone Carol I think, Mavis?'

Mavis dialed the office.

'WISE Enquiries, how may I help?'

'It's us, Carol,' said Mavis, 'you're on the speakerphone. We're calling in for updates and briefings, if now's a good time to do that.'

'Hullo everyone,' said Carol, dropping her pseudo-English accent, which she used as her 'telephone voice', and reverting to her natural Welsh lilt.

'Anything happened since we left?' asked Annie, leaning as far forward in her seat as possible, but still shouting.

'Quite a lot, actually,' said Carol. She sounded as surprised to be saying it as her colleagues were to hear it.

'What?' asked Annie with excitement.

'The Serious Crimes people called from Brixton about Mrs Monckton, the money and her nephew,' said Carol.

'Again? What do they want now?' asked Annie in exasperation. 'I've given them a full statement already. Twice. What more do they want?'

'Well, that's the thing,' said Carol mysteriously. 'I think that there's more to it than you might think.'

56

'Out with it, Carol,' said Mavis.

'All right then,' replied Carol, obviously disappointed that she wouldn't be able to string her colleagues along for longer. 'You know that detective sergeant you've been dealing with from the Brixton police station, Annie?'

'I certainly do,' piped up Annie, quite perky now. 'Six foot two of sex on a stick. Dark, brooding and a smile as wide as the Thames at Greenwich. What's he want? I hope it's me.' She giggled throatily.

'I think your luck might be in, Annie,' said Carol, a chuckle in her voice. 'He did all he could to get your personal mobile number from me, but you know I wouldn't give it to him without your say-so. I told him that if he needs to speak to you about the case then he can keep phoning the office and I'll keep asking you to phone him back. But I didn't get the impression it was official business he wanted to talk to you about. I'll text you his number so you can phone him if and when you like.'

Annie glowed as she listened. 'Oh, come off it, Car. I haven't got a snowball's chance with him. Bill. Funny that a man named Bill would, in fact, join the Old Bill.'

'So,' pressed Carol, 'do you want me to give him your mobile number or not?'

'Yes. Feel free.' Annie snapped more than she'd meant to.

'OK, thanks,' said Carol, sounding exasperated. 'Other than acting like some sort of virtual matchmaker, I've emailed the contracts to His Grace the Duke, and he's signed them and faxed them back. I've booked you three a family room at the Coach and Horses Inn at Talgarth. It'll sleep up to six, is a reasonable rate, and they proudly promote the fact that they have Wi-Fi in the room, though you'll have to buy the password for twenty-four hours' use. They serve dinner in the pub there until ten o'clock. After that there are sandwiches at the bar. Breakfast is also served in the pub, and it's included. Checkout is eleven o'clock. Annie, there's a bus from Talgarth to Anwen-by-Wye that goes from right outside the pub you're staying in tonight, to almost outside the pub where you'll be staying in Anwen-by-Wye tomorrow night, which, oddly enough, is also called the Coach and Horses. I've booked you in there for two nights as Annie Parker, as agreed. Use the credit card that doesn't have the company name on it. And don't forget to get receipts. For everything. All of you, but especially you, Annie. All you need is some sort of little pouch, like a separate purse, to keep them in. It's not that difficult, and I can't charge them to the client if you don't give me the receipt. Either that, or I have to spend ages getting duplicates, or additional information from the credit card company. So, charge everything you reasonably can to the cards you have, and keep receipts for the cash you spend. Right?'

'Yes,' said Annie as though responding to a nagging parent.

'Good. Now the bus you'll be catching, Annie, leaves Talgarth at half past ten tomorrow morning, and will get you to Anwen-by-Wye at twenty past two. Mavis, Christine needs to drop you off at Hereford station, where you can be collected by the dowager's handyman, Ian, in her car. The train you would have arrived on is due at the station at eleven twenty-two a.m. Christine, I suggest you get Mavis to the station by eleven a.m. so she can be inside and check on the arrival of the train, before the driver arrives, so that her cover is complete. OK?'

The three women in the speeding vehicle chorused, 'Yes.'

'Good girls,' quipped Carol. 'Other than the logistics, I've also managed to gather a lot of information about the Twyst family, Chellingworth Hall, the background of Anwen-by-Wye, a little about the village itself and some of the people who live there. That's where I need to do some more digging, and I'll get onto that as soon as I hang up here. I've emailed everything to all of you. Annie, did you remember your charger for your tablet?'

'Yes,' said Annie, sounding bored.

'And your charger for your phone?'

'Why do you always pick on me?' asked Annie, sounding hurt.

'Because you forget things dear,' replied Mavis, on Carol's behalf.

Annie made a noise that spoke volumes as Carol continued, 'So, what else can I do for you three before I head off home?'

'Any news on any other cases?' asked Mavis.

'Yes, actually, there is a bit. We finally got paid by Mr Mumbai's Curry-in-a-Hurry chain for all of the mystery dining we did. Well, you three did. You'll be pleased to know he said he'd recommend us for any future work of the same type. He especially mentioned your uncovering of how one of his chefs was sneaking meat off the premises and replacing it with more vegetables, Mavis.'

'Aye, well, if you're going to charge a Scot for lamb and give them mostly potatoes, you'd best be a lot better at it than that man was,' replied Mavis, smiling proudly.

'I'll deposit the money in the bank on my way home,' added Carol. 'And that's that. I'll be off then. I'll have my phone on while I'm on the Tube, so you can try to reach me there, though you all know how bad the reception can be, and then I'll hook up everything when I get home and be available all weekend. I've told David what's happening, and I'll be at your beck and call whenever you want. I thought I'd stay at home on Monday and work from there, then meet you all back at the office on Tuesday for debriefing and billing. With receipts, all right?'

'Yes, Carol,' chorused the travelling team.

FIVE

The journey to Talgarth continued unremarkably, though it took longer than they had all hoped. Christine and Mavis listened to BBC Radio 4 while Annie plugged in her headphones and nodded her head to the sixties soul music which provided the soundtrack to her life. By the time they arrived at the ancient market town, nestling beneath the Black Mountains which formed a natural barrier along the border between Wales and England, it was dark.

Uncurling herself from the back seat of the Range Rover, Annie Parker groaned. 'Oh, Gordon Bennett, stiff as a flamin' board I am.'

'You wee things have no idea what it's like to age,' replied Mavis as she began to pull bags from inside the tailgate.

Christine stretched, arching her back like a cat. 'We've been sitting for a long time, Mavis, and you know Annie's a martyr to her back.' She winked at her colleague as she spoke.

Annie's head shot up as she heard her own frequently used phrase being thrown in her direction. 'Oi, you, no poking fun.' She pointed the tip of her tongue at Christine, then put it back where it belonged when she caught Mavis's stern expression.

'Let's get checked in, some food in our stomachs, with not too much alcohol to wash it down' – Mavis directed her gaze toward Annie as she spoke – 'and let's find out what Carol's sent us. Then I suggest an early night.'

'Good plan,' replied Christine, and the three women made their way into the eighteenth-century building that was to be their home for the night.

By the time they finally settled into their surprisingly comfortable beds, they were all full of good, if stodgy, home-made food, tired and ready to sleep, but, as Mavis pointed out, they needed to read their briefing notes before they slept, so they each opened their electronic devices and scrolled to the document Carol had sent them earlier in the day. Silent reading ensued.

TO: AP, MM, CW-S
FROM: CH
CASE: #27 DOTTY DOWAGER
REF: BACKGROUND BRIEFING

1.a)   Contact is Henry Twyst, 18th Duke of Chellingworth, Powys. Age 55. Single. Second son of Harold Twyst, 17th Duke of Chellingworth (died 10 years ago).

b)   Older brother, Devereaux, died aged 47 (12 years ago), no wife, no children.

c)   Henry has one sister, Clementine, aged 52. She has use of their house in London and a suite at the hall. Moves between the two, but mostly in London.

d)   Mother Althea, Dowager Duchess, aged 79. Second wife of 17th Duke, whose first wife died giving birth to older son. Althea Wright wasn't from a titled family (I am looking into this – can't seem to find out much about her for now). She popped out a spare (our client, Henry) and then a daughter very quickly.

e)   When his brother died, Henry (our client) was called back to

62

Chellingworth Hall from an artists' commune near Arles, France, where he was living and painting. Clementine was there with him, but she stayed on in France when he returned. Henry only had a couple of years to come to terms with becoming the next duke, rather than not having to do anything much with his life, which is what he seemed to be doing.

2. Staff at Dower House: (NB: there was no dowager immediately before Althea. The 17th duke's mother died when she was quite young, so didn't survive her husband to become a dowager. Thus, the Dower House was opened up, and staffed, after the death of the 17th duke, to accommodate Althea, his wife. This was about 9 years ago. After it was agreed that the house should be reopened, it cost a fair bit to spruce it up, because it had to be brought up to new building codes, so it took a while.)

a) The cook, Mrs Mary Wilson. Widow. Lives in. Been there since it was staffed, so 9 years. Aged 63. Relatively local, from Hay-on-Wye. Duties include planning menus, cooking, etc.

b) The handyman/factotum, Ian Cottesloe. 27. Single. Lives in. Born and raised on the estate.

First language Welsh, speaks perfect English. Does anything and everything from driving to gardening to maintenance. Father and grandfather did the same before him.

c) Lady's aide, Jennifer Newbury, 33. Single. Lives in. Originally from Swindon, I think. I'm looking into this again. She says she's from Swindon, but I can't find a record of her at all. I have found something for a Jennifer Newbury of the same age from Leytonstone, but I have to dig around a bit more. Is a general helper for the dowager in all her personal needs.

d) A company from the village provides cleaners on an as-needed basis, and they also work at the hall. Am awaiting a roster of details from the Estates Manager – see below.

3. Staff at Chellingworth Hall:

a) Estates Manager is Bob Fernley. 60. Lives in a house on the estate. Married, no children. Wife is Elizabeth. Very involved with the village. Originally from Stourbridge, Wiltshire. Was appointed by 17th duke and kept on by 18th. Runs the farming operations on the Chellingworth

Estate, plus oversees the maintenance of the fabric of the hall, the Dower House, all the various buildings, etc.

b) Public Operations Manager is Stephanie Timbers. 32. Lives in a cottage in the village, owned by the estate. Single. Ex-PR person from a London agency. Events, public access, marketing communications, etc. New appointment by 18th duke, been there 3 years.

c) Housekeeper is Mrs Violet Davies. Widow. 58. From village. Lives in since husband's death. Appointed by 17th duke and kept by 18th duke. She has staffers who come to help when needed, help with catering for tea room at hall, etc. She oversees all this, as well as looking after duke. Also in charge of cleaning staff, list to be obtained from Estates Manager, above.

d) Various farm-workers live on the estate, but rarely have occasion to visit either the hall or the Dower House, with the exception of delivering any fruit, vegetables, eggs, etc. Usually such deliveries are made to both properties by the wife of the Estates Manager, Elizabeth Fernley, but sometimes they are brought directly by the producer to each dwelling.

4. The village of Anwen-by-Wye, and history: (Anwen means 'very fair' or 'beautiful' and it's close to the River Wye)

a) Population of about 175. It's in Powys, which is on the Welsh side of the Wales-England border. Land owned by the Chellingworth Estate. There used to be a sheep market there, but it isn't held any longer, though the Market Hall, built circa 1565, remains. The village was established in 1490. The earliest building was the village church, St David's, which was begun in 1490, and finished in 1515. There are three pubs, one church, one post office. Otherwise it's largely a development of homes around the crossroads which forms the village, all four roads leading to the common at the heart of the village. This is still common grazing ground, and there's a right of way into and out of the village for anyone wanting their animals to use it.

b) The Twyst family was granted the dukedom in 1459 by Henry Tudor, Henry VII, in recognition of services rendered in supporting him with Welsh troops that allowed him to successfully overcome Richard III at the Battle of

Bosworth. The Twysts supported Henry Tudor because he was Welsh-born. Their star rose with his. When his son, Henry VIII, acceded to the throne, the then Duke of Chellingworth, Devereaux Twyst, was one of the young king's trusted advisors. The Twysts made their early fortune from wool (sheep). The name of Chellingworth is used for the estate and dukedom because the original Twyst married a Chellingworth, so they used both names, one for the family, one for the dukedom.

c) I can't find out much about the people who live in the village at this short notice, though the Coach and Horses is the biggest pub there, and seems to be quite the social center. It looks like most people who live there make their living from the Chellingworth Estate in some way. That said, there's an antique shop, a couple of tea rooms, and a list of activities that take place on the common mainly in the summer months. It's never won anything like 'Prettiest Village', but the photos show it as being very nice, but not overly primped. There seem to be a lot of meetings at the church hall about property prices in the area, and the village seems to be facing the problems that are common for such places – there's not enough housing stock for the young people who want to stay, so they leave, then only older folks are left behind. Because the Twysts own the village and many people rent, they are able to stay, but farmers who own surrounding lands are now selling up and new housing estates, as well as fancy executive developments, are getting closer to the Chellingworth lands.

d) You said that the duke had referred this case to the local police. There's a mobile police station that operates in this area, part of the new austerity measures. Because of the rural setting, they use Police Community Support Officers (PCSOs) in the region. They are the ones who are visible in the communities, keep in contact with local community leaders to understand which people might be likely to display problem behavior, or understand possible times or places where trouble might be expected. They liaise with members of the police force proper. In this area that's the

Dyfed-Powys Police. Powys is the largest county in Wales, covering about a quarter of the landmass of Wales, but has pretty much the lowest crime rate in the entire UK. It's very sparsely populated. Nearest police station is Hay-on-Wye, and Divisional HQ is in Brecon. The duke told me he dealt with PCSO Davies to begin with, then got referred to PC David Thomas, then to Sergeant Rosie Price, then to Inspector Phillip Phillips. That seems to be as far as it went, though I have to say I suspect that the local inspector would probably have got in touch with Divisional HQ about the bobble hat, given that we're talking about the duke and the dowager.

Have fun in Wales, and don't drink too much beer, Annie – talk soon! Carol

'It sounds like we've all got our work cut out for us, with all these people to investigate,' said Christine pensively.

'At least you two have got a starting point,' grumped Annie. 'There's nothing here to speak of about the village, except a load of history.'

'All the more fun for you if the landlord of the pub is to be your fount of all wisdom,' said Mavis as she turned off the bedside lamp. 'Now sleep, girls. We have a lot to do tomorrow.'

SIX

David Hill stretched out his arm to brush his wife's hair from her eyes. He loved to watch her sleep. The duvet squashed her face into wrinkly, beautiful mounds, and he even loved the way her nose was pushed sideways by the pillow. He found it hard to believe that inside this person he loved so much was another person, yet to be met, held, loved, played with and enjoyed.

Carol Hill snuffled and rubbed her hand through her hair. She snuggled herself deeper into the bedding and began to snore. David smiled. Still five months to go before he could hold his child and tell him, or her, about their wonderful mother. A woman who'd dragged herself up from a poor little farm in west Wales to hold down one of the top systems management jobs in the City of London. A woman who'd used her wits and her brains to allow men to see her as something more than a secretary. A woman who never had a bad word to say about anyone, even when they were belittling her in front of others. A woman who didn't need to be cruel to prove a point, she'd just prove it, by her actions, and move on.

David could hardly believe that she'd fallen for him. He was just a worker bee. She was the queen. But she had, and here they were. He was still scurrying off to the City every day, and Carol was now an enquiry agent. An *agent*!

David rolled onto his back, and his wife mirrored his actions. They each wriggled a little until they found the perfect distribution of limbs within the bed.

Staring at the ceiling, David contemplated Carol's new life, and began to fret. He knew she was always safe, because the other three made her stay at the office. And he knew she enjoyed what she did, that it gave her a sense of purpose. But he still worried. David worried that someone might bump into Carol when she was on the Tube. Hurt the baby somehow. He told himself that was ridiculous, and squeezed his eyes shut.

Please let the baby be all right. Please let the baby be all right.

David sighed as quietly as he could, trying not to disturb his wife. He glanced over at her heaving figure. Now on her back, she was snoring more loudly and rhythmically. He loved it. She was being so careful to do everything right for the baby. They'd both read volumes about how she should eat, exercise, drink, look after her skin, prepare for the birth and so on. It had taken them five years to get pregnant, and they both knew this might be their only chance, ever, to have a child, because Carol was thirty-five, after all.

Please let the baby be all right. Please let my wife be all right. Please let them both be all right.

David wished there was more he could do. He felt so helpless, as though he'd contributed all he could to the process, and now his wife had to do everything else. It wasn't fair. He wanted to be a part of it all. Both he and Carol were aware of the hormonal changes they could expect during her pregnancy, and he could spot the moments when she counted to ten to stop herself from snapping at him when he was being maybe a little too attentive, trying to be a little too helpful. But David couldn't stop himself sometimes. He needed to be useful.

He wondered if they'd ever find somewhere new to live before the baby came along. They'd both hoped they could find somewhere a bit less urban to raise their firstborn, but, apparently, so did half the world's population. Anything good, that they could afford, was snapped up before they'd even had a chance to view it. Things weren't looking too good. Carol's income was down to nothing, and he was sticking with his job in the City because they needed the good money he was earning. But he wasn't happy there. Since Carol had left the company, things just hadn't been the same. He missed his wife. They'd met because they worked together, then they'd become a couple, then they'd married, and had been so happy to be in each other's company all day, every day. He knew that wasn't every-one's cup of tea, but it had worked for them. But the stress had been too much for her, so now she did this. If only he'd had the guts to go it alone when Carol had. But now wasn't the time to take the risk. Now was the time to put his head down and be the breadwinner.

Carol's steady breathing finally lulled her husband to a happier place. He loved it that she thrived on the work she did with the other 'WISE

Women' as he called them. Nice women. Good company for Carol, and it gave her a chance to keep doing something she was good at. But, as Carol had said as they enjoyed sharing their dinner together that evening, a baby changes every life it touches, directly and indirectly. They saw it in the faces of the first-timers they'd seen at the meeting at the clinic. Varying levels of panic, or denial. Each couple facing a common life experience, but from a different place, with different challenges ahead.

Instead of sleeping, David ran through his list of chores for the weekend. Carol would be working through, so he'd have to get the shopping done, and take care of her. He liked that. In fact, the idea that, in a year or so, he might resign and Carol could go back to her much-higher-paid job in the City didn't appall him. He'd make a good house-husband, and Carol was the one with the better earning potential. They hadn't talked about that option. But would Carol ever turn her back on her enquiring counterparts? He doubted it.

SEVEN

Alexander Bright alighted from a black cab in Savoy Court and enjoyed sensing the excitement of the early crowds entering the Savoy Theatre for that evening's performance. Pushing his way into the adjoining hotel through the wooden

73

revolving doors, he felt quite at home as he crossed the dramatic black and white marble floor, surrounded by the mixture of Edwardian and Art Deco elegance at which the Savoy excelled.

He was pleased that the renovations had managed to allow the place to still feel the same as it always had, yet also have a refreshed air. Crossing the Thames Court, with its unique iron-work gazebo and stunning grand piano, he was looking forward to his meeting, and the chance to enjoy a couple of drinks at his favorite London watering hole.

Luxurious carpeting sprung beneath his hand-made shoes, and he smiled inwardly that a ragged little street urchin from the worst estate in Brixton was now able to feel comfortable in such surroundings. The Savoy had been one of the first places he'd visited to study how to act correctly in proper society. He'd watched with fascination as people ordered, ate and drank. He'd seen how accommodating the staff members were to those for whom visiting the illustrious hotel was, clearly, either a one-off experience, or at least a new one. He was grateful that, during those early visits, he'd never once been made to feel inadequate, or intimidated by the history and culture surrounding him – something he suspected might be the result of the place having a back-ground steeped in theatrical history. He'd been impressed by the fact that, of all the people they could have chosen, the Savoy had selected the wonderful Stephen Fry to be the first guest to officially check in following their multi-million pound restoration project. The man who'd made him laugh in countless episodes of *Blackadder* and, before that, in *Jeeves and Wooster* and *Fry and Laurie*. A funny man. A delightfully well-read and eloquent man. Alexander had learned a lot from watching and listening to him over the years.

As he entered the American Bar, Alexander looked around for the man he hoped was going to be able to arrange an invitation for him to see the Chellingworth collection of antique dentures. Since Bill Coggins had mentioned its existence, he'd done some digging and, if the reports were to be believed, it would be a joy to see.

He was a few minutes early for his seven p.m. appointment, and the bar was still bustling with people who'd stopped in for a drink after work, or were rushing to get away to theaters where curtains would rise at seven thirty. He could also spot the tourists for whom visiting the famed bar was on their 'must-do' list. More casually dressed than the office or theater crowd, he wondered what it would be like to be one of them; to have someone with whom he could share time away from work, away from home – away from the realities of life. He suspected it would be a delight to have someone with whom he could be himself – his complete self, not the manufactured and studied person he had become in order to allow his chameleon existence to continue. Settling on a stool at the bar, he considered his order while enjoying the excellent skills and artistry of the pianist who was putting the iconic, gleaming white Steinway piano through its paces.

By the time his carefully acquired acquaintance, Jeremy Linwood, arrived, Alexander was enjoying the bittersweet taste of a Negroni and contemplating his opening gambit.

EIGHT

'Mother, will you please sit down. I'd like to do so, but I cannot if you will not.'

'Don't be silly, Henry, it's perfectly acceptable for you to sit in the presence of a woman who has been given adequate opportunities to take a seat but has clearly chosen not to do so.'

'I don't mean that such an action would wound societal norms, Mother, what I mean is that I cannot be comfortable with you pacing about all the time. Please sit a little while? We are in a sitting room, after all. I need to go through some of the details for the weekend with you.'

Althea Twyst perched on the edge of a straight-backed chair which was upholstered in an alarming shade of green. Not sage. Not leaf. Just plain bilious. Henry's artistic eye was further affronted because the dowager was dressed in beige and purple, which he felt drained her of any color. 'Go on then,' she urged, as she wriggled.

Henry addressed his watch. 'They'll be here before too long. Ian will collect Mavis MacDonald from the railway station and deliver her here to the Dower House, and Christine Wilson-Smythe will arrive at the hall in her own vehicle. Can you remember all that we discussed about who this MacDonald woman is supposed to be?'

Althea Twyst shook her head sadly. 'Henry, you are such a worrier. Of course I remember. Mavis is a nurse who attended me when we were all up at the Scottish estate some years ago. For some reason, not defined by you, we became friends – which I have to say I think would be highly unlikely. In any case, we have kept in touch, and I have invited her to stay with me for the weekend. Do I have it right?'

Henry nodded. Now that his mother had settled herself in a chair, or rather on one, he himself stood and began to pace. The sitting room was as snug and cozy as it could be given its massive dimensions, and paltry heating.

'It is imperative that not one single member of the staff knows we have made these arrangements in order to ascertain the origins of the blood-stained bobble hat. If this all . . .' Henry searched for the right way to express his worries about his mother's mental capacities. 'If this all comes to nothing, we don't want them getting upset that we were considering one of them as possibly guilty of some sort of wrongdoing. It wouldn't be fair.'

'But spending all this time implying that I am senile is perfectly acceptable, is it, dear?' asked Althea quietly. Her tone implied stoicism rather than annoyance.

Henry gazed through the window at the copse at the bottom of the hill, dithering over his response for so long that his mother turned her attention to McFli, who, ever at her feet, was seeking attention by nudging her ankle. The dowager bent to scratch behind his ear, which caused him to groan with pleasure and set his tiny tail beating against the leg of the chair.

Henry continued to stare out of the window as he said, 'I have never used that word, Mother.'

Althea Twyst looked at the back of her son's head and replied, 'You don't have to say it, Henry, I can hear you think it.'

She stood up, tapped her thigh to indicate that McFli should accompany her, and moved to stand beside her son. She reached up, put her hand on his shoulder, and patted him gently. They looked at each other, anxiety on the face of the son, comfort on the face of the mother.

'I know it's hard for you to believe, Henry, but I did see what I saw. And, somehow, we'll find out what happened. I'm getting on, and I'm not the woman I once was. I know I have often found myself wondering why I have stood, or walked into a room, or cannot find my spectacles. But these are normal parts of the aging process, my dear. If you examine your own life I am sure you'll be able to think of occasions when something similar has happened to you. After all, not even you are getting any younger. But I *am* still in possession of my faculties, Henry.'

'Yes, Mother,' replied the worried son, anxious that he should sound convincing. He liked the feeling of his mother's hand upon his shoulder; the warmth of her touch comforted him. He wondered about what his life would be like without her, and realized immediately that was not something he wanted to countenance.

When her son had taken his leave, Althea Twyst informed Cook that she would like tea to be served upon the arrival of her guest, then settled herself on her favorite couch with a giant book of crossword puzzles. McFli jumped up beside her, circled a few times, then rested his back against his mistress's thigh, stretching his four paws as far away from his body as possible, and making little snuffling sounds. The companions remained this way for the next forty minutes or so, until Althea heard the sound of an arrival in the entry hall. Setting aside her reading glasses, she stood. McFli trotted beside her as she prepared to act her way through greeting a woman she'd never so much as set eyes upon as though she were a long-lost friend. But she found that she needn't have worried, as the diminutive figure beside Young Ian turned to her with such an open, welcoming visage, that her own immediately mirrored it. Anyone seeing the women's expressions would have interpreted them as joyful.

'My dear Mavis,' said the dowager warmly.

'Duchess,' replied Mavis, very properly.

'I have told you before, it is Althea to you, my dear,' replied the dowager. The two women embraced.

Ian Cottesloe, who'd refrained from making small talk with his passenger on the journey from the railway station, stood patiently holding Mavis MacDonald's bags. He noted that the small Scottish woman was a couple of inches taller than his now-tiny mistress, but that both women seemed extraordinarily pleased to see each other. He wondered how they had come to be so close, given that he'd never met any other friends of the dowager's. He'd rather assumed they must all be dead.

'I'll take these bags to your room,' said Ian as he slipped past the women, who were heading to the sitting room.

'Please tell Cook she can send up tea now,' said Althea Twyst, still beaming at Mavis.

'Och, that's very kind of you, Althea,' replied Mavis. 'I could kill for a cuppa. And something sweet.'

'Madeira cake, I believe,' replied the dowager as she steered her 'friend' toward the desired room.

'Perfect,' exclaimed Mavis, as Althea closed the door to the hall behind them.

Once alone the women regarded each other with smiles playing about their lips.

'You're very good, Your Grace,' said Mavis.

Althea grinned. 'You too. And it really is Althea, even when we're alone. I think I'm rather looking forward to this. You're not at all what I expected a detective to be.'

'That would be because I'm an enquiry agent, Althea, not a detective.'

'And what would be the difference between those two things, exactly?' asked the dowager, settling onto the sofa and indicating that Mavis should choose a spot in which to sit.

'Well, I realize it might seem like a nicety of semantics, but my personal opinion is that the term "enquiry agent" is more British. I cannot help but feel that the word "detective" has become endowed with all sorts of American overtones. And you won't find a more British group of women than we four. We represent each of the four proud nations that comprise the United Kingdom, and we are all able to bring our own national, as well as uber-national, sensibilities to bear upon a case. We are a unique group, Althea, and British to the core. Of course, there's the ribbing between us that I am sure you can understand, living so close to the border as you do. But we all work well together, and, though we are four women of very different ages and from very different social backgrounds, we are exceptionally good, loyal and reliable friends to each other, as well as being colleagues.'

Althea took a moment to reply, but, when she did, she took Mavis by surprise. 'I'm pleased to hear that you have developed a sense of sisterhood, but I have to say that, over my not inconsiderable lifetime, I have come to find I prefer the company of dogs, then horses, then men, then, least of all, women.'

Mavis MacDonald's green eyes twinkled as she replied, 'Well, maybe you just haven't met the right women, Althea.'

McFli yapped, as though he'd understood every word, and both women smiled at him, Althea rubbing his ear. It was this picture of pleasant companionship which greeted the arrival of Jennifer Newbury, who entered pushing a wheeled tea trolley laden with crockery, silverware and a perfect loaf of golden cake.

'My word, but that looks good,' exclaimed Mavis.

'Cook is second to none when it comes to cake, isn't that right, Jennifer?' said Althea proudly.

'You're quite right, Your Grace,' replied Jennifer as she began to serve the cake and tea.

While the young woman busied herself, Mavis MacDonald observed silently. Dark haired and eyed, Jenifer Newbury was a well-built young woman. Mavis was pleased to see that here was one young person, at least, who understood that it was perfectly acceptable for a woman to weigh more than a child and still be attractive. Her hair was glossy, and tied back in a classic chignon. She wore comfortable shoes, a dark, sensible two-piece suit and a powder-blue blouse. It wasn't exactly a uniform, but it hinted at such. Her skirt skimmed her knees, her legs were bare, she wore just simple pearl stud earrings and a fine gold chain at her neck. No rings. Clean hands. No polish on her short nails. She looked clean, and Mavis noticed her light floral perfume. Good teeth. Sturdy, not willowy. Even features, not much make-up. A pretty smile, thought Mavis. She wondered why she'd chosen the life she had, and determined to find out.

'You must be the Jennifer I've heard so much about,' said Mavis. Althea looked somewhat taken aback, but Jennifer beamed.

'I hope it was all good,' said the young woman. Mavis knew she had to get her to say more than that, then maybe she'd be able to detect an accent. Carol's note had said she couldn't place the woman in Swindon, but that maybe she came from Leytonstone. Mavis decided to be direct.

'And where is it you come from originally?' she asked, accepting a cup and saucer.

If the young lady's aide was surprised to be asked such a question she certainly didn't let it show. Smiling she replied, 'My family was from Swindon, but we moved when I was quite young to an area outside London. I tried working in London at first, but I didn't like the hustle and bustle. The country life suits me much better.'

'She hasn't always been a maid, have you, Jennifer?' said Althea quietly.

'You mean aide, Your Grace,' replied Jennifer.

'Do I?' responded the dowager.

Mavis sipped her scalding hot tea to try to cover her smile, then said, 'What line were you in before you came here, dear?' Mavis added a little extra Scottish lilt to her voice, which she always felt endeared her to people.

Jennifer smiled. 'I worked in a jewelry shop for a while, in Hatton Garden, as a sales assistant. Then in an antique shop that specialized in estate sales of jewelry, just off the Portobello Road. Then I decided that I'd prefer to work with living people rather than just things, so I got some qualifications and started to work as an aide at a place where older folks lived. Then I came here.'

'Fascinating,' said Mavis. And she meant it. 'And are you preferring it, dear?'

'Preferring what?' asked Jennifer Newbury, looking puzzled.

'Working with the living, rather than grubby old jewelry and ancient antiques,' replied Mavis in a patient tone.

Jennifer smiled. 'Oh, yes. Absolutely. Her Grace is a joy to be with and, of course, I get to live in this wonderfully quiet home.'

'And yet still surrounded by beautiful antiques,' added Mavis.

'But of course. My surroundings are both peaceful and beautiful,' responded the young woman without taking her eyes off the cake she was cutting. 'It's the most wonderful place to live. I can breathe freely, and am able to see exquisite workmanship in every corner of every room in the house. And when we visit the hall – have you ever been there?' She finally glanced in Mavis's direction. Mavis shook her head. 'Well, when you have the chance to visit it, do take it. It has the most wonderful paintings, sculptures and artifacts. Are you interested in art at all?'

Mavis noted that the young woman had skilfully managed to turn the conversation, and wondered if this was something she did naturally, as a means of engaging her charge and the dowager's guests, or whether it was because she wanted to hide something. Mavis decided that the aide with the background in jewelry and antiques was someone about whom she wanted to discover more. But it appeared that it would not be upon this occasion, because Jennifer served the cake, and left the room.

'There's no jewelry missing, I checked,' said Althea as soon as the door closed.

Mavis gazed thoughtfully over the rim of her cup. 'Ach, so your mind went there too.'

The dowager nodded and continued, 'And I've snooped about in all the drawers and corners since IT happened, and I can tell you that nothing at all is missing. Even the ivory Japanese netsuke collection, which is very old, and very valuable, and would be by far the easiest thing to lift, each item being so small, is untouched.' Althea Twyst sounded disappointed.

'*Lift?*' queried Mavis.

'I do watch television, you know,' replied the dowager. 'I am not adrift in this place without a tether to the twenty-first century. I watch my fair share of criminal investigation dramas. I know very well that a body found with petechial hemorrhages of the eyes means that someone's been strangled or suffocated. I am also fully aware of what Luminol does, and I could probably explain lividity to you if I needed to. I am not the geriatric idiot I suspect my son has led you believe me to be. I keep my mind alert at all times. In fact, I believe I could beat Henry at chess today, or at any given crossword. Unless all the clues were about art, then I know he'd beat me. I never had much time for art, but it's all that he and his sister seem to care about. Very different types of art, of course, but what they choose to call art.'

Mavis was enjoying the moistness of the cake in her mouth, and hoped she'd have time to savor the creamy flavor and dense, yet yielding texture, for at least a few moments. Luckily for Mavis, Althea seemed to be on something of a roll, so she munched happily as her hostess chattered away, absently petting McFli, whose nose was quivering in the direction of the cake plate.

'I like art when it serves a purpose. The portraits in my entryway, for example. All good, no-nonsense pictures of people. No cameras. So there was a reason for them. A record of the family, dear dogs and horses, special farm animals, and so forth. I don't mind paintings of fruit and flowers, or even a nice scene of the landscape, but Henry? He likes watercolors. Wishy-washy things, all of them. No substance. A bit like him. But at least you can, usually, make out what they are. As for Clemmie? Well, I have no idea why what she likes is even called art. What's artistic about splattering a bit of paint on an old broken chair or two, and balancing them on top of each other?'

Mavis noted that Althea didn't seem to expect an answer, though she did at least pause to draw breath.

The dowager continued, 'I think it's all a big con. Remember that pile of bricks they bought at the Tate back in the 1970s? Same sort of thing. Utter rubbish. But that's what Clemmie likes. I've told her not to expect to be able to put any of her "installation" things on display here. She says the public will love it. We've agreed to disagree. Fortunately, Henry is on my side, though I think she's been working on him about some sort of sculpture garden. Probably a collection of hideous lumps of rock and iron. Nothing with a recognizable shape, I suspect. In any case, she tends to keep her interest in London, which is where she spends most of her time. We have the house there, you know, so she lives there, I live here, and Henry's up at the hall. No one to live at the Scottish estate anymore, so it's just run as a farm with the house on constant standby.'

'It sounds like a very peculiar way to live to me,' dared Mavis.

Althea Twyst sipped her tea. 'You're right, of course. Over the decades, I've come to accept it as normal. Though it's very different from my own background.'

'And what was that?' asked Mavis between mouthfuls of cake.

Placing her cup and saucer on the trolley Althea sat very upright and said, 'I was the second wife of Harold, the seventeenth duke. His first wife died giving birth to my son Henry's older brother, Devereaux. Very sad. I have been told she was a bright and lively woman, though she never enjoyed the best of health. After a year or so of mourning her, the seventeenth duke took it upon himself to seek out a new wife. One who could provide him with another son; a "spare". He found me in the chorus of a musical revue at the Strand Theatre called *For Adults Only*.'

Watched by Althea as she sipped her tea, Mavis was pretty sure that the dowager was waiting for a look of surprise. She suspected that Althea enjoyed playing the 'shock angle', but she had decided to remain unblinking

'It wasn't as risqué as its title implies,' added Althea after a couple of seconds, 'and the cast was stuffed with people who were quite well known at the time, and went on to become household names. Wonderful times, though my professional career lasted exactly two weeks. The night that Chelly – that's what I called him, which was frowned upon in certain circles – visited the theater I fell and broke my ankle. And that was that. Or so I thought. I didn't know that the man with the kind eyes who offered to wait with me

87

until the ambulance arrived to take me to the hospital was a duke. He visited me, with flowers. Even made sure to call on me at my tiny little bedsit in Finsbury Park. He was a treasure. I fell for him before I found out who he was. I tried to say no to him, but we made a go of it. Something of a scandal at the time. But we had many good years together and, of course, Henry and Clementine – Clemmie – came along.'

Mavis nodded. 'Where in Finsbury Park?'

Althea smiled. 'Given what I've just told you, that does seem to be an extraordinary question. Queens Drive. Why?'

'I'm on Wilberforce Road, just a street away,' replied Mavis with a smile.

'Good heavens.' Althea picked up her cup and raised it toward Mavis. 'Neighbors.'

Mavis mirrored Althea's actions. 'In a manner of speaking.' She grinned.

As she sipped her tea, Mavis MacDonald was quite certain that Althea Twyst, Dowager Duchess of Chellingworth, ex-revue chorus girl, breeder of dogs, rider of horses and finder of dead bodies, was certainly not losing her faculties. Which made the case of the bloodied bobble hat even more puzzling.

'So what happened to Henry's older brother?' asked Mavis bluntly.

Shaking her head sadly, the aged duchess answered quietly. 'Measles, when he was in his forties. It took all of us by surprise. It seems that, in the depth of mourning his first wife's loss, Henry didn't attend to his son's immunization. Devereaux traveled a great deal, and he must have picked up the disease on the last trip he took, to Indiana in America. None of us thought anything of it, but it seems they had an outbreak of measles while he was there. When he returned to Chellingworth Hall he fell ill. We all thought he had the flu. By the time the doctors realized what was happening, it was too late. He died of complications as a result of pneumonia.'

'That's a very unusual thing to happen, you know,' commented Mavis. Reacting to Althea's quizzical expression, Mavis added, 'Nurse. Thirty years.'

Althea nodded. 'Ah.'

Mavis continued, 'It's a disease that used to kill so many children, but the immunization program has all but wiped it out. Here, I mean. Not everywhere, of course. Very sad. So your wee Henry was never supposed to take the title then?'

Althea smiled ruefully. 'Henry? No. Devereaux was a strapping man. Full of vim and vigor, as you might say. He seemed to be constantly in motion. Always getting something done. His father groomed him for his role, and he would have been a dynamic duke.'

Althea and Mavis shared a grin at the phrase.

'How long ago did he die?' asked Mavis.

'About twelve years ago. Just short of two years before his father passed. So poor Henry only had a little time to get used to the idea that he'd be taking over the family business, which was how his father always referred to the dukedom.'

'And how's he doing?' ventured Mavis.

Settling herself in her seat, Althea thought about

her answer for a moment. 'Not as badly as I'd feared, but not as well as I'd hoped. He's not a businessman, and that's what our type need in a family these days.'

'*Our* type?' said Mavis with a cheeky cock of the head.

Althea grinned and winked. 'Touché my dear, touché. I might not have been born to it, but after almost sixty years of being a duchess, I believe I am, now, pretty well embedded in the upper echelons. Henry wanted to be an artist. Indeed, he spent his life wandering Europe seeking inspiration, and producing his watercolors very nicely. But his father called him away from that life, to this. Of course I love him, and it was simply awful for me to see the light of happiness die in his eyes, to be replaced by an expression of constant anxiety. I tried to help. Still do. His sister is no use to him at all. And then there's the question of inheritance. He's really getting to be of an age where there might be no one who will have him.' Althea paused, and Mavis realized that the duchess had been speaking to her as one woman to another, not as a client to an investigator.

'I understand,' said Mavis simply, hooking her hair behind her ears.

'Yes, I think you do,' replied the aged woman.

'So, now that we've established some trust,' said Mavis quietly, 'tell me exactly what happened on the night in question.'

The women exchanged a guarded glance.

'Very well,' said Althea. 'From my point of view, it began when McFli began to bark. He

90

doesn't usually do that at night. He's a very well trained animal, even if I do say so myself.'

McFli cocked his head at the sound of his name, and looked at each of the women in turn, seeming to know that he was being spoken about.

'He does seem to be a very well behaved wee creature,' said Mavis, smiling down at the dog, who wagged his diminutive tail.

'I knew something was wrong immediately I awoke.' Althea smiled. 'It's not that I have any extra senses, but I do trust my instincts. I pulled on my robe and made my way to my door. Upon opening it I heard a sound downstairs. McFli raced off ahead of me. I had to make a decision; should I wake a member of my household, or should I investigate myself. I'm sure that Henry thinks I'm a stupid old woman, but I am well aware that my home is fitted with a very expensive alarm system, and it was not sounding, so I just assumed . . .' Althea Twyst paused and gave her next words some thought. 'I think I assumed that one of the other people who lives here was moving about, though I do not recall formulating a reason for anyone to be doing that. I turned on the lights before descending the stairs – I saw no reason not to – and when I walked into the dining room I saw the body.'

'Now let me stop you there for a moment, Althea,' interrupted Mavis. 'Were the lights in the dining room on or off?'

'Off. I turned them on.'

'And was the door to the dining room open or closed?'

'Closed. I had to open it.'

'Then what was it that made you go to the dining room first? Or did you go to another room first, then the dining room?'

'I went directly to the dining room,' replied Althea with certainty. 'You're right. Why did I do that?'

Mavis waited in silence.

'The smell,' said Althea with a look of discovery on her face. 'Good heavens, I hadn't thought of that. It was the smell. Coming from the direction of the dining room.'

'And what smell was that?' asked Mavis, fascinated.

Again Althea paused. Her expression told Mavis she was grasping at threads of her memory. She shook her head. 'It wasn't a smell that resembled anything except that I seemed to know that something was hot. Nothing specific. Not plastic, or rubber, or coal or . . . no, it was definitely something hot. That's all I can say. Not like ironing, but sort of similar. You know the way that the odor of hot clothes hangs in the air after you've ironed something?' Althea's eyes appealed to Mavis.

'Indeed, I do,' replied Mavis, 'though I'd not have thought it an occupation with which you'd be overly familiar,' she added, smiling a little.

'Childhood smells, my dear,' winked Althea. 'Never forgotten. Though, you're correct, it's been many a year since I stood behind an ironing board. But it was that sort of a smell. Not something one would expect. Hot.'

'Very odd,' noted Mavis. 'Did you have any fires lit in the house that evening?'

Althea Twyst shook her head. 'It was cool enough for me to need to pull a shawl around my shoulders, but not so cold that we needed to light the fires, or even turn on the central heating for the radiators.'

'So you entered the dining room, turned on the light and – what exactly?'

'When I take you to the room you'll see that, standing at the door, one can see the fireplace. It is to the right of the dining table. In front of it is a particularly fine rug. Upon that rug lay a body.'

'Now be thoughtful about your words, Althea. I know you've spoken of this to the police, and that it was several days ago, but think about it as though it's happening right now. Close your eyes for a wee moment. Think back to how you felt. Were you warm, or cold? How was McFli acting? Other than the smell of something hot, did you smell, or sense, anything else? You know it's important, so take your time.'

Althea Twyst squeezed her eyes shut and gripped the edge of her chair with both hands. McFli whimpered and nuzzled into his mistress's leg.

'He was scratching at the door when I got to the bottom of the stairs,' said Althea. 'That's why I went to the dining room. It wasn't just a funny smell. McFli was at that door.'

'Good. Go on. Use all of those lovely senses you have.'

'It's chilly. Colder in the entry hall than in my room.'

'Good.'

'McFli knows he's not to scratch at doors, so I reprimand him. Then I open the door, smell the smell, and turn on the lights. So the smell wasn't in the hallway after all. Oh, I say, this is very useful. Now, what do I see? Ah, yes, Jennifer hasn't put the chairs back beneath the table correctly after dinner. I must mention that to her. Then I see the body. I don't know what it is to begin with, but it only takes two steps for me to see that it's a person. McFli is sniffing at it. He's running around the head part, then the feet. The body has very large feet. The soles of his shoes are facing me. No . . . they aren't shoes. They are little booties. Red, with a thick white edge on the sole. Everything else is black.'

'Do you know what sort of clothes he's wearing?'

'Yes. The policeman asked me that, too. Black trousers, but like jeans. Tight. A black hooded thing, with the hood over the back of his head. But I can see blood. His face is looking at me. His mouth is open. I can see blood on the side of his forehead. His eyes are open. When I see that, I know he is dead. Yes, I know it, and it frightens me. I call McFli. I can't see him. He runs from behind me and knocks into me. I walk toward the young man. Mavis, he's very young. He cannot be more than twenty, or so. Not white. Not black. Brown. Clean shaven. A few darker spots on his cheek. And blood.' Althea opened her eyes and looked directly at Mavis. 'He wasn't breathing. I am sure of that.'

'How close did you get to him?'

'I walked right up to him. I was standing on

94

the rug looking down at him. That's when I saw the bobble hat. It was lying between him and the fireplace. I walked around his feet, bent down to pick it up, then I picked up the poker as well. I remember I thought that whoever had done this might still be in the house.'

'Good. Now, tell me, why didn't you call your staff at that time?'

Althea looked confused. Her eyes darted to McFli, then back to Mavis. 'I don't know. I felt alone. Scared. I left the dining room and picked up the telephone handset from the entry hall, returned to my room with it, shut the door, and I telephoned Henry. He told me to go back to my room, which didn't make sense, because I was already there. So I sat on the bed and held McFli, and the poker, very tight.'

Mavis studied Althea Twyst very carefully. Even the recounting of her experience had rattled the woman.

'It doesn't make sense, does it?' asked Althea, shaking her head. 'Maybe Henry has a point after all. Any sane person would have called for help. All I had to do was scream and I'd have wakened the entire household. Or at least I might have telephoned the police. But I phoned Henry instead. What on earth did I think he could achieve?' Althea Twyst shook her head. 'I didn't act at all logically. Maybe I am losing my marbles.'

'I think you'd had a tremendous shock, and didn't quite know what you were doing, my dear,' replied Mavis calmly. She paused for a moment, then continued, 'Did you hear anything else? Did McFli bark again at all?'

'No, he was very well behaved. He didn't even bark when Henry was approaching. I could hear him crunching along the driveway. Then McFli began to squirm, I turned on my bedside lamp, and shortly afterwards Henry knocked at my bedroom door. We discovered that the body had gone. But I still had the hat.'

Mavis nodded. 'I assume the police kept the hat?'

'Yes. But I took photographs.'

'You did?' Mavis sounded as surprised as she was.

'I thought that if the hat disappeared somehow, no one would believe anything I said. So I took photographs of it as soon as I got back to my bedroom. Oh! I forgot that bit, but, there, I've told you now. I have a little digital camera that I use to take photos of the birds I see, and the garden I have just begun to grow. It's amazing to see things poke through the earth that way. I'm sorry I always dismissed gardening. I've left it very late to experience the joy it brings.'

'May I see the photos?'

'Of course.'

'Good. Now, would you be so kind as to take me to the dining room, then I'd like to see the alarm. And I would also like to take a thorough look around the entire Dower House, upstairs and down, if you don't mind.'

'I don't mind at all,' replied the dowager quietly. 'You do believe me, don't you?' She sounded worried.

Mavis nodded. 'I believe that you believe it, Althea. Now I have to help the WISE Enquiries

Agency try to find out if something really happened and, if it did, what it was.'

Althea's 'Thank you,' was almost a whisper.

Mavis allowed herself to enjoy her final mouthful of cake, but knew that, very soon, she'd be seeking a way to examine the security systems in the Dower House, under the guise of being a very nervous guest who wanted to know exactly how safe she'd be in her bed at night. She decided that Ian Cottesloe would be her next target. Surly he might be, but she felt if she could get him alone, and not behind the wheel of a car, he might open up to a little old Scottish lady who was worried about her safety. Before Althea summoned the factotum, Mavis sent a text to Carol, outlining areas suitable for further enquiries, then looked forward to enjoying the company of a strapping young man. It was a poor substitute for spending time with one of her two sons, but she always felt more connected to them when she chatted with men of roughly their age.

NINE

Annie Parker slipped on the bottom step of the bus as she was getting off and almost twisted her ankle. Luckily for her, the man who'd alighted just ahead of her was large and slow-moving, so, instead of falling flat on her face, she toppled forward onto him, and he, in turn, lurched into other folks who had foolishly assumed that a bus stop was unlikely to be somewhere where they'd suffer a bodily injury.

Thus, Annie's arrival in Anwen-by-Wye was greeted by a chorus of 'Oi! What do you think you're doing?', and even one or two guttural Welsh phrases which she suspected might be quite insulting. She thanked everyone, then apologized to everyone, grabbed up her bags and took in her surroundings. A wide expanse of grass that looked as though it could easily serve as a full-sized football pitch was surrounded on all four sides by detached houses that seemed to have been built at various times throughout the past five hundred years. Annie quickly spotted that three pubs and a large church anchored the four corners of the square. There were only three thatched cottages, which disappointed Annie. She'd hoped for more. Only two aspects of country life appealed to Annie: chocolate-box cottages and indulgent, lengthy pub lunches.

Annie disliked the countryside, in general terms. She was convinced that her DNA was a mixture of asphalt, exhaust fumes, shredded bus tickets, Cabernet Sauvignon, nicotine, sauces made almost entirely of capsicum, butter, jerk spices and bacon fat. She regularly drew acid comments from Carol, who claimed she only had to smell the vinegar wafting from a bag of chips to put on weight, because Annie Parker really could eat anything she wanted without so much as gaining an ounce. She got a bit bloated after too many pints of beer – about six – but that was it. Her beloved Eustelle had told her, when she was a very small girl, that the addition of hot sauce to any item of food meant that the body ate up the calories it contained. Annie had never had reason to doubt her mother's wisdom, and always carried a bottle about her person, in case there wasn't any on offer.

Just like Eustelle, Annie was about five ten, weighed around 120 pounds, and couldn't do anything about it. Eustelle's theory was that they both had bones like birds – light and brittle – and metabolisms that ran at full pelt because of the hot sauce. It was true that Annie had broken at least half a dozen bones in her lifetime, but she reckoned that wasn't so bad, considering she had hundreds of them. Besides, her body was so angular that she kept knocking into things, so a few bruises and chipped bones were to be expected. And as for a body that could burn anything off? She reckoned that was why she was always so sweaty.

As she breathed in a couple of lungsful of fresh country air, Annie Parker began to cough heartily. Dropping her luggage to politely cover her mouth, she heard an ominous crack come from inside the softer of the two bags. Still threatening to hack up a lung, she quickly realized that the bag had contained a new bottle of perfume, and her favorite sauce. She suspected it now contained a puddle of one or the other. Typical!

Nattering to herself that there was nothing she could do about it at that moment, she caught sight of the Coach and Horses pub. Annie tutted with resignation as she realized that she was directly opposite the corner where she wanted to be, and she weighed up walking along the pavement around the outer edge of the square to reach her goal, or whether she should simply tramp across the large grassy common. There were no paths, and she didn't want to soak her shoes as soon as she got off the bus, so she decided to stick to the asphalt, which was her preferred surface upon which to walk in any case.

There wasn't much traffic and, once the bus had chugged out of the village, it was very quiet. At least, Annie thought it was quiet because she lived in a flat that overlooked eight lanes of traffic. Gradually, as her ears acclimatized to their new surroundings, she heard birds singing, the odd lawn mower rattling around, the annoying tsst-thump-tsst-thump-tsst-thump of a rock anthem somewhere far in the distance, and one of those bells that jangles when a shop door opens. The bell was ringing behind her. She looked around and noticed an antiques shop that she'd wandered past, and she drifted back to peer inside.

Sitting in the Georgian bow window was a small table flanked by two chairs. Exquisitely inlaid with marquetry in a variety of shades and types of woods, the pieces complemented each other in scale, style and age. Most of Annie's knowledge of antiques came from twenty years of watching *Antiques Roadshow* on the BBC and guessing the prices with Eustelle on the phone. They'd always watched it that way, both in their own flats, each with a cup of tea in one hand, and a telephone in the other. They enjoyed it. But Annie knew what she liked, and she liked these pieces.

'Caught your eye, did they?'

Annie hadn't noticed the man at all, then he was right beside her. She jumped, dropping one of her bags on the man's foot.

'I'm most terribly sorry,' he said quickly. 'Here, allow me.' He picked up the bag from his injured appendage and handed it to a very surprised Annie.

'Ta, doll,' was all she could summon. *Why's he apologizing to me?* she thought.

'You're most welcome,' said the man. Annie noted that he looked as though he was wearing someone else's teeth, plus his own; there seemed to be altogether too many of them in his mouth. They spilled out, forming an aggressive point. It made Annie think of horses, which she really didn't care for, and she knew she was leaning away from the man.

Wishing he would stop smiling at her, Annie introduced herself, by way of a distraction. 'Annie Parker. Here for the weekend,' she said, extending an arm as far as she could, and hoping he'd move away to shake her hand. Instead, he grasped it and moved even closer to her. He was almost as tall as Annie, and almost as skinny, but, whereas her locks were shorn close, this man had a wild mop of gray hair that sat on top of his head like a couple of frosted Shredded Wheats. Annie tried not to stare, but it was mesmerizing; it was quite obvious that his hairdo was kept in place with hairspray.

'Tristan Thomas,' he said with an immediately obvious Welsh accent, shaking Annie's hand as though he were trying to start a car with a crank.

'At your service,' he added, alarming Annie even further. Then the penny dropped.

'Your shop?' she asked, jerking her head at the window.

'Indeed it is,' he effused. Annie smelled licorice on his breath, and noticed black spittle squelching in the corners of his mouth. She withdrew her hand as gently as she could, his grip sliding along her long fingers.

'A pleasure,' she lied.

'Maybe you'd like to come and take a look at what else I have to offer?' He grinned.

Annie noted that the man's accent was a good deal heavier that Carol's, which, she supposed, had lessened as the years she lived in London increased. It hadn't occurred to Annie that understanding what people were saying in the little Welsh village might be a challenge. She felt a bit uncertain of herself, but was utterly convinced about her opinion of this man.

Everything in Annie recoiled from him; she couldn't help herself. She resorted to an unusually sheepish grin as she replied, 'Well, you see, I've only just got off the bus, and I'd like to dump me bags really, doll, so, if you don't mind, I might come back later.' She started to walk away, determined to shake off the man's unwanted attention.

Tristan Thomas followed, stretching a worryingly long arm toward her. 'My card,' he said, thrusting his hand toward her face.

Annie stopped, put a bag on the ground, took the card, put it in her pocket, picked up her bag – all in about a second – then continued on her way, calling, 'Ta, doll!' over her shoulder. She walked as quickly as she could, and didn't look back, though she could feel a pair of watery brown eyes boring into her back. She looked neither right nor left, but kept her head high and shoulders down, and congratulated herself that long legs meant she could cover a lot of ground very quickly.

Arriving at the pub felt like reaching sanctuary. Annie strode inside, walked up to the bar and said to the barman, 'G and T please, doll. And make it a double. Ta.'

As she settled herself on a bar stool, her bags at her feet, the man behind the bar looked her up and down, then set about preparing her drink. Annie shoved a five-pound note in his direction, which he took, replacing it with a worryingly small amount of change. She drank deeply.

'Up from London?' asked the barman as she replaced her half-empty glass on the bar.

Annie nodded, her hackles rising. 'How can you tell? Not many of us lot around these parts?'

The barman smiled. 'Yeah, it is a bit milky hereabouts, but it's not that. Accent, love. Recognized it right off. East End somewhere?'

'Mile End, but me mum and dad moved us out to Plaistow. Now I live in Wandsworth.'

'Posh,' replied the man with a grin, pretending to polish a glass.

'You?' said Annie.

'Bethnal Green,' said the man smiling.

'You must have been away a long time,' remarked Annie. 'You said that as though it's spelled with a "th" not an "f".'

The man picked up a glass from behind the bar containing what looked like Scotch, and raised it toward Annie.

The toast, and the gulp that followed, led Annie to order another drink and produce another note.

'On the house,' said the man. 'John James, landlord,' he added, 'but they call me Jacko.'

'Of course they do,' replied Annie. 'Annie Parker. They call me Annie.'

'Not "Nosey"?' quipped the landlord.

'Not if they know what's good for 'em,' replied Annie, giving him a look that could freeze lava.

'And what brings a nice cockney girl like you to Welsh Wales this weekend, I wonder,' said Jacko, now leaning on the beer taps, there being no other customers waiting to be served.

'I dunno,' mused Annie, 'I thought I'd just get away for a few days. You know, fill me lungs with some fresh air before it starts to rain for the whole winter. Just have a bit of a wander, really.' She wanted to sound vague, but it seemed she'd gone too far.

'Picked a bit of a funny place to wander. Not much in these parts, except the hall. Got off the bus, right?'

Annie nodded. Maybe the kerfuffle she'd caused at the bus stop had drawn some unwanted attention after all. 'Well, if you're going to leave town you might as well leave it good and proper. I just want to sit and be. Maybe walk a bit, you know?'

Jacko didn't look convinced. 'Where are you staying?'

Annie was surprised. 'Here. A friend of mine booked me in. A bit last minute.'

'Haven't got no one booked in this weekend,' replied Jacko. 'At least, not that I know of. Hang on a mo . . .' He walked to the end of the bar and poked his head around the corner. Annie noticed the bottom of a set of stairs up which he shouted, 'Del? Delyth? You up there?'

A distant female voice replied, 'Yeah?'

'Did you take a booking for this weekend?'

'Yeah. Tonight and tomorrow. I told you last night.'

'No, you didn't.'

The female voice drew closer and sounded more exasperated. 'Yes, I did, Jacko. Told you after closing, I did. Standing right there, behind the bar, we was.'

A woman of about fifty appeared at the foot of the stairs. Her clothes were bingo chic, her hair the color and texture of dried grass, and her complexion that of someone as familiar with alcohol as the cask in which Scotch has been aged.

'My lady-wife, Delyth,' said Jacko to Annie, by way of an introduction. The woman nodded. 'Delyth, my lamb, this is Ms Annie Parker, who believes she's staying here for the weekend.'

Delyth James looked Annie over, registered some surprise, then seemed to lose interest in her immediately, and replied, 'Yeah, she is.' She turned as she said, 'Room's ready. Wanna come up?'

Annie was relieved that at least she didn't feel she needed a knife to cut this particular Welsh woman's accent, looked longingly at her full glass on the bar, but felt she should follow her hostess.

'No one'll touch it,' said the landlord, clearly noting Annie's glance. 'If you unpack later you can come straight back down and keep me company.' He cast his eyes around the pub, where only two other patrons were huddled at two separate tables nursing half-pints. 'I could do with it,' he said with a shrug.

'OK,' said Annie, and she did just that. It wasn't difficult to drag herself away from her rented room: miniscule, with uneven floorboards, luridly matching curtains and bedspread – refugees from a 1980s attempt at interior design – it wasn't exactly a home away from home, so she was happy to return to the comparative cheeriness of the almost empty pub. Annie had never seen the appeal of beams upon which she could bump her head, or horse brasses that would require constant buffing, so the décor of the pub left much to be desired in her eyes, but she supposed it was what the tourists expected, and the locals had learned to ignore, so she understood why it looked the way it did.

Settling onto her stool once again, she took her chance to begin to pump the landlord. 'Get many tourists this time of year?' she asked. She felt it was the sort of opening gambit any landlord might expect.

Jacko drew close once again and said, 'Not enough.'

'A lot of locals, then?'

'Not really.' He nodded toward the almost empty pub.

Annie wondered if Jacko wanted company with whom he could be silent, but decided to give it another go.

'Got to be tough keeping going then, I'd have thought. What brought you all the way out here, from Bethnal Green?'

'Her upstairs.' He nodded. 'She's from just up the way near Hay-on-Wye, and her old man set us up with this place when we got married. Wanted to keep her close by. And if your father-in-law tells you he's going to buy you a pub, well, what's a man to say?'

Annie nodded sagely. 'Kids?'

'A boy. Well, you know, young man now. Though young layabout would be a better way to describe him. I mean, I know Delyth's old man gave us this place, but before that I had a trade. And we've worked hard at running this place too. Him? All the get up and go of a slug, that one. I've told him to get a trade, even helped him get an apprenticeship, but he didn't stick to it. Too much like hard work for him. Told him and told him. But no, he'd rather hang about with his mates. At least they're family, I suppose.'

'Hereabouts?'

'Nah, back home. Cousins, mainly.'

A very old man, who Annie fancied smelled of linseed oil, ambled up to the bar, distracting Jacko for a few moments as he silently poured another half pint of mild ale, which the man sipped, then took back to his table.

'Not the chattiest, is he? Nor the other one,' said Annie quietly.

Jacko smiled, looking tired. 'Them two? In here every day, regular as you like, from about eleven thirty till about two. Each of them'll have three halves of mild. They each sit at their own table staring into space. But will they ever talk to each other? No. Known each other all their lives, they have. Grew up here, had families here, worked the estate their whole lives. Then they sit there. Like that. You'd think they'd want to talk, you know, like about old times or summat. But nothing. I tried a few times to get them going, but they don't want to do it.'

Annie gave the matter some thought. She knew two men in their eighties just like these two who sat at separate tables in her local pub in Wandsworth. She'd never fathomed them, either.

'Each to their own,' she said.

'True,' replied Jacko, washing the used half pint glass.

'What's the estate you mentioned?' asked Annie as innocently as she could.

'The Chellingworth Estate. Just up the way there. Duke of Chellingworth lives at Chellingworth Hall. Owns pretty much every-thing hereabouts. Thought you might be here to visit the place. They let the likes of us in there these days, so long as we pay up for the privilege.'

'Maybe I will,' mused Annie. 'But if they own everything around here, how come you own this pub?' asked Annie. She was curious.

Jacko smiled. 'Something to do with the bloke who ran the pub when it was still owned by the Twyst family giving Charles the first a load of beer for his troops. So Charlie-Boy tells the then duke he has to give the pub to the bloke running it. Land, stock, building, the lot. And it's stayed that way ever since. You know, in private hands, like. Doesn't make a lot of sense to me, 'cos as far as I know Charles the first didn't ever come by this way. Nearest he got was Shrewsbury, which was a lot farther away in those days, if you know what I mean.'

Annie nodded. She wasn't desperately interested in ancient history, so tried to get her enquiries back on course. 'Nice people round here, are they?'

Jacko looked thoughtful. 'Usual mix. Some tossers, but mainly steady country types. Course, there's them posh houses out past the ring road. One of the farmers sold off his land and they built some of them "executive estate" houses. Load of rich twits from all over. Call themselves Londoners, some of 'em do. But only one or two really are. Got some of the posh Welsh and the posh English there. Hideous places. You know – all fur coat and no knickers type of houses. See, I like the old places, me. Really old stuff. You?'

'Marks and Sparks is fine by me,' said Annie honestly.

'Like her upstairs,' said Jacko. 'You women. If we have any more pillows on our bed there won't be room for me. And changes them all the time, she does.'

'Happy wife, happy life,' said Annie, quoting something she'd seen on TV.

'Happy flamin' credit card company, more like,' replied Jacko, sounding tired.

'No lorries round here for stuff to fall off the back of then?' winked Annie.

Jacko stood upright and began to polish the

beer taps. 'Not so you'd notice,' he replied. Annie spotted that his tone had become guarded.

'Doin' all right over there, David?' he called to the customer who hadn't moved yet. The man looked surprised to be addressed at all, and Annie detected a distraction on the part of Jacko.

She looked at her glass and decided she'd have to sip more slowly. 'So what did you do before the pub?' she asked cheerily.

Sensing he was on safer ground, Jacko replied just as brightly, 'Sparks, me. You know, electrician. Good job. Worked me own hours, and I might have made a good go of it, but we were young, and we spent most of our time down the pub anyway, so we thought it would be fun to run one. Didn't have any idea how hard it would be, but we worked at it, and it did well. Well, it did back then, anyway. The no smoking thing's done for us.'

'I saw you've got some tables outside,' said Annie. 'I can smoke out there, can't I?'

Jacko nodded. 'Yes. Not so bad in the summer, but the winter? This is Wales. Start smoking when they're about ten around here, so now they all stock up at the supermarkets in Brecon, or Builth Wells, and drink and smoke at home. The young ones play those stupid game things, and the old ones sit around and moan about how the pub isn't the place it once was. Of course, the tourists who want to eat here love it, but they're only here a few months, then it gets pretty dismal. As you can see.'

'Well, I'll have another,' said Annie, draining her glass, 'but just a single this time, ta. And I insist upon paying.'

Jacko prepared her drink. 'I won't say no. But you're not going to sit here all day, are you? What about the peace and quiet of the countryside just outside my doors?'

'Well, I was thinking I should eat something,' said Annie, realizing the time. 'Have you got a menu?'

Jacko looked embarrassed. 'I have, but it's just her and me right now. We're not one of those gastro pubs, and I'm not as good in the kitchen as Delyth. But she's got a bit of a headache today, so if you want much more than a sandwich, you might be out of luck.' He tried a winning grin as he passed a slightly slimy plastic-encased card to Annie, and she was wondering how she'd manage without something in her stomach to soak up the gin.

'Put her down, Jacko, you don't know where she's been,' boomed a cracked voice from behind Annie. Annie turned from the bar to see a silhouette approaching her from the open doorway.

'Oh my Good Gawd! It's you, innit?' said the small, round shape.

Annie peered, but couldn't make out any features. 'Sorry?' she said.

'You're Eustelle's girl. Eustelle Parker's girl. Whatsyourname?'

'Annie?' said Annie hesitantly.

'That's right. Annie. That's your name. Remember me? Well, I dare say you wouldn't. Too young, I s'pose. Though maybe not. I'm Wayne's mother, Olive. Olive Saxby. Remember? Mile End infants? Tower Hamlets juniors? In school with Wayne, you was. Remember?'

Annie chewed the inside of her cheek as she trawled through her childhood memories. Wayne? Wayne Saxby?

'Got it!' Annie exclaimed. 'Had nits all the time and played for the school football team. Right? Are you his mum then?'

Finally the light settled on the woman's face and Annie could see a person, rather than a blob. No bells rang. She could have sworn she'd never seen this woman before. And, even if she had recognized her, she wondered what on earth she was doing in a pub in the Welsh countryside. She looked to be about Eustelle's age, so around her mid-seventies, and was dressed in a countryside uniform of a long Barbour coat and a pair of Hunter wellies. A headscarf was doing its best to contain a head of dyed hair set in a springy perm. It was failing.

'A pleasure to meet you, Mrs Saxby,' said Annie, extending a hand.

'Don't be silly,' said the little, round woman, 'come here love, it's Olive.' She reached up to Annie, who had stood upon the woman's arrival, and hugged her somewhere around her middle. Annie looked taken aback, as did Jacko.

'Know each other then?' Jacko's tone had returned to its 'suspicion' setting.

'Course we do,' said Olive Saxby. 'She and Wayne were joined at the hip as youngsters, weren't you?'

Annie didn't recall being attached to anyone by any part of her anatomy when she was a child, but she decided that smiling was the best response.

'So, what brings you to this part of the world?'

112

said Annie, feeling somewhat bemused, and becoming increasingly alarmed that this woman might know something, somehow, about her real employment.

'I think I should be the one asking you that,' replied Olive Saxby jovially. 'I live here. Well, not far from here. With Wayne. Bought a place out here he did. With one of those granny apartments. Lovely, it is. Looks after his old mum a treat, he does. How's Eustelle, by the way, dear? Still the right side of the grass?'

Annie nodded. 'Yes. Eustelle's doing just fine, thanks. Living in Putney Hill now,' she added, though she wasn't sure why.

'I'd forgotten you did that. Always called her Eustelle, ever since you was this big.' Olive indicated a very small child indeed. 'I don't know how she put up with it. But there you are. So why are *you* here? We're very close to the middle of nowhere here, you know.'

'That was the attraction,' said Annie. 'Though I didn't expect to bump into a pub landlord from Bethnal Green and you from the Mile End Road. I was thinking more Welsh beer and sheep.'

Olive drew close and lowered her voice to a conspiratorial level. 'I'd give both of those things a very wide berth, if I were you,' she whispered. 'So how about I drive you out to see Wayne? He'd be tickled pink to see you again. Come and have dinner. Come and stay. Or am I trying to take business away from you, Jacko?'

Embarrassed looks flew between Annie and Jacko.

Annie tried desperately to think of some way

by which she could remain in the village to fulfil her snooping duties, but she couldn't think of anything that would hold any water, in the face of Olive's kind, though utterly unwanted, invitation. She wanted the chance to find out why Jacko had tensed up when she'd mentioned stolen goods; she wanted to find out more about people in and around the village who might be up to no good. But here was this woman from her past trying to drag her off.

'There would be the matter of not being able to *not* charge for the booking,' said Jacko firmly.

Annie was immediately grateful for a glimmer of a chance to redeem her situation.

'Yes, of course,' she replied quickly. 'It might be nice to pop out for a bite, but I really should get back here this evening. You know, not too late. I haven't even unpacked. And I'm not really dressed for—'

Olive held up her hand. 'Sorted. I'll drive you out, and back. I don't drink anymore, see? Can't. But I'm fine to drive after dark, even at my age. I'll get you back early. And no one will care what you look like. Never were a fashion plate in any case, as I recall.' She looked Annie up and down. 'Not much point really. Not married, I see.'

Annie looked at her left hand, where Olive's gaze had landed with a deafening thump. 'No. Not yet,' she said brightly.

Olive smiled. 'Ah, bless. Still hoping, are you love?' she said scathingly. 'Come on then. The trusty steed is just outside.'

'Good luck,' called Jacko, as Olive pulled Annie toward the door.

Annie's terror that there might be horses involved with her imminent means of conveyance dissolved as she spied a battered old Land Rover parked at something of an angle to the grass verge. But her mind was still whirring. She couldn't ignore her work responsibilities entirely.

Just as they approached the vehicle Annie said, 'Just a mo, Olive. Look, if you don't mind waiting, I think I'd better pop to the loo before we go bobbing along the country lanes, and I wouldn't mind a quick ciggie, too. I haven't had a chance to have one since I got off the bus, and I don't suppose for one minute that I could—'

Once again Olive Saxby cut her off, which was not something with which the voluble Annie Parker was overly familiar. 'Ah now, I might not drink no more, but I still smoke meself, love, so don't worry. Smoke your head off while we drive, and at the house too. Wayne's into them big old cigars these days, but he's always leaving them everywhere, so there's no shortage of ashtrays. He says an Englishman's home is his castle, and no government busybody is going to tell him what he can and can't do in his own home. So go and have a tinkle, by all means, but then we'll get going. Okey dokey?'

Annie nodded, and waved as she rushed back into the pub.

'Jacko, before I go, where's the ladies, please?' called Annie, drawing raised eyebrows from the two octogenarian patrons.

Jacko pointed toward the staircase, 'Along the bottom, on the right,' he said.

As soon as Annie sat, she punched the speed-dial button for Carol's home phone.

'Hiya, Annie, how's it going? Nice village?' said Carol as she answered.

'Imagine a mixture of *Midsomer Murders*, *Lovejoy* country, and a more than healthy dose of *EastEnders* and you've just about got it,' replied Annie.

'*EastEnders*?' said Carol, sounding surprised.

'Yeah – long story. Too long. Look, I haven't got much time, and I've got to keep my voice down, so listen and take notes, all right?'

'Ready,' replied Carol seriously.

'OK, John James, known as Jacko, landlord of the Coach and Horses, from Bethnal Green. Wife Delyth, from Hay-on-Wye. Find out all you can. My nose says he's not as straight as he makes out.' Annie scrambled in her pocket. 'Tristan Thomas, of A Taste of Time. Antiques shop over-looking the common. His card says he's the proprietor and valuer. Slimeball. Also check out Wayne Saxby. Used to live in Mile End, now he's living here somewhere, in some fancy house, probably a newish-build. I used to be in school with him. His mother just spotted me, but I don't think my cover's blown. Hope not, anyway. I'm off to have dinner there, with the Saxby clan. I can't get out of it. But I'll come back tonight and be on the case, promise, doll. Any news for me?'

'Not yet,' replied Carol.

Annie flushed. 'All right. Gotta go, I'll phone later, when I get back to the pub.'

'You're sure you'll be all right?' asked Carol.

116

'''Course,' replied Annie, dragging paper towels from a wall-mounted holder.

'Take care,' said Carol. 'You never know who might take a dislike to what we're doing,' she added.

'Car, you do fuss,' said Annie, 'talk later, doll.'

As she dashed from the loo, Annie Parker noticed that Tristan Thomas had arrived in the pub and she overheard what he was saying to Jacko: '. . . midnight tonight, round the back . . .'

As soon as he caught sight of Annie he shut up, and his equine features settled into a broad grin. Annie acted as though she hadn't noticed anything untoward and waved cheerily at both men.

'See you later,' she called as she headed to the door. As she made her way to Olive's vehicle, she wondered what the revolting antiques dealer had been talking about so conspiratorially with the pub landlord, then she threw herself into the Land Rover, winding her legs and arms about her as she squirmed to buckle her seatbelt.

Her apprehension about her journey returned as Olive Saxby merrily ground her way through the gears with one hand, and swung the steering wheel about with her other, which also held a cigarette. The vehicle bounced onto the road with a lurch, the back wheels throwing up stones. Annie grabbed onto the door and wondered if she had enough courage to let go, so she could light up and have a smoke. It was a difficult decision.

TEN

Almost every member of staff at Chellingworth Hall did their best to get to a window as the arrival of the duke's weekend guest became imminent. Some were able to do this quite unobtrusively, others had to make a supreme effort, but most managed it. The last of the members of the public had to be out of the hall by four on the dot, and Christine had arranged to arrive at four thirty.

The rush to prepare the most palatial guest room, the requests for special meals, the necessity for the visitor to be given every courtesy and treated as a most honored guest – all this had piqued the interest of those who knew very well that Henry Twyst never, ever, received lone females at his home.

Seemingly oblivious to the attention that quivered behind the glittering windows of Chellingworth Hall, the Honorable Christine Wilson-Smythe, only daughter of the Viscount and Viscountess of Loch Carraghie and Ballinclare, alighted demurely from her vehicle, and was greeted by Henry Devereaux Twyst, eighteenth Duke of Chellingworth, with a handshake which was warm and friendly. Having already decided on her role, Christine embraced him and pecked him on the cheek, which sent staff of all types and ranks scurrying away from their watching posts with a great deal of grist for the rumor mill, which was just what Christine had planned.

Henry Twyst blushed and stammered, 'Good to see you again, Christine.'

'You too, Henry,' said Christine loudly enough that the suited and booted man waiting to take her bags from her car could hear her. 'It's so wonderful to be back at Chellingworth. It's such a pretty place.'

Henry looked up at his two-hundred-and-sixty-eight-room Jacobean pile with Georgian wings as though with fresh eyes. 'Pretty?' He'd never heard it described as such before. 'Handsome, I've always thought,' he replied.

Christine looked again at the house that filled her view. She knew that parts of it had been built in the fifteenth century, and that Elizabeth I had visited. Indeed, a dozen royal visits had occurred between 1565 and 1635. The weathered stone was now a fairly uniform buttery-gray, but she noted the differences between the Jacobean central section, the Georgian wings, and the brick-built Victorian buildings she'd passed as she drove through the 6,000-acre estate.

'I agree,' she responded. 'Handsome. Good choice of word, Henry. You've hit the nail on the head as usual.'

Henry blushed again. 'Shall we?' he asked, holding out his arm.

Christine took the proffered limb, nodded, and the couple proceeded to mount the sweeping stone steps that led to an ornate main entrance.

Waving Christine ahead of him, Henry

119

acknowledged his butler, Edward, as they entered, as did Christine.

'Miss Wilson-Smythe is in the blue room, I believe, Edward,' said Henry. 'Would you like to go up right away?' asked Henry of his guest.

Christine smiled. 'Not right away, thank you, Henry. I thought we might have a cup, or a glass of something, first?'

Henry stammered, 'B-but of course.'

'This way, ma'am,' said Edward, bowing a little and leading Christine across the cavernous marbled hall toward an open door, through which she spied a delightfully decorated sitting room. Pushed to one side at the door was a velvet rope strung between two brass posts.

'Your guests don't come in here?' asked Christine, walking confidently into the bright, welcoming room.

'They are allowed to peer, but not enter. It's the ceiling. Those who know, tell me that it's in a perilous state. The plaster might begin to drop on to us at any moment.'

'They're always telling Daddy that about the house in Ireland,' replied Christine laughing. 'He just ignores them. But I dare say there's a question of liability, so it's best to keep them out.'

Henry nodded. 'If enough of them come to visit, I can get it fixed. Big job, they say, but what can one do?'

'Exactly,' replied Christine. She wanted Henry to feel as comfortable as possible in her company – given the circumstances – and also wanted to signal to the staff that she was his friend. His 'almost equal'. If she knew anything about living in a home with staff, it was that the gossip would have begun long before she'd arrived, and that she'd be under a very discreet microscope every moment she was at Chellingworth.

Tea was served, along with tiny almond cakes, and Henry and Christine were left to themselves, the door being closed silently as Edward withdrew.

As soon as they were quite alone, Henry sprang from his chair and began to stride about. 'This is much more stressful than I'd thought it would be,' he said, wiping his brow with a large silk square which he pulled from the pocket of his rather snugly fitting Prince of Wales checked jacket.

Christine stood too, and approached Henry. She knew she had to calm him. 'Henry, don't worry. You'll get used to it. Look at it this way; I really am an old friend just coming to visit. All you need to do is act as though that's all this is, and I will do the rest. You don't have to snoop, or pry, or even really lie. Just let's be who we are, and I will take it from there. But we do need some opportunities for me to mix with, and be able to get to quiz, the staff. So I suggest a tour of your home. Now, be honest, do you think there's any chance at all that Edward could be mixed up in whatever might have caused a bloodied bobble hat to appear at your mother's house?'

'Good heavens, no!' exclaimed Henry, shocked. 'There's absolutely no way that Edward could be involved. He was my father's man, and now he's mine. He's almost a Twyst himself. No, no. No question. Not Edward.'

'Any suspicions at all about anyone else, since I've asked you to think about it?' pressed Christine.

Henry looked thoughtful. He stood gazing through the ancient windowpanes, which always pleasantly distorted the outside world just a little. He seemed to be searching for the right words. Christine waited patiently.

'I do not feel adequate to the task of pointing the finger of suspicion at anyone,' said Henry, without turning around. 'It is not in my nature to be a suspicious person.' He turned to face Christine, and she could see the anguish in his expression. She also noted the family resemblance between Henry and the fourteenth duke, who stood, fully regaled in his ducal robes, in a defiant pose beside what must have been a favorite steed. The portrait of him was fully twenty feet high and dwarfed the mere mortal who stood beneath it.

'I understand,' said Christine quietly. She sensed the weight of history upon the man's shoulders. She'd seen it in her own father, on occasion, when being a viscount required responsibilities of him that he found difficult. 'But I need something to go on, Henry. If I am to be able to help you, that is.'

'Yes, yes,' replied Henry, tersely. 'But I find it challenging to believe that someone I know here would be mixed up in – whatever it is.'

'Did you make a list, as I asked?' Christine hoped he had.

Henry nodded and pulled a piece of paper from his waistcoat pocket. He held it toward Christine, seemingly reluctant to hand it over. Understanding she'd have to take the lead, she grasped the paper and sat down to read Henry's notes.

'Should I assume that all those listed under "not possible" are those you know well, and those under "maybe" are those you know less well?'

Henry nodded. Christine had suspected that that was how this would play out. She knew how it felt to believe that one knew one's staff as though they were family members, their being so much a part of one's daily life. But she also knew, from sad experience, that this was not always the case. She'd had to point out to her father that his valued and trusted driver of many years was listening to his private conversations and passing on information about deals he was brokering in the City to others, for a financial reward. It had shaken her father's trust in every member of his staff, and they'd both agreed to keep it from her mother.

'I propose that you begin to take me around Chellingworth, Henry and, under the guise of showing off the place to me, you find a way to introduce me to each of the persons you have listed as possibly being able to come under suspicion, as well as your trusted staff. I propose we begin immediately, because it's quite a task.'

As Henry led Christine from the sitting room, he explained that some of the people listed had already left the hall for the day, some worked in other buildings on the estate, and some lived in the village. Christine felt less worried about the village-dwellers, because she knew that Annie

123

was covering that angle, and she determined to try to come up with some sort of plan that would allow for Mavis to help out with those who lived on the estate.

'Who's first?' she whispered to Henry as they entered the grand, pillared hall.

'I have no idea,' replied Henry, sounding lost.

Christine stifled a sigh. Why was every man she'd ever met of her class either a buffoon or an ass? 'Well, let's begin in the kitchens. I can have a cogent conversation about tonight's dinner and meet everyone there. How about that? If my experience is anything to go by, the people who work in the kitchen know everything about everyone in a household.'

'Whatever you say, Christine,' he replied quietly.

ELEVEN

David Hill entered the small living room of the flat he shared with his wife to discover her sitting with her beloved calico cat, Bunty, on her lap, a mug of steaming tea at her side and tapping away at her laptop.

'Sorry, Carol, I didn't mean to sleep in,' he spluttered.

Carol looked up from her screen. 'Aw, you looked so lovely there so fast, fast asleep, that I didn't like to disturb you. You've had a busy week. You must have needed the sleep. There's tea in the pot. Should be all right. Can you manage?'

David grinned at his wife and set off to get himself some tea and toast.

Carol returned her attention to her screen. She had a list of things to do before the rest of the team members were likely to check in with her and she wanted to get ahead of the game. The rosters of casual staff at Chellingworth Hall had arrived first thing, and she was carrying out what checks she could on the people listed. She was grateful that full addresses had been provided, because every other person seemed to be a Jones, Williams, Thomas or Davies, which, being Welsh herself, she realized would be the norm in the area. She'd already been at it for over an hour and hadn't found anything amiss with anyone so far.

She wasn't hopeful that emails she'd sent regarding Jennifer Newbury's, and the Dower House's cook, Mary Wilson's, previous employment would get a response on a Saturday morning, but she'd tried in any case. She'd put out a few feelers about Ian Cottesloe and his volunteering with the local Scout troop but, again, didn't expect much to happen until Monday at the earliest. That was going to be her main problem, with the girls being away at the weekend.

By the time her husband came back into the sitting room with his breakfast tray, Carol knew she was able to take a break, so she pushed the laptop away, and snuggled Bunty, who deigned to arch her back and return Carol's petting with a long, slow stretch.

125

'How are you this morning? All right?' asked David anxiously.

'Not too bad,' replied his wife with a smile. She felt wretched, but she didn't like to complain about her nausea, because it didn't help anyone.

'Did you eat?'

'Had some toast.'

David nodded as he crunched into his own, the thick layer of butter and Marmite squelching and dripping onto his plate as he did so. 'Mmmm . . .' he mumbled.

Carol smiled, winked and swallowed with a dry throat.

'Anything much happening yet?' mumbled David through his toast.

Carol looked at the clock and her sleepy-headed beloved husband, then shook her head. 'It's early yet. They're all on the move to their locations. I've got a few bits I can be doing, but I need more information from them to be able to help. I don't think there'll be much until this afternoon. We could fit in the grocery shopping after breakfast, and come back for a late lunch, then I can start. But, in the meantime, maybe you could jump online and start hunting down some suitable places for us to live when we're three? You know, something that's got more than a cupboard as a second bedroom, and doesn't mean either of us has to sacrifice a limb to be able to afford it. How about that?'

David nodded, and began to look through the listings of houses for sale on his own laptop.

TWELVE

When Alexander Bright presented his invitation at the door of the starkly white art gallery on Hoxton Square on Saturday evening, he was greeted with a wan smile by the woman with the lank hair who took it from him. A server, who he suspected had been hired for the evening, managed a wider beam as he offered Alexander a glass of champagne. Finally, a girl he placed in her late twenties with a strong Eastern European accent, managed a genuine grin when she offered him, 'a savory treat without fish', which seemed, to Alexander at least, to be an odd way to describe a canapé.

Wandering among the startling sculptural works, which all combined reclaimed wood and barbed wire in some sort of configuration, Alexander tried to look interested, which he wasn't. He yearned for art which was beautiful, spoke to the soul, or at least employed fine skills. But he spotted his mark for the evening, and gradually worked his way toward her.

Lady Clementine Twyst had been described to Alex as being vivacious, which he'd often heard used as a euphemism for plain, but noisy. He quickly realized that the word was hardly adequate to describe the woman he was regarding. Dressed entirely in black, with a gash of red lipstick and a vivid purple head of bobbed hair, Clementine

Twyst's appearance screamed 'art hipster'. Sadly, although she certainly did give off an aura of intense positivity, she was about fifty, so a few decades too old for the look she espoused, and the clique which surrounded her seemed to comprise very young men in worn, shoddy clothes, who looked as though they needed a good bath and a decent meal.

Alexander was disappointed, though he immediately realized that the task ahead of him would be easier than he'd feared. Launching a major charm offensive, he approached, introduced himself, mentioned the names of a few people who knew Clementine and, within five minutes the couple was alone, with Alexander allowing himself to be entranced by 'Clemmie's' explanation of why the works in the room spoke to her.

Alexander noticed how Clemmie drank. It wasn't how much she drank, but the way that she drank, that was familiar to him. It was how his mother had drunk, though she'd never had to bother with the social niceties.

An hour later they were eating plates of charcuterie in a supposedly cool restaurant on Wadeson Street, which had the appeal of only being accessible via a rather forlorn alley. Clemmie nibbled, as did Alexander, but she continued to drink, whereas he sipped Earl Grey tea.

By the time Alexander poured Clemmie Twyst into his Aston Martin to deliver her to her substantial home just off Knightsbridge, they had a plan for him to collect her at ten the next morning to drive to see her family's collection of antique dentures.

Finally feeling the cool, clean, 600-thread-count sheets of his own pillow, Alexander allowed himself a moment of joy. He'd achieved what he'd set out to do; he was about to be taken to see one of the most comprehensive aggregations of antique dentures in the world. If all the rumors about what he would have the chance to see at Chellingworth Hall were true, not even the British Dental Association, or even the Hunterian Museum, had managed to accumulate such a selection. He wondered if the Twyst collection really did contain a spare set of Winston Churchill's dentures, as many sets of Waterloo Teeth as he'd been led to believe, and even ancient Egyptian, Indian, Japanese and American teeth too.

Turning onto his side he contemplated, once again, why he felt so connected to dentures, then he dreamed of his mother and of his elocution coach and tried to stop all his own teeth from flying out of his mouth as he slept.

THIRTEEN

As Olive Saxby's driving descended into mere torture, Annie Parker began to pray for her life. She also prayed that the red-brick monstrosity that they were approaching was their destination and was relieved when Olive said, 'Nearly there.'

Looking like a cross between a Victorian school and a local authority office block, the building outside which Olive scraped the Land Rover to a shuddering halt lacked any grace whatsoever. The brick was harsh and new, the windows classlessly plastic and the stone lions, rampant, at the front door made Annie think of a downmarket restaurant, rather than a palatial home. The scale of the place was grandiose, but it looked as though it had been built by a child who wanted a giant dollhouse.

'Just wait till he sees you. I bet he'll be speechless,' enthused Olive as she jumped down onto the coral pink gravel.

Without waiting for Annie, the woman raced to the front door, as quickly as her septuagenarian legs could carry her, then she began to remove her wellies. Hopping about, as best she could, she turned to Annie, who was dutifully trying her best to catch up, and said, 'Shoes off, love. He don't like people wearin' shoes in the house.'

Annie was horrified. She hated her feet being on display and bemoaned the fact, silently, that she was wearing men's socks inside her trainers. But she had little choice but to accede to her host's wishes.

Once inside, Annie became even more apprehensive. The entryway soared two stories above her and a staircase swooped up both sides, making a meal of gold-embossed ironwork as it did so. The patterned wooden floor looked as inviting as an ice-rink to Annie, who envisaged her sock-clad feet slithering away from beneath her. Walking gingerly at first, she tried sliding her feet rather than striding out, and wondered how long she'd be able to remain upright.

The front door closed behind them, Olive Saxby called out, with a powerful and raucous voice, 'Wayne? Wayne, love, where are you?'

'In the kitchen, Mum. And don't scream,' replied a gruff voice, just as loudly.

Olive grinned at Annie. 'Ooo, I can hardly wait!' She hugged Annie and indicated that she should follow her lead. Annie did. Tentatively. The long corridor stretched ahead of them, and Annie noted large rooms on either side as she made her cautious way behind Olive.

Just as they approached a wide archway at the back of the house, Olive announced, 'I've brought you a surprise, Wayne. A visitor. I'll bet you'll never guess who.' She turned to Annie. 'Come on in, love, he don't bite.'

Annie walked into a kitchen-cum-sitting room that was about the same size as her entire flat, and saw a man and woman sitting on a sofa beneath the biggest television screen she'd ever seen. The man didn't look at all familiar, and his expression suggested he felt the same way about Annie.

Wayne Saxby looked at Annie, then his mother. He held up his hands in confusion.

'And this is?' he said, sounding annoyed.

'Oh, come on, love. You know her. You do. She knows you, don't you?' Olive looked at Annie with a mixture of apprehension and hope.

Annie thought it best to cut to the chase. 'Annie Parker,' she said brightly. 'Mile End?'

A glimmer of recognition crept into Wayne's eyes. He stood and took off the spectacles he'd been using to read the newspaper. Annie noted that he was a strapping man, though not flabby. He'd managed to hold on to most of his hair, too. Peering at each other, they both said, in chorus, 'Oh, yeah, I see it now,' and then they laughed.

'Annie Parker. As I live and breathe,' said Wayne. His wife was looking up at him with a surprised expression. 'Annie and I were in school together, Merle,' he explained. 'Annie, my wife, Merle. Merle, meet the only girl who ever gave me a black eye. Remember?'

Annie grinned. 'Not on purpose, doll. If you recall, I was trying to do a handstand against the wall of the school but I lost me balance and caught you a cropper on the way down. Maybe if you hadn't been so interested in trying to untuck my dress from inside my knickers you wouldn't have got clobbered, eh?'

Back patting and hugging ensued and pretty soon Annie was settled on the sofa with a gin and tonic and an opportunity to relive many old memories. A slight sense of guilt nibbled at her conscience as she chatted happily about old classmates and shared or gleaned information about what had become of them. The same process for beloved, or hated, teachers, then for old out-of-school friends and contacts. Eventually, Merle Saxby took her leave to busy herself in the kitchen, with Olive's help, and their call to join them at the table in the dining room was met by Annie and Wayne with a cheer.

Settling herself at the table, with a fresh gin and tonic and a glass of good Cabernet Sauvignon in front of her, Annie felt it appropriate to raise her glass to her hosts. Her smile was genuine when she spoke.

'Well, I'd never have guessed I'd be doing this tonight. I came here to Wales expecting to be eating pie and chips in the pub, on me own, having yomped about the countryside a bit, and here I am thinking about being the blackboard monitor at Mile End Juniors and breakin' me arm when I tried to play football against twinkle-toes Saxby here.' She raised her glass toward Wayne. 'Took me out like I was a boy, you did, and I know that was one of the reasons we were such good friends afterwards. Never treated me any different because I was the tallest in the class, boy or girl, and never made fun of me feet, me big bum, or me skin color. Ta, doll.'

Wayne grinned.

Annie next raised her glass toward her host's mother. 'I don't know why you were in the Coach and Horses today, Olive, but I'm glad you were, and that you recognized me and invited me here. And thanks for this lovely dinner, Merle. Roast beef and Yorkshire pud is just about my favorite meal. And the promise of spotted dick for afters has got me mouth watering already. What a treat on a Saturday night. But what will you have tomorrow, if you're having this fancy roast on a Saturday night?'

'Sunday is sports in this house,' replied Merle. 'No time for a big meal, so I always do one on Saturday. Right, love?'

Wayne nodded.

Annie thought it a bit odd, but was grateful for

the strange habit, nonetheless. 'Cheers to you all,' she said, raising her glass. 'Bottoms up!'

'Cheers! Bottoms up!'

They all drank.

Silence, punctuated by Annie's 'mmmm's' and 'lovely gravy' were all that followed for several minutes, then the conversation renewed.

'I wonder what Eustelle would think of this,' mused Annie.

'We could phone her when we've finished here,' said Olive. 'Love to hear her voice again, I would. That lovely Caribbean accent. I can see her now, plain as day, standing at the gates of the infants' school on your first day, Annie. Cried like a baby, she did. You didn't look back once, just ran into the doors and you was gone.'

'I don't remember that,' admitted Annie with a pang of guilt. *Poor Eustelle.* 'I do remember Mr Locklear, though. I dare say he wasn't really that big, or that old, but he seemed it to me. Remember him, Wayne?'

Wayne nodded and washed down a mouthful of roast potato with a gulp of wine.

His mother answered Annie as he drank. 'He was the only male teacher at that school of yours. Funny that. Terrible what happened to him. Did you hear about it?'

Annie shook her head.

Olive shook her head heavily. 'His house burned down. Him in it. About ten – no, twenty years ago now. Very sad.'

Annie was taken aback. She didn't know anyone who had died in such a tragic way. 'Oh, Gordon Bennett! That's awful. What happened?'

134

'No one knew,' replied Olive. 'Went up in minutes, the paper said. Nothing anyone could do. His cat got out and that was that. Saved the houses either side, though they were flooded, of course. All the water. Still, lucky no one else was killed. Tore down the whole row in the end, they did. Wasn't that one of the early lots you bought, love?' she asked her son.

'Yeah. Weird, really,' said Wayne thoughtfully. 'I managed to get a row of six houses for a knock-down price, literally, and it made a real difference to the business at the time. I had no idea until later that Mr Locklear was the one who'd been killed.'

'Yes, you did, love,' replied his mother. 'I remember at the time you said what a shame it was. You even knew that man who adopted his cat. Gilbert, wasn't it? The cat, not the man. Don't know his name.'

Wayne rolled his eyes toward Annie. 'I think you're misremembering, Mum,' he said, smiling.

Olive concentrated on slicing a piece of beef and muttered, 'I expect so, Wayne. If you say so, love.'

'More of anything for you, Annie?' asked Merle, flicking her lustrous dark hair that showed not a strand of gray, despite what Annie reckoned to be her forty-odd years.

'No, ta, Merle. I think I'd better save some room for afters.'

As post-dining relaxation ensued, Annie thought about telephoning her mother. Eustelle would enjoy talking to Olive, she thought, and it couldn't do any harm. So, after a large, steaming spotted dick had been served and heaped with glistening custard, then consumed, she dialed her mother's number, told her where she was, mentioned, as discreetly as she could, that her mother shouldn't talk about Annie's work, and passed the handset to Olive.

'Eustelle? Eustelle Parker? Ooo, how lovely . . .' began Olive Saxby, giggling.

'Let me show you around the place, while Merle's clearing up,' said Wayne close to Annie's ear. 'Mum'll be on the phone for ages. I hope your mum manages to get a word in edgeways.'

Annie laughed. 'I talk a lot, doll, but it's Eustelle who taught me how. I think she'll give as good as she gets. And, yes, I'd love to see the place. Looks like a big house. But I should help Merle with things, first.'

'No, I insist you go with Wayne,' replied his wife. 'It won't take me long to clear this lot into the dishwasher, then I'm going to make some coffee. Decaf all right for you, Annie?'

Annie hated decaffeinated coffee. She didn't see the point of drinking it, but, to be polite, she agreed it would be just smashing.

'Come on then,' urged Wayne. 'Let's start upstairs and work our way back down.'

'I could do with moving around a bit to let that lovely meal go down,' said Annie to Merle as her host led her out of the kitchen and back toward the front door.

Clambering up the stairs, Annie knew she was hankering for a smoke, but she told herself she'd have to wait. It occurred to her that she might

136

get some insights into the local community from Wayne, so she formulated her attack and began.

'So, if you've been here five years, you must know a lot of the people hereabouts,' she began, addressing Wayne's back as he scaled the stairs ahead of her.

He half turned as he climbed and said, 'Not too many. We don't mix too much locally. There's a nice bloke on this estate who comes from Northamptonshire and made a pile running a private minibus and coach company. His wife and Merle get along fine. Go off to this little spa type of place in Hay-on-Wye, they do. You know, get everything waxed and painted, or buffed and bronzed. He and I have been known to enjoy the odd brandy or two together when the girls are off primping. But we don't go into the village much. Mum likes to, so she does things like going to the post office for us, and so forth.'

'I see that landlord at the Coach and Horses is from Bethnal Green,' said Annie brightly as they reached the topmost landing. 'Small world, innit?'

Wayne laughed. 'Yeah, now that was a turn up for the books. Never knew him back in London, but he seems a decent sort. Jacko, right?'

Annie nodded. *Decent sort?*

'This is ours,' said Wayne opening a double door. 'It's worth taking a look just for the view,' he added as Annie peered inside.

She stepped into a sumptuous room in which a king-size bed was dwarfed. Trying to ignore the massive television, the two chaises and the open door which showed her a marble-clad en suite bathroom, she walked to the floor-to-ceiling

137

window which looked out from the back of the house, in the same direction as the floor-to-ceiling windows in the kitchen area. Because of the three-story height, the view was quite different. Instead of looking into the delightful garden of the house, here she had a view from the crest of the hill toward what she guessed must be Chellingworth Hall. Set to one side of the main edifice was a smaller building on a lower hillock. She guessed that must be the Dower House. Neither building was floodlit, but she could clearly see lights at windows, suggesting life inside the buildings. She imagined Mavis and Christine working hard on their investigative tasks and a chill of guilt ran down her spine.

'What's that?' she asked innocently. 'Or should I say where's that?'

'Chellingworth Hall on the left, the Dower House on the Chellingworth Estate on the right. Owned by the idiot duke. Henry Twyst. Nut job.'

'A duke? Have you met him?' Annie feigned excitement.

'Yeah, a few times. Mainly at charity things they have there. You know the sort of thing – marquees in the grounds. God forbid we'd be allowed to actually eat inside the hallowed place itself. They open it to the public, but they never welcome people with open arms. They're sitting on a gold mine, if only they knew it. The things I could do with that place, given half a chance.'

'Like?' asked Annie, feeling truly curious.

A light began to shine in Wayne's eyes as he gazed into the deepening darkness. 'Not just events, like weddings and so forth, but a wonderful hotel and country club. Six thousand acres they've got and none of it used much. They've got a bit of farming there, you know the sort of stuff, with wild boars, goats for fancy cheeses, that sort of thing, but it's so underused. All they'd have to do would be get a bit of planning permission here, and put up a few temporary structures there, and they could really rake it in.'

He looked at Annie and said, 'Got no kids, he hasn't. Not likely to either. He's a weird one. His sister's one of them artsy types and his mother's as daft as a brush. Batty as hell the lot of 'em. And when they go, well, I don't think there's anyone left of their lot. The title will die and I'm betting they'll sell off the estate.'

Annie smiled. 'They haven't got some distant cousin somewhere who'll get the lot? You know, like on *Downton Abbey*?'

Wayne looked puzzled. 'Why'd you say that?' he asked, an edge to his voice.

''Cos I watch *Downton Abbey*,' said Annie in as matter-of-fact a tone as she could muster. She wondered why he'd bitten her head off.

Wayne shrugged. 'Ah, right. Not my cup of tea, that. Haven't got any long-lost relatives that I know of. Though that type breed like rabbits, don't they?'

'Well, not the present ones, by the sound of it,' replied Annie, smiling. 'Really mad, are they? Or just, you know, posh barking?'

Wayne grinned. 'What's the difference? The old one's the worst. But I reckon the son's not far behind.' Wayne walked away from the window and added, 'But that's enough about the Twyst family, come and see my sports room. It's just across the landing.'

Annie smiled politely, though she couldn't imagine it would be very interesting. Wayne marched across the landing that straddled the entire top of the staircase and threw open another set of double doors. This time, clever lighting revealed what Annie could only imagine was a male paradise: a billiard table, dart board, large button-backed leather chairs and the biggest TV screen she'd yet seen in the house, plus a well-stocked bar.

'Doesn't Merle mind you having this on the same floor as your bedroom?' Annie was genuinely puzzled.

'One of the reasons Merle and me got together was because she loves all this as much as I do. Besides, we neither of us want to risk having to go up or down any stairs when we're done in here and want to hit the hay. So it's perfect.'

Annie wandered around the room making suitable noises. She looked at the photographs and trophies that lined the walls, of which her host was obviously very proud. Some of the team photos were old enough that she could spot Wayne in his football-playing days. Others were clearly more recent.

'Look, there's someone I recognize,' said Annie, pointing to the toothsome vision of Tristan Thomas.

Wayne laughed. 'Oh, yeah, that Thomas bloke from the antiques shop in the village. He's always around,' he said wearily.

Annie did a double take at one photograph,

then looked back at another. 'Is this bloke in two different teams?' she asked.

Wayne joined Annie in front of the photographs, looked at where she was pointing and said, 'Oh, yeah. That team's the one I sponsor in the village, and that's one I sponsor at the Hoop and Stick in Mile End. You know it?'

Annie shook her head.

'Nah, probably not,' he replied. 'They did it up and renamed it. It used to be The George. On Bancroft Road.'

'The one along from Mile End hospital?'

Wayne nodded. 'They managed to keep most of the character of the place and the football team there brings people who work at the hospital together with the local community – such as it is these days. I bung 'em a few quid now and again and they all buy me a drink when I drop in.'

'So who's the bloke who's in both teams? And how'd he manage that?' asked Annie.

Wayne peered at the photos. 'Well, you've got sharp eyes, I'll give you that. It's Mickey James. Son of the landlord at the place you're staying. He used to play here. Now he plays there.'

'Oh right. Jacko mentioned something about him having cousins around Bethnal Green and his son being there these days. You got anyone still living in that neck of the woods now, Wayne?'

Wayne shook his head. 'Nah. Little Connie, my girl that I was telling you about earlier, she lives in the States. Me brother's dead and his wife remarried some bloke out in Essex. His kids are still somewhere in the old place, but I don't hear much about 'em. Anyway, enough about all that, let me show you the guest facilities on the floor below. Pretty swish they are, even if I do say so meself. Merle's to thank for all the decorating, of course, not me. She's good at it, ain't she?'

Annie nodded as Wayne closed up his surprisingly fascinating sports room, and tried to think of how she was going to get out of Wayne Saxby's house and back to the Coach and Horses as quickly as she could, so that she could tell Carol that there was a pub football team in Mile End that wore black tracksuits and black woolen hats sporting blue bobbles.

FOURTEEN

FROM: CH
TO: MM, AP, CW-S
REF: RESPONSE TO ALL YOUR DAY ONE QUERIES

1.ANNIE QUERIES:
NOTE TO TEAM: ANNIE NOW LOCATED AT HOME OF WAYNE SAXBY, UNTIL SHE RETURNS TO COACH AND HORSES PUB OVERNIGHT SATURDAY/SUNDAY
a) John James (Jacko) 57, landlord of Coach and Horse pub in Anwen-by-Wye, Delyth James (wife) of same address: he's been in trouble for receiving stolen goods, but not

142

since he turned twenty. An electrician employed by a sub-contractor in Tower Hamlets for ten years. Nothing on her. Business seems clean, but reduced profits in past three years. No local news stories, except when the pub hosts charity or fundraising events. Delyth James, 52, is the daughter of Mr Stanley and Mrs Florence Davies, of Hay-on-Wye. (NB: Newspaper story about him buying the pub for his daughter. He made his money in haulage into and out of the port of Manchester. He sold up in 1963, when the port was the third largest in the UK, and 'retired' to Hay-on-Wye.) Jacko and Delyth have a son, Michael James, 23. Left school at 16, been in trouble a lot with the Dyfed-Powys police. A few drugs charges and problems with causing a fracas – three times, but never at his father's pub. The lad seems to have a temper. He's also been in court in London; he seems to spend a good deal of time back in his father's old haunts in the East End with some members of extended family. Not a good family. They pop up all over east London. Checking a range of names I've uncovered, as a family group they seem to be into all sorts,

143

including petty theft and some semi-organized shoplifting. The son's not been pulled in in connection with any of that.

b) Tristan Thomas, 46, antiques dealer with a shop in Anwen-by-Wye. Interesting man. Seems to have had a wide variety of jobs, none of which had anything to do with art or antiques until about ten years ago. He holds a lease on the shop A TASTE OF TIME in the village for another five years. It's owned by the Chellingworth Estate. Looks like a marginally profitable business, but turnover is down in last five years to about a third of what it was before. No qualifications of any sort that I can find. Just popped up and started calling himself a valuer. Often questioned by police about stolen goods (maybe to be expected in his line of business?). Never charged with anything. Originally from Cardiff. Ex-wife still lives there. Divorced and single now.

c) Wayne Saxby, 54. Originally from Mile End, London. Owns house in Highridge Estate, which is made up of new executive homes on land just outside Anwen-by-Wye. Married to second wife, Merle Saxby. He made a pile in real estate, as one of the moving forces behind the gentrification of London's East End. Sounds like a lot of his old 'friends' weren't sorry to see him move to Wales. Newspaper and online stories about him sticking to the letter of the law, but not to the spirit of it, nor being a good or trustworthy neighbor. Seems he bought up a lot of properties very cheap, then either developed them himself, or flipped them to others to do the same thing. 'Community displacement' is a phrase people use when they write about him. One daughter from first marriage, Connie Shulman married an American property developer Stephen Shulman and lives in Miami. Two kids. Doesn't visit her family much. Wayne's mother, Olive Saxby, lives with him at the Welsh house. He met his second wife when she became his personal assistant, at the property development company. He was still married to wife #1 at the time, but not for long. She didn't wipe him out, due to some clever legal footwork on his part, and now she's remarried. They don't keep in touch. From local Welsh press clippings I gather he's a pillar of the local community around Anwen-by-Wye. He supports a lot of charities and sends money to, rather than taking part in, local fundraising efforts. Seems to be a pretty big supporter of local football clubs. Still owns a fair amount of property in the Mile End/Bethnal Green area, mainly rentals. Not known as a slum-landlord, but not far from it. Multi-millionaire, solid invest-ments, property speculation.

2. MAVIS'S QUERIES
   a) Photos of the bobble hat (thank Her Grace for taking photos of the label as well as the hat!) mean I've been able to track it. Good news – it's made in the UK. The manufacturer is near Birmingham. I will talk to them on Monday – there's no one there who can help me until then. Their website says their smallest order is for 250 items, but they can make thousands. Will get back to you when I find out more. Let's hope they didn't make thousands of this design!
   b) The information about the alarm system at the Dower House is avail-able on the website of the manu-facturing company (which I find odd, but there you go!), but here's what you need to know. It's a good system and the information you gave me about the installers, Mavis, tells me it was well installed. No

cowboys involved. I've studied the specifications. There is no easy way to disarm the system without the codes, or significant knowledge of electronic circuitry. However, can you please check and send photos of how the power is hooked up to the system? It's supposed to have a back-up battery, which should kick in if the power goes off, but the website suggests a few ways of using a back-up generator as well. I'm going to check with the installation company on Monday about the specific people who installed the system. Not impossible to bypass, with the right knowledge, it seems.

c) Jennifer Newbury is telling the truth. I've identified her correctly and she has an online CV that tallies with her work at an old folks' home and before that. Nothing else on her right now. No red flags. Social media suggests she had a boyfriend during her pre-old folks' home years, but not since.

d) Ian Cottesloe has received every clearance required to work with at-risk youth and appears in local press as a keen supporter of, and volunteer with, local youth groups, scouts, football, rugby and cricket teams. No other apparent interests. All social media activity seems to be linked to these groups. No apparent girlfriend.

e) Mary Wilson, cook, has a CV that goes back about thirty years and is accessible through the website of the agency that found her for the Dower House. I'll speak to the agency on Monday morning.

3. CHRISTINE'S QUERIES
I need some feedback, Christine! Annie and Mavis have checked in. It's seven on Saturday evening. I'm going to phone you. What are you doing?

MORE:
Having just spoken to Christine I will send this email to you all anyway. NOTE TO TEAM: Christine is dining with our client and will check in via email tonight. My mobile will be beside me – now I'm going to put my feet up. I wish you all a very pleasant and productive evening. Call me if you need me.

FIFTEEN

Christine Wilson-Smythe picked up the Waterford crystal champagne flute and toasted Henry Twyst. It was quite clear to her that he'd made special arrangements for their pre-dinner drinks, because a fire was roaring in what was obviously an under-used fireplace in the paneled library.

The evening light was all but gone beyond the windows of Chellingworth Hall and there was a definite chill in the air.

'Daddy's always moaning about how much it costs to keep our place in Ireland warm, but you do a splendid job here, Henry. My room is delightfully cozy and this fire's a treat.'

Henry glowed with more than the warmth of the flames behind him. Christine noticed, as he stood at the hearth, that his suit was a little tight around his middle and he couldn't move his arms as easily as she suspected he'd been able to when the suit had been new and had fitted him.

She perched comfortably on a delightful example of Jacobean needlepoint upholstery and observed, 'You seem to have very effective staff, Henry. The place is very well kept. I adore the flowers. From your borders?'

Henry nodded. He didn't seem to be blessed with the ability to converse at all, which worried Christine. If she was to draw him out about the people on his list, she needed him to open up to her. Noticing that he'd already drained his glass, Christine said, 'Don't wait for me to finish before taking some more, Henry. I like to see a man enjoy himself. Go ahead, please.'

As she'd suspected, Henry gleefully replenished his glass and refreshed hers by half an inch. Christine wondered if she'd found the way to loosen his tongue. After yet another glass of champagne, dinner was announced and Henry took Christine's arm to lead her to the dining room. Using the seat at the head of the table, and the one to its right, Christine noted from the setting that several courses were to be served, and she hoped that none of them would be too heavy.

As the first course arrived, then the second, Christine tried to enjoy the ambience of the green brocade-walled room and the small talk that she managed to winkle out of her host. Eventually her ploy of encouraging Henry to drink more than herself began to bear fruit. After the fish course, by which time Henry was well into his second bottle of total consumption, Christine began to list names and Henry began to react.

Responding to her first query, he sounded flustered as he began, 'I cannot believe that Bob Fernley has anything to do with my mother finding a wretched bobble hat in her dining room. He managed the estate for my father and I trust him totally. He runs the entire farm business for heaven's sake. And his wife, Elizabeth? She's a pillar of the local community. Without her doing what she does – much of which is what would be expected of my wife, if I had one – the whole fabric of estate and village life would start to unravel.'

Christine couldn't help but wonder how much pride Elizabeth Fernley might derive from being seen in such a flattering light within the local environs.

'And your housekeeper, Violet Davies?' pressed Christine.

Henry looked flabbergasted. 'You met her when we visited the office. What on earth would a woman like that be doing in possession of a bobble hat?'

Christine had to admit that Henry made a valid point. Mrs Violet Davies was in her late fifties and built on the classic Welsh chassis, styled after a cottage loaf. Her nylon, belted housecoat was anything but flattering and Christine had noticed that the woman had a very small head. She was convinced that this wasn't an illusion created by the girth of the rest of the woman's body, and recalled that Carol was always bemoaning the fact that no hats ever fitted her because they were always too big for her. Christine wondered if there was some strange Welsh gene that endowed people of that race with particularly small heads, then decided that was foolish. In any case, the bobble hat found by Henry's mother had been a medium size, and she was sure it wouldn't have fitted Mrs Davies, even if she could have come up with some bizarre reason for the woman wanting to don such an item.

As Henry rattled on about how no one in his household could possibly come under suspicion for whatever had happened, Christine began to become more convinced that, in all probability, the bobble hat had belonged to the disappearing corpse. She hoped that Mavis was having better luck than she at finding out if anyone inside the Dower House might have been likely to disarm the alarm to allow an intruder, or intruders, to enter the premises.

'Tell me again what the police said about the drugging of your mother's household,' she said.

Henry's gaping mouth told her that she'd raised

the topic out of the blue and that he'd twigged to the fact that she hadn't been listening to him at all. He looked sulky as he refilled his glass with the last of the wine from the decanter that had arrived to accompany the lamb course. Christine felt guilty, but impatient. Henry had invited her here to work for him, after all, yet he seemed content to poo-poo all her questions.

Finally realizing that she was waiting for an answer, Henry put down his glass and looked Christine straight in the eye. 'I sent all the information I had to your office. The woman I spoke to on the telephone there told me that she would disseminate it to your team. What more can I tell you?'

Christine sat forward in her seat, leaning toward Henry. 'I gathered that an assumption was made about drugging, but that there was no proof. Is that correct?'

Henry nodded. 'Yes. Everything used to prepare and serve the stew that was eaten that night had been washed up and put away before anyone retired. The assumption of the staff having been drugged was based upon their statements that they each felt tired as the evening wore on, they all therefore went to their rooms earlier than usual and all slept very soundly. No one has any idea what might have been put in the stew to make this happen.'

'Were any tests, such as blood tests, conducted to try to ascertain the nature of the drug?'

'The police didn't think it necessary,' replied Henry dryly.

'And have the local police given you any

information as a result of their testing of various foodstuffs they removed from the kitchen after the event?'

'No, but I don't see how they could, given that all the stew had been eaten or washed away. They only took a few carrots and an onion or two. It seems ridiculous that they could find anything amiss with a selection of random root vegetables.'

Christine tried to not show her irritation as she changed to a different approach. 'Was it unusual for your mother to not eat dinner?'

Henry wriggled his shoulders uncomfortably. Christine had noticed that this was a normal affectation for Henry when he felt he was being blamed for something. 'Not that I am aware of,' was his telling reply.

Christine tried not to sigh. Henry was obviously concerned about his mother, but he had made it pretty clear to her that he looked to her staff to take primary responsibility for her wellbeing.

'I haven't met your mother, Henry, at least, not since I was very young. I know she had a reputation as a fine horsewoman and was a well-known breeder and trainer of Jack Russell terriers. Tell me, have there been any other changes in her behavior about which you are not telling me?'

Again, Henry did the shoulder thing.

He replied grudgingly, 'She's been seen talking to herself and she ignores people when they speak to her. As though they were not there. Mother's never been like that before.' He spoke quietly, disquiet lacing his voice. 'I've overheard the staff mention it. I haven't seen it myself.

And . . . well, there was the incident with the mushrooms.'

'What incident with the mushrooms?' asked Christine calmly. *Poison? An attempt on her life?*

'It was at the shop in the village. There is only one. It's a post office and a general store thingy. Mother was there one day. She insists upon walking into the village on occasion, despite her years. Anyway, one day she threw all the mushrooms onto the pavement, outside the shop. It caused quite a commotion. Ian had to be sent to fetch her back to the Dower House in the car.'

It wasn't what Christine had expected.

'Did she explain her actions?'

Henry wriggled. 'She said that no one should have to eat the mushrooms.' He sounded mortally wounded. 'I paid for them, of course.'

'Anything else?' asked Christine with trepidation.

'The herb garden.'

Christine didn't need to do more than raise her eyebrows to force Henry to elaborate.

'Mother has never, ever, shown the slightest interest in anything that grows. Animals, she loves them all, but plants, flowers, trees – they have never interested her. To her, they are just *there*. Then, about a year ago, she insisted that Ian dig up a whole section of her walled garden to plant a herb garden. And she's been tending it herself. It's extraordinary. She insists that everything she grows is used up here at the hall and in the tea rooms, and so forth, as well as in her own kitchens. The cooks are very happy to accommodate her and I have to say that her efforts have resulted in some cost-saving for us. But mother working the soil? Tending crops? It's bizarre.'

Christine gave Henry's comments some thought, then returned to her original point.

'The police established that the stew was unattended in the kitchen for quite some time, allowing access to the pot by anyone in the household, and that, on that particular day, several people were known to have visited the Dower House. Correct?'

'Yes,' said Henry, looking at his empty glass sadly. 'Elizabeth Fernley called in with some eggs. Mrs Davies, my cook, visited Mrs Wilson, mother's cook, to take tea. Stephanie Timbers and a chap from the pub in the village had an appointment with mother to discuss plans for the harvest supper at St David's Church. We provide the food for the supper, and he cooks it.'

'Which pub?'

'I believe it's the Coach and Horses. Yes, that's it.'

'Tell me about Stephanie,' said Christine.

'Look, I know you said you didn't want dessert, but would you mind if we moved to the library where I can smoke?' said Henry plaintively.

'It would be my pleasure,' said Christine. Henry helped her from her seat and they returned to the library. The fire had been stoked, a bottle of port, a humidor and a large crystal ashtray had been set on a small table beside the fire, and Henry motioned for Christine to sit. She felt quite at home, so she wafted her black chiffon to one side, so that she could pull her feet up onto the chair. Henry's raised eyebrows descended as he poured drinks, lit a very large cigar, and settled into what was obviously his favorite, very well-worn leather seat. Christine imagined that his father might have felt the same way about it.

'So, you were going to tell me about Stephanie Timbers,' said Christine, enjoying the fumes of her port, but merely sipping from her glass.

'Fine woman,' said Henry expansively.

Christine was taken aback. Intrigued, even. This was the first time she'd seen Henry Twyst exhibit anything but a polite warmth for a member of the staff at the hall.

'Full of energy and a good brain too. A little older than you, dear . . .' He was now beginning to sound patronizing, and Christine began to worry about how much was too much for Henry to drink to be useful to her. 'She has brought a new vitality to this place since she arrived,' he enthused. 'Been here a few years now and we've really noticed the difference. Very good CV. Lots of experience in the world of commerce, you see. Lots of big clients. Not that we are big, and we certainly don't have the sort of money she'd like us to spend on what she calls targeted communications, but a good egg. Not a very illustrious past in terms of upbringing, but her energy and intelligence have brought her a long way.'

'So you don't think she could be—' Christine didn't get any further.

'I won't hear of it!' exclaimed Henry, almost dropping his cigar. 'Stephanie Timbers is a first-class type. Don't libel her here.' Christine noted that Henry was quite pink in the face, though she couldn't be certain if that was because of a special feeling he might have toward Stephanie Timbers, or the amount of alcohol he'd consumed during the evening and his closeness to the fire.

'It would be slander,' muttered Christine, 'but I know what you mean. And I didn't intend to imply that—'

Once again she was interrupted by her host, who ground his cigar into the ashtray and plopped his glass of port onto the table. 'I won't hear of it, I say,' he snapped. 'I did not invite you here to make accusations against people I like.' He seemed to suddenly be aware of what he'd said and wriggled his shoulders. 'These are the people I trust most in this world. I'll thank you to not besmirch their character. I believe it is time I retired and I'll be so bold as to suggest you do the same.'

Christine decided that, despite the fact that this man was both her client and her host, she had to regain control of the situation. He might be almost twice her age, but she suspected he was far more than twice as intoxicated as she.

Christine stood. 'Thank you for a delightful evening, Henry. I think you've made a very good suggestion. I shall go to my room now and look forward to pursuing my investigation first thing in the morning. I've arranged for coffee to be brought up to me early, but I will join you for breakfast. Until then . . .' She held out her hand to Henry, who looked as though he'd been smacked in the face by a large haddock.

Saving any alternative, Henry shook Christine's hand and she left the library, seeking the solace

157

of her own room and a chance to catch up on any messages that Carol had sent. She fumed silently as she mounted the grand staircase. If Henry Devereaux Twyst didn't want her help, she wondered, why had he approached her? By the time she reached the top of the stairs she had her answer: he wanted her to explain away the bobble hat, not find out why it had come into his mother's hands. She hoped that Mavis had good news about the woman's state of mind. Henry's tales about some particularly dotty behavior had Christine concerned, but she felt more determined than ever to get to the bottom of it all.

SIXTEEN

Mavis MacDonald settled herself into her magnificent bed and pushed her reading glasses onto her nose. She was looking forward to reading what Carol had sent by way of research, so powered up her tablet device, downloaded the email attachments to a message and opened up the document.

As she read, she made pencil notes in a little pad beside her, smiling at the fact that her handwriting was so illegible – to anyone but herself – that many doctors with whom she'd worked at the beginning of her nursing career had decried its form. Mavis, therefore, had two distinct varieties of cursive upon which she could call: her natural scrawl – ideal for her work as an enquiry agent when she needed secrecy, and her legible form – which she reserved for those occasions when it was essential that others could read what she had written.

Once she had read, she began to type. She'd insisted that her tablet had a real keyboard, because she just couldn't cope with typing little letters on a screen, so her speed and accuracy were adequate.

She reported back to Carol, copying in her two other colleagues, that she had now met the three members of the dowager's household. Many of her questions about Jennifer Newbury had already been answered by the results of Carol's research, as had her interest in Ian Cottesloe's involvement with local youth groups, about which he'd enthused when she'd been wandering the servants' quarters with him. She requested that Carol try to find out more about Mary Wilson, to whom Mavis had taken an instant dislike.

'I cannot find it in me to condemn a woman who cooks so well, but she has the most acid of tongues and an unpleasant nature. I know you'll appreciate that I am attempting to not be overly judgmental when I say she has an edge to her that could slice a girder. I suspect you'll find pointers in her past, because a woman brimming with so much anger and spite could not have lived her entire life without one or two wee incidents somewhere along the line. I suggest you also check her maiden name, Mary Vaughan. She's a very large woman, in all dimensions, and I will admit that I find her intimidating, but that's not the issue. She has a temper and a sense of

159

entitlement, and those do not sit well together, in my experience.'

Mavis continued to read her penciled notes, this time, the ones she'd made earlier in the day. She quite happily spoke aloud as she read and formulated her requests and notes.

'Althea Twyst seems to be in generally good physical shape, though it is clear from the way that her clothing sits upon her frame that she is losing height and girth. It is not unusual for a woman of her age, and it would appear to be a gradual decline. Her bowed back is, I suspect, the result of the natural aging process. She suffers from arthritic pain, largely in parts of her body where bones have been broken as the result of riding accidents. Her eyesight is, I believe, very good for one of her age. I see no signs of cataracts and she wears spectacles to allow for easier reading. Her mid- and long-distance sight seems good. I do not detect any signs of depression, and her medicine cabinet shows she is on few medications, save statins and, when necessary, over-the-counter painkillers. I have noted no signs of dementia, to date, though that is a condition which can present in many forms and might only be detected over a period of time. Her wits and brain seem sharp.'

Mavis thought for a moment about what she had gleaned about the night in question, reread her notes from her two major discussions with Althea, then began to type. As usual she tried to convey to Carol and, through her, to her other colleagues, the reasons why she was saying what she was.

If her brain and eyes are sound, then the question remains, what did she see that night? I have now had a chance to take her through her experiences twice: once before, and once after, dinner. On both occasions her story remained the same, but there were some interesting details that I would like to put to you all for consideration.

a) I believe that her wee dog, McFli, played a greater part in the proceedings that we had been led to believe. It was he who awakened his mistress, it was also he who drew her attention to the dining room, rather than any of the other rooms. According to Althea, McFli showed considerable interest in the body, which is to be expected, but she mentioned that he was darting about in the dining room while she gave her attention to the figure on the floor. I believe there is every possibility that the bobble hat she found might not have originally been lying where she discovered it. McFli might have picked it up from anywhere in the room, or possibly even another room, then dropped it between the body and the fireplace, which is where it lay, according to Althea.

b) On both occasions, Althea spoke of a 'hot smell' in the dining room. She cannot be more specific. I am

161

going to try some experiments (I shall burn and extinguish candles, for example) tomorrow, to see if I can recreate the aroma, so I will give you more information if I can. But please bear this in mind when making your enquiries. I'm sorry to be so vague, but I only have her words to work with.

c) I believe that all three members of the dowager's household would be capable of lying about being fast asleep that night, and all three have the ability to disarm, and rearm, the alarm system. I will investigate the power supply to the alarm first thing in the morning, as requested by Carol, and will report back via text.

Mavis stopped typing and gave her report some thought. It had been a long and largely productive day, but she was tired. She looked over at the folding alarm clock she took with her on every trip away from her home. She'd long ago learned that it was foolish to rely upon unknown alarm clocks, or even an electronic device, so always packed the small, collapsible clock that her younger son, James, had given her as a gift for a long-ago Mothering Sunday. Behind the face, in the half of the shell that could just be seen when it was opened, she'd carefully inserted a photograph of the entire family, taken when the boys were small, before her poor, dear husband's early death. The faded colors, sunburned faces, summer clothes and a backdrop of the Lake District's picturesque landscape always made her smile. It was happy memories of a too-short but joyful marriage, and the knowledge that both her boys were now, themselves, settled with supportive wives with bonnie children, that soothed Mavis MacDonald to sleep that night, though in her dreams her three grandsons appeared to her wearing hoodies and bobble hats, and running about with wee dogs tucked beneath their arms as they raided a jewelry shop in London for a collection of fire irons which turned out to be the plants, Red Hot Pokers, which she recalled her grannie used to grow in great clumps in the front garden of her slate-roofed bungalow in Dumfries.

SEVENTEEN

Hello Girls – Annie here, as if you couldn't guess. Sorry I'm so late reporting in. You'll never guess what – I thought my cover was blown today, but I think I got away with it. DON'T PANIC, Mavis, cos I know you will. It all went OK. I'll tell you. So, I got off the bus and went to the pub. Met a bloke on the way who turned my tummy with his teeth. Tristan Thomas – Carol put him in her report. Antiques dealer, he SAYS, but I think he's dodgy. Not because of his teeth, though, frankly, they're enough, but I saw him later in a photo . . . right, let me tell you. Sorry. No, I'm not redoing all this, just follow along.

Before I got to the pub this antiques dealer introduced himself, more about him later. At the pub I met the landlord and his wife. They have a son. They are all in Carol's report. My impressions? He looks the part, but he acts like a fish out of water, even after all the years he's been running the pub. Doesn't fit. She's a local, but looks like she dresses from the markets. Welsh. Bottle blonde. Chip on her shoulder about something. Possibly him. They've got a son, like I said, but he's back in London with family. More about him later too.

Anyway, I was chatting to Jacko, the landlord, when this blast from the past shows up and recognized me. Olive Saxby was friends with Eustelle back in our Mile End days. I was in school with Wayne, her son. He's only living in that posh estate up on the hill here. Had to go there for dinner. I couldn't get out of it. Big house. Mansion, really. Ugly as sin and decorated in early Hammer Horror. Plus bling. On his second wife. She's all right. Merle. Good cook. Quiet. Likes her drink. Olive doesn't anymore, and I think I know why. Diabetes. Anyway, Wayne was showing me around and – drum roll please – I think I found the bobble hats! Yeah, me! I know ☺

Wayne's into football and sponsors the Coach and Horses pub team here in Anwen-by-Wye, AND a team at the Hoop and Stick pub in Mile End. The kid from the pub here belongs to both teams. Mickey James, he goes by. Michael. And the team at the Stick and Hoop wears black tracksuits and those black and blue bobble hats. There you go. Sorted. Someone from that football team left their hat at the Dower House. My money's on the kid from the pub, even though his dad says he's back in London. It's a link, right? And all because Olive asked me to dinner.

I've been thinking about it, and Wayne didn't seem too pleased that I'd noticed that Mickey James was on both teams. And that Toothy Thomas antiques bloke also sponsors the team here in the village, so him and Wayne must know each other, though Wayne came over all vague when I asked him about it. And Wayne Saxby isn't vague about anything. I noticed.

So that's good. Right? I got some solid intel, as they say. Tomorrow I'm going to try to find out more about Mickey James, the links back to the East End, and if the bloke, Ian, who works at the Dower House, is part of the football team in the village. If your notes are right, Carol (and I'm sure they are) then he's happy to kick a ball about with anyone, so I think he might be. He could be another link. A real insider.

One more thing, Carol. If you've got any time, and I know it's not a priority, could you look up some info about an old teacher of mine. Mr Locklear taught the reception class at Mile End Infants. Seems he died in a fire at his home back in the 1990s. I liked him. I remember him as very kind. I didn't even know he was dead. I don't know why, but I've got a horrible feeling that the fire in which he died might not have started innocently. If you haven't got the time, don't worry, I'll do it myself when I get back. Ta, anyway.

OK. Bed now. I'm knackered. Must be all this fresh air. Up and at 'em in the morning, even though it's Sunday. Hope you're all OK. Night night.

EIGHTEEN

As midnight on Saturday became one a.m. on Sunday, Carol Hill lay awake listening to her husband snoring. If she didn't know better she'd have sworn she'd eaten a plate of bricks for dinner. She couldn't get comfortable. Wondering how she'd feel in a few months' time, when the baby was bigger than an orange – which she knew it was, at four months gone – she sat up and decided that going downstairs and walking around a bit was her best option. She didn't want to disturb David, so she rolled out of bed, as far as she could, then carried her slippers and dressing gown down with her.

Bunty was curled up on the top of the back of the sofa, her favorite spot, but awoke when Carol closed the door to the sitting room, stretched, then wound her way between Carol's feet as she stubbed them into her slippers. Tying the belt of her dressing gown, Carol silently grieved the loss of her waist and wondered if it would ever return.

Rubbing her tummy and stretching her back, Carol tried to make herself burp, to no avail. A hot cup of tea? She wondered if she could manage it without waking her husband, but, feeling as she did, she decided to give it a go.

Waiting for the kettle to boil, Carol grabbed her laptop from the dining-room table, and set it on the kitchen counter. With Bunty safely at her side, she shut the kitchen door and opened up her inbox. Nothing.

Knowing that when the internet wasn't available to them, the girls communicated by sending attachments to phone messages, Carol checked that method. She downloaded all the feedback that had been sent since she and David had decided that an early night had been in order.

A steaming mug beside her screen, Carol read everything she'd received and made a mental list of what she'd have to tackle first thing in the morning.

Bunty leaped onto the counter, and Carol pushed her down. 'You're not allowed, and you know it,' she chided. Bunty looked up at Carol with a distinct expression of sulkiness. 'Understand every word, don't you?' said Carol. Bunty mewed that she did.

Bunty rubbed herself against the kitchen door just as Carol belched. 'Oh, that's better,' she announced. 'Let's try to get some sleep now?'

Bunty agreed it was a good plan and padded up the stairs behind Carol, then assumed her second favorite position on the foot of the bed. Carol knew it was only a matter of time before Bunty worked her way up to the pillows, but she didn't care. Her indigestion had cleared and she was tired.

NINETEEN

Alexander Bright stripped off his shorts, dropped them onto the floor and stepped into the shower. He'd had a good workout, watching the Sunday morning traffic crossing Tower Bridge from his windows, and was ready to face the day ahead. The idea that he was about to visit a rarely seen, museum-quality collection of odontological wonders excited him more than he'd thought possible.

Impeccably dressed, in a manner suitable for a day motoring to a stately home, and with a small overnight bag and a suit carrier, he made his way, via his personal lift, to the parking garage beneath his building. He'd allowed himself ample time to collect Clementine Twyst and still arrive at Chellingworth Hall for tea, as had been the plan.

However, it was later than he'd hoped when he and his 'hostess' finally reached the M4, because Clemmie had slept in, then had forgotten all about their arrangements. He'd employed some fancy maneuvers to get her back on track, and put his foot down once he could.

As the London skyline disappeared behind them, to be replaced by the Slough countryside, then the turrets of Windsor Castle, the Aston purred beneath his hands. Clemmie looked suitably impressed, almost leering at him. The sight was made more alarming by the fact that she'd chosen to dress all in purple – to match her hair, he assumed. He wondered how the day would progress. The Wiltshire countryside mounded around them, the cornfields that flashed past were bare and settling down for the winter ahead. The ribboning road was relatively quiet, and, although he knew he should keep an eye open for police cars, Alexander pushed his sleek vehicle almost to her limits in an effort to make up the time they had lost while Clemmie ambled around her London house trying to find cosmetics and accessories he couldn't imagine she'd need for one overnight stay in her own, other, home.

The drive was painless, until they hit the M32 interchange for Bristol, when everything slowed to a crawl until they were past the M5 junction. It was the first time that they'd talked at any length, Clemmie having been listening to her iPod, and Alexander preferring BBC Radio 4. Lowering the volume on *The World This Weekend* Alexander watched as Clemmie dropped her ear buds onto her lap and lit a cigarette, which she dangled out of the window.

'So what about this brother of yours?' asked Alexander. 'Is he anything like you?'

Clemmie laughed. Alexander thought he detected a note of cruelty in her tone. 'Henry? Well, we look nothing alike and we don't share any interests. Very country is Henry. I can't stand it there. Nothing to do. No one to mix with, which he doesn't seem to mind. Totally wrapped up in Chellingworth, is Henry. Otherwise, we're like two peas in a pod.'

'Has he a good head for business?' asked Alexander, thinking about a documentary he'd recently watched about the plight of British stately homes.

Clemmie guffawed. 'Henry? Oh, do me a favor, dearie. Couldn't run a knees-up in a brewery. Hopeless at it all. But then, to be fair to him, he wasn't trained for it. Mother thought that he and I could be allowed to follow our muses, because Dev would do all the business and ducal stuff.'

'Dev? Who's that?'

'Our older brother, Devereaux. Well, half-brother actually. My mother, Althea, was the second wife. Henry and I had an older brother by our father's first wife. But he died. Of measles, of all things. So Henry had to step up.' Clemmie flicked her ash out of the window and took a long drag on her cigarette.

'Must have been tough for you, losing a brother.'

'I didn't know him terribly well,' replied Clemmie. 'He was away in school when I was young and, by the time I was old enough to get to know Devereaux, he was off traveling the world. Very active, he was. Always yomping about doing something or other. Father indulged him, of course. Encouraged him, even. Said he had to get it out of his system before he settled down to take the title. But he died before Father did. Father was very upset, of course, and Henry and I were dragged back to the stately pile to be read the riot act. Henry stayed, but I drifted off. No one needs a girl about the place, so I mainly live in the house in London. Mother doesn't seem to mind, and Henry couldn't care less. After all, what could I possibly do there?'

Alexander knew enough about the responsibilities of wives, sisters and mothers in the titled classes to believe that there was a good deal that Clemmie could have been doing within the community surrounding her family's estate, but he bit his tongue. It certainly wasn't his business to be telling her what she should be doing, and he reminded himself that striking up a friendship with her was merely a means to an end. In fact, he found her quite annoying and living down to his expectations of the worst sort of attitude he'd come across while mixing with those for whom titles, land ownership and a leisurely lifestyle were the norm. He wasn't at all surprised that she had remained single. He couldn't imagine any man being prepared to put up with her self-absorption for long. He sighed with irritation, but his passenger didn't seem to notice because she was reinserting her ear buds as they picked up speed, heading for the Severn Bridge.

Once in Wales, the traffic seemed to disappear, though it immediately started to rain. Alexander pushed on until the turn off onto the A roads which took them through Pontypool, then Abergavenny, out to Talgarth, and finally onto what, to his mind, should have been designated B roads, so narrow and winding were they. Unfamiliar with the route, he took things more slowly, and he listened to Clemmie rattle on about galleries, artists, social acquaintances and parties until he wanted to throttle her. But he gritted his teeth, and pretended he was smiling. It seemed to Alexander that Clemmie spent most of her life in the newly burgeoning East End art scene and a range of converted warehouses and old pubs which now served to attract the hip artsy crowd, like the place they'd eaten the night before, where industrial lighting and whitewash paint seemed to be all the rage.

Negotiating the lavish ironwork gates to the Chellingworth Estate, Alexander steeled himself for what lay ahead. He pulled up in front of the short, bald man who was the ticket seller for the estate. As soon as the man spotted Clemmie, Alexander noted that he seemed to search for a non-existent forelock to tug, then waved the car through.

'Beastly, don't you think?' said Clemmie, sulking.

'What?' asked Alexander, wondering if she was referring to the man in the high-visibility vest they'd just passed.

'All these . . . you know, people. Plebs. All running about the place. I don't know how Henry puts up with it. There must be some other way to make some money out of the place. We can't even use the main body of the house anymore. We have to live in just one wing.'

Alexander resisted the temptation to point out that Clemmie didn't live there at all, but in a house in London probably valued at millions of pounds and stuffed to the rafters with art and artifacts worth just as much again. Instead, he allowed himself a sweet moment or two of anticipation, as he stayed clear of a minivan ahead of him that was throwing up pea gravel.

As the high, brick-built walls of the Chellingworth Estate disappeared behind them, Alexander allowed himself to enjoy the view. The rain had cleared, giving way to patches of blue sky between fluffy clouds and the sweeping landscape didn't disappoint. Verdant pastures, strategically placed copses, ha-has to enclose the animals. It was quite idyllic. He'd read up on the history of the Twysts and of the estate. Capability Brown himself had had a hand in the design of the landscape and Alexander felt the touch of genius all about him. Ahead of him, on higher ground, was Chellingworth Hall itself. Of course, he'd seen photographs of it on the internet, but they didn't do justice to the scale and symmetrical beauty of the place.

As every other vehicle pulled into a driveway that led to the parking area, Alexander negotiated a narrower part of the approach, which he had to share with pedestrians. The car, and its occupants, drew a great deal of interest. As it finally crunched to a stop at the bottom of the stone stairs which led to the front door, it gathered quite a crowd. Alexander opened Clemmie's door for her, and the two ascended the stairs, to be met, halfway up, by a flustered man in a dark suit.

'Edward, how lovely to see you,' cried Clemmie. 'This is my guest, Mr Alexander Bright. We thought we'd overnight. The bags are in the boot, such as it is in that little beauty.' She nodded toward the Aston, which had been almost engulfed by a group of men, all of whom were being dragged at by wives and girlfriends.

'Lady Clementine, what a delightful surprise,' said the man.

Alexander was immediately sure of three things: the man was well past his prime and probably suffered from some sort of heart complaint, and that he was anything but delighted to see Clemmie.

'Mr Bright,' said the man politely.

'Alexander, please.'

'Mr Alexander, if I might have the keys, I'll have your bags brought in and the car moved to the stable block. It will not be accessible to the public there,' he noted.

Alexander felt a pang of panic every time someone else drove his car, but it was something he'd had to get used to since he so often used valet services. One thing he'd never be able to get used to, however, was the idea that someone would handle all his personal items while unpacking for him, and he'd discovered that it was perfectly acceptable, in good society, to say so.

'Thank you, Edward,' he replied, handing over the keys. 'I prefer to unpack myself. A foible.'

'I understand, sir,' replied Edward in a neutral tone.

'Come on, let's find Henry,' called Clemmie as she all but ran into Chellingworth Hall, startling the members of the public who were milling about whispering. 'Follow me,' she said, unhooking a thick red velvet rope, allowing the brass end to clang loudly against the brass pole from which it hung. 'I expect he's skulking in his private rooms,' she called.

Alexander carefully replaced the rope and noticed the glances of barely concealed surprise and jealousy as he turned to join Clemmie. Adept as he was at mixing with all sorts of people, he had never experienced this before, and he felt a tingle of anticipation as he realized that he, Alex Bright, from the back streets of Brixton, was about to enter a world that was new and usually closed, to him.

TWENTY

After just one day at the Dower House, Mavis MacDonald could sympathize exactly with how Althea Twyst felt about having members of the public roaming across the Chellingworth Estate. Having always lived in close quarters with others, either during her nursing days, or at her mid-terrace flat in north London, she found it odd that she should feel the presence of hundreds of strangers in a landscape that she neither knew, nor owned, so oppressive.

From its vantage point on a hillock, the Dower House had an excellent view of the hall, as well as the beautiful landscape that comprised the estate. Before the gates had opened that Sunday morning to allow public access, the verdant, gently rolling pastures glistened with dew, and mist wreathed sinuously into and out of the dips and copses. Mavis had been awestruck by the beauty to such an extent that she'd sat at her bedroom window for more than an hour just looking at it all, and allowing it to bathe her with its overwhelming gift of peaceful solitude.

Then the cars had begun to make their way along the winding drive. Then the coaches. Then more cars. Then, possibly worst of all, the people had begun to appear. Satiated on art and architecture at the hall, they began to wander, aimlessly, in the previously unpopulated landscape. Their voices carried in an alarming manner, especially those belonging to small children.

Usually, Mavis adored the sound of a child's laughter. Indeed, she thought there were few more joyful sounds in the world. But this? Why was this different to hearing the sound of her next-door neighbor's children playing in the back garden? Why was it so much worse than being cheek by jowl with the hordes on the summer beaches?

Mavis couldn't fathom it. But she knew she felt it.

When she joined Althea for coffee, she had a new understanding of the woman.

'It must be very difficult for you, having people roam your estate like this,' she observed as she filled her cup in the morning room.

Althea didn't look up from her newspaper. 'Ah, the poor old landed gentry bemoaning the arrival of the plebian crowds?' she quipped.

'No,' said Mavis gently. 'I mean the loss of the truly profound peace you must feel when it's just you, alone, with the land.'

Althea's head came up, a strange expression on her face. 'You've felt the magic already?' she asked sharply. 'It usually takes longer. But I'm glad. Henry doesn't feel it until he leaves it. He doesn't value it as I do. And I have learned to appreciate it even more in the past few years. I sometimes wonder if this is how heaven will be.'

'With hell being the days when visitors overwhelm the estate?' asked Mavis, smiling.

Althea nodded. 'Precisely.'

McFli yapped his way across the room toward the door.

'Who is it, my dear wee man?' asked Mavis, drawing a smile from the dowager.

A knock was followed immediately by Jennifer Newbury's head appearing around the door. 'There's a telephone call for you, ma'am. It's His Grace, the duke. Shall I bring in the handset?'

Mavis thought it was a very peculiar question. Althea nodded and Jennifer did as she was told.

Althea took the handset and put it to her ear. 'Speak,' she said loudly. She paused, listening. 'Yes, both of us. Very well, at seven,' she said,

177

then handed the instrument back to Jennifer, who took it and disconnected the line. 'That will be all for now, Jennifer, but please make sure that my emerald crepe is ready for me to dress at six.' She paused and thought for a moment. 'Pearls, I think. Thank you.'

Jennifer left the room as Althea returned her attention to Mavis.

'Did you bring anything suitable for dinner?' asked the dowager. 'Henry has invited us to join them at the hall later on.'

Mavis nodded. 'I have a black dress that suits most occasions,' she replied. 'Though I left my pearls at home, I'm afraid.' She winked at the dowager.

'Pearls are not a requirement,' replied her hostess with an impish grin. 'I like you, Mavis MacDonald,' she added.

'I'm glad,' replied Mavis, 'because I don't imagine you're a person I'd enjoy having as an enemy.'

'How very perceptive of you.'

'I've never been accused of being blind to the obvious.'

The two women raised their coffee cups toward each other and drank.

For several moments a comfortable silence filled the room. Althea returned her attention to the newspaper, and Mavis stood to admire the borders in the walled garden beyond the windows. She watched Ian Cottesloe as he moved easily between the tall plants, pulling at the odd weed and resetting stakes as he moved from one end of the pathway to the other. Mavis considered his role with the local youth and especially the football teams.

She'd spent some time with him as he'd shown her around the property the previous day, and she'd warmed to him. What she'd read as surliness as he drove her from the railway station had, she believed, been a product of the fact that he wasn't sure of her status in the household. Once Mavis had made it clear to him that she had nursed the dowager, many years previously, while she was visiting the Scottish estate, he seemed to open up. He finally appeared to be able to relate to her within his world view. Mavis wondered what it must have been like to grow up on the Chellingworth Estate as the son, and grandson, of men who had performed the same duties. Concepts such as continuity, a pride in the achievements of previous generations, and a sure knowledge of one's future and past seemed, to Mavis at least, to be in short supply in the modern world.

Ian Cottesloe was not a young man struggling to find himself by wandering the world with a backpack; he knew who he was, and what was expected of him, and he'd made it abundantly clear to Mavis that he was more than happy with his lot. When Mavis had sought to draw him out about those he knew within the local environs, eager to understand if there was a person, or people, in his life who might entice him or encourage him to allow them access to the Dower House, his demeanor had suggested to Mavis that, while he was tied to the local community in many ways, they were not ties that would bind him in such a way that he would break the trust that had existed between his family and the Twysts for three generations.

He had no girlfriend, that much she had established. In fact, Ian had laughed when she'd asked him about a young woman being in his life, and had responded that he was happy to wait to meet his wife, as his father had been to meet his mother. He told Mavis about how his mother had come to the estate as a kitchen maid and how she and his father had finally married when she became the under-cook. Ian was good looking, there was no question, and his very demanding work meant that he was in excellent physical shape. But Mavis wondered if a modern woman would be able to cope with the life he clearly wanted to lead.

'A penny for them,' said Althea as she pushed her folded newspaper to one side.

Mavis turned. 'Ach, I'm a Scot, Althea. How about I charge you a pound and we call it quits?'

'Do you think Ian had anything to do with it?' asked Althea, glancing beyond Mavis to the garden. 'I do hope not. He's a treasure. Like something from a lost age,' she added wistfully. 'Very much like his father, in many ways.'

Mavis sat opposite the dowager and weighed her words carefully. She sighed. 'I realize this must be difficult for you, and I don't want to speak out of turn. But, if someone came into your home, and managed to do so without setting off the alarm system, then I'm afraid it's most likely that they received help from an insider. Now, to be sure, that person might not be one of your staff. My colleague at the office, Carol, will pursue enquiries into the people who installed the alarm and, as you know, we're also checking into the backgrounds and local links not just of the permanent staff here and at the hall, but also of the more casual workers.'

'But not Ian,' said Althea quietly.

'I don't think so,' replied Mavis. 'His roots here run very deep.'

'And what about Mary? She's a very good cook, you know.'

Mavis smiled. 'Dinner last night proved that, Althea. And I know that Carol is continuing to check into her background. But I have to say that I found her most unhelpful when I spoke with her. At least, when I tried to speak with her. Now, to be fair, she was preparing our food while I attempted to engage her in a revealing conversational topic or two, but, in terms of her general approach to life I'd say she's a person who sees the glass as more than half empty, and has little desire to see it refilled, for fear she'll have nothing to complain about.'

Althea smiled. 'Did she try to tell you about all the ailments she's suffered?'

'Aye, she did. But I cut her off. Believe me, as a nurse, I've had more than my fill of that type over the years. She's one of those women for whom a hangnail would be interpreted as requiring the immediate amputation of a limb, probably without an anesthetic, and a simple cold would be perceived as some dreaded tropical disease. When she spoke to me about being drugged that night – which she did quite openly by the way, despite the fact that she has no idea that I am here carrying out enquiries – she had at least a dozen possible means and methods by which her unnaturally deep sleep could have been induced. I listened to that part of her conversation at least, but had to give her the benefit of my experience when she began to claim that the after effects were still being felt.'

'Did anything she said make sense at all?' asked Althea, leaning toward Mavis with her elbows on the table.

'Maybe,' replied Mavis enigmatically. 'She was at great pains to explain how the stew was unattended in the kitchen for long periods, and she was keen to tell me, as far as she was aware, of everybody's comings and goings that day. One thing she did mention, that maybe you can illuminate for me, is the question of whether it is, in fact, possible for any uninvited members of the public to gain access to this place. I've seen the wall that surrounds this house, and the locked gates within it, with my own eyes. I gather from Mary that Mrs Fernley has a key to the rear gate and that a warning telephone call, plus the use of a pull-bell at the gate, will mean that Mary will open the gate from the inside to allow those without a key to enter. Is that the case? Do you know whether Mary has ever left an unlocked gate unattended?'

Althea rose from the table and walked to the window. 'Such a beautiful day,' she said, 'though it looks like we might have rain soon. Maybe a shower will send everyone running back to the hall.' She turned and added, 'If Mary left a gate open, she wouldn't tell me, Mavis. She is a good cook, but I am not blind to her nature. She works for me. She would be afraid that she would lose her position for such an oversight. Henry has made it abundantly clear to my staff that they are responsible for my wellbeing, and my safety. Not that I imagine my son has ever suspected my life to be in peril in my own home.'

'And Jennifer Newbury? Is she merely an employee, looking out for herself?'

Again Althea gave the matter some thought. 'Ultimately, yes.'

Mavis nodded. 'I see.'

Pulling her notebook from the pocket of her cardigan, Mavis flicked through its pages. She paused. 'Althea?'

The dowager turned. 'Yes?'

'I wonder if I could talk to you just one more time about that night,' said Mavis.

Althea sighed. 'If you must. Though to what end I don't know. I cannot imagine there is anymore I can say. We've been over it several times already.'

'It was something you didn't say that I wanted to talk to you about,' replied Mavis.

Althea resumed her seat at the table. 'I'm intrigued.'

Mavis smiled. 'You told me that the young man lying on the floor had a hood over his head, but that you could see blood on the side of his face.'

Althea nodded.

'I wonder if I could ask you to close your eyes once more and picture the scene again?'

Althea did as she was asked.

'You're standing above the young man. You're

close to him, as close as you ever came. McFli is causing a commotion behind you, as you told me, and you notice the blood. Can you describe that to me?'

Althea's head tilted, her eyelids flickering. Mavis heard her breathing slow, and she could tell that the woman was willing herself back to the moment in question.

'He's lying on his front, prone,' began Althea, 'but his face is toward me. The hood is on the back of his head, not covering his entire head. The blood is . . . the blood seems to have begun its journey beneath his hood and to have run down from his hairline, onto the side of his forehead, and then his cheek.'

'Would you say it looks as though gravity has done this, in that the blood is in one stream, or is the blood smeared?'

'One stream. Yes, it looks as though it has rolled down, not been brushed down.'

'Good. Now tell me about his hair.'

'I can't. I didn't notice his hair,' replied Althea quickly.

'All right,' said Mavis quietly, 'let's go back to the blood. You say it's come from his hairline onto his forehead. Let's focus there. Can you see his hair now, Althea?'

'It's dark. It's not very short and it's not very long. It's flat, but it's very black.'

'Good. And now his skin, dear. I know you told me he was brown-skinned, but is his skin very dark? Or is he a lighter brown?'

'Mid-brown. Like strong, not very milky coffee.'

'Good. And now, finally, tell me about his eyes.'

'They're open. No, *it's* open. I can only see one. He's like a fish on a plate, just one eye. It's glassy.'

'And what color is it?'

'Black. Well, a little bit brown, very dark brown, but mainly black. And dead.' Althea opened her eyes and, once again, Mavis could see the fear in them.

'You did very well, Althea.'

Althea picked up her coffee cup and drained the few last drops. 'Good,' she said dryly, 'because I don't want to have to do that again. It's very unnerving.'

'I know, dear,' said Mavis, 'but it was very helpful. I'm just going to phone Carol at her home so that she can refine her research into missing persons to focus on non-Caucasian, possibly Asian, or mixed-race young men, which could save her a good deal of effort. You remembered much more than the other times, Althea. Good job. I'll just pop up to my room, now, if you don't mind. I'll join you for lunch later, how about that?'

Althea nodded and McFli barked his agreement.

TWENTY-ONE

Christine was exhausted and she'd only just finished a light Sunday lunch. She'd been up early, to get going before the public was allowed to enter the hall, and had spent the entire morning working her way from one staff member to another, raising topics of conversation which could then be turned to her advantage. She had no doubt that many of the people she'd spoken to would end up gossiping with each other about how strange she was, but she couldn't care about that.

Her efforts had revealed two things: most of the staff were viewing her as a possible future duchess and sizing her up in their own way, and not one of them seemed to have the slightest inkling about a bobble hat having been found in the Dower House. True, most had heard about the dowager's 'funny turn' almost a fortnight earlier, but it seemed that the staff at the Dower House, and the local police, had at least managed to remain tight-lipped about the bloodied bobble hat.

Lunch with Henry had been excruciating. He really had few topics of conversation except those which concerned the running of the hall, which Christine accepted was a major undertaking. However, Henry appeared to now view her as some sort of confidante, and was clearly glad that he had someone with whom he could share his deep despair that the hall would ever fund its own renovations. Though she would not reveal her anxieties to her colleagues, Christine was also beginning to panic that Henry Twyst might not, after all, come up with the readies to pay them for their time and effort.

A wave of relief washed over Christine when Henry told her that he had an important meeting to attend after lunch, and invited her to join him.

She saw a chance for escape, but, on the point of declining Henry's offer, she changed her mind when she realized it would give her a chance to make her assessment of someone she'd not been able to corner thus far: Stephanie Timbers.

The meeting took place in the estate office, to which Henry led Christine via a circuitous route, which avoided any areas open to the public. Stephanie's delighted expression upon seeing Henry enter the office altered more than subtly when she spotted Christine behind him. Almost immediately the young woman managed to rearrange her features to present a welcoming front, but Christine had seen what she'd seen, and was sure of one thing: Stephanie Timbers was keen on Henry Twyst. That, when taken with the way Henry had defended Stephanie the night before, meant that Christine was determined to pay particular attention to the public relations professional who'd, apparently, walked away from a successful career in London to become the head of a non-existent marketing and promotional 'department' at Chellingworth Hall.

Accepting a rickety seat, and pulling it to an angle from which she could observe both the duke and his employee, Christine decided to allow the meeting to go ahead as planned and to become an observer. Stephanie was attractive, but not in the pretty sense. Christine noted pale skin, glossy, naturally very dark brunette hair, an aquiline nose, a strong, determined brow and a hint of the regally horsey about her. She didn't smack of jolly hockey sticks, but Christine could see how she'd fit in – in an unremarkable way

– with the county set. Of course, her English accent meant she'd stick out like a sore thumb with the locals, but it would matter less if she were to find herself mixing with tourists. In terms of her build she was short, stocky and had a not unpleasant figure, but she'd probably never look blousy, even in an evening gown. Christine reckoned she was in her early thirties, so a little older than herself, but with several good child-bearing years ahead of her.

As the meeting progressed it became clear to Christine that Henry and Stephanie were very comfortable in each other's company; their body language showed how relaxed they were, and yet they shared a common energy, as though everything that was transpiring between them bore a little edge, which made it more exciting, even if they were having a rather hum-drum conversation about the selection of jams being served at the tea shop.

'I wonder what your guest thinks?' said Stephanie quite pointedly. 'Which would you prefer to take home?'

Christine blinked with embarrassment. 'Sorry? I just wasn't listening for a moment there. Could you repeat the question?'

Possibly taken aback by such honesty, Stephanie repeated her query. 'Henry and I were wondering about the comparative merits of serving the estate honey versus the local honey from the Builth Wells Country Market in the tea room. The one from the market is pretty local too, so they both fit our brand proposition. You see, the problem is, we can sell our honey for a good profit in the little shop, where people like to buy it as a souvenir for themselves, or even take it as a gift for others. Or we can put it on the tables in the tea shop for people to use. We don't produce enough to do both, properly. I feel we should be growing the offering we have under the Chellingworth Estates brand, and that works better when people take it home, in a labelled jar. Henry's not so sure. What do you think?'

Christine decided to give the matter some serious thought. 'I'd say sell your stuff in the shop, use the locally produced stuff on the tables. People will remember this place when they see the jar at home, and it'll get the name about if they give it as a gift. But, if honey's such a good seller, then maybe make some plans to be able to produce more?' She'd given it her best shot, and felt satisfied.

Henry looked at her with disdain. 'So, exactly what Stephanie said.' He seemed to be damning Christine for some dreadful type of plagiarism, but beamed at Stephanie and said, 'I agree with you, Stephanie. Let's do that.'

Oh, yes, they're more than a little keen on each other, thought Christine. *I wonder what's holding them back? Their professional relationship, or is Henry that much of a snob?*

Aloud, she said, 'Well, I'm glad to have been of some little service.' The couple's glances told her they didn't think she had been, but they were both far too polite to say so.

Christine looked at her watch. The day was slipping away from her and she felt she'd learned all she could about Stephanie Timbers; a woman so smitten with the duke probably wouldn't threaten any possible future relationship by aiding and abetting someone in their desire to gain access to the Dower House. 'I wonder if I might excuse myself?' she added. 'I have some phone calls to make.'

Henry raised himself from his seat in anticipation of Christine doing likewise, and she quite rightly took this as a sign that he'd be happy for her to leave. The gleam of relief in Stephanie's eyes told her she'd be glad to see the back of Christine – whom she, possibly, viewed as a challenger for Henry's affections.

Having told a white lie to get out of the dingy office, Christine decided to settle herself in the sitting room to write up her reports. Wandering back the way Henry had brought her, she eventually found her safe hiding place and, having bumped into Edward on the way, she settled herself, poured herself a cup of tea from the supplies brought along by the butler, then went so far as to close her eyes and allow the afternoon sunlight to warm her skin after she'd shut up her laptop. She all but drifted off into a semi-peaceful nap.

Rousing herself with a start when Edward arrived to clear the tea tray, Christine decided to take her laptop back to her room and bring down her boots to be able to take a walk outside to clear her head, once the public had left for the day.

'Who the hell are you?' asked a short, pale woman with a shock of purple hair as she all but ran into Christine as she was exiting the sitting room.

'I'm a guest of His Grace,' replied Christine properly, unsure as to the woman's identity. The tiny woman encased in purple clothes seemed to vibrate with excitement, but the surprise on her face suggested to Christine that she was shocked to find an unknown woman on the premises.

'I'm his sister, Clementine. Where is he?'

'I'm Christine Wilson-Smythe, Lady Clementine,' replied Christine calmly. 'His Grace is taking a meeting with Stephanie Timbers in the estate office. I left them to discuss something to do with the harvest supper at the local church.'

Clementine Twyst gave Christine a good look up, then down. 'A guest of Henry's, eh? He doesn't have many of them. You're about right for it, I suppose. Typical of Henry. And it's Clemmie. I can't stand all that "Lady" stuff. Makes me feel as though I'm a hundred years old. Well, not unless it gets me a better table at a restaurant, of course,' quipped Clemmie. 'This is Alexander. Henry can wait. I need a drink.'

It became immediately clear to both Alexander and Christine that Clemmie was far more interested in imbibing than carrying out proper introductions, so Alexander stepped up.

'Alexander Bright. An acquaintance of Clemmie's,' he said.

Christine shook his extended hand. 'As I said, Christine Wilson-Smythe. An acquaintance of Henry's. I'm here for the weekend. You?'

'Just overnight,' replied Alexander.

'Since Clemmie has left us to our own devices, allow me,' said Christine.

'The sun's low enough that it must be past quite

a few yardarms, besides, it's Sunday afternoon. What's Sunday good for but a few drinks and a general lounge-about?' said Clemmie as she sloshed the contents of a decanter into fine crystal. 'What about you, Alexander? Fancy a snifter?'

'Tea has just been cleared away,' said Christine to Alexander with more reserve, 'but I'm sure more could be brought, if you'd prefer.'

'I wouldn't mind a G and T, if that's possible,' he replied.

Christine smiled. 'Shall we help ourselves?' she asked of Clemmie, who shrugged her response and threw herself into a chair that sat in full sunshine, dangling her legs over one of the stuffed and tufted arms.

Henry Twyst bustled into the room with Stephanie as Christine was pouring tonic into Alexander's gin. It was clear to Christine that he'd invited the woman for a drink and wasn't impressed by what he found

'Clemmie? What are you doing here? Were we expecting you? Oh, hello,' he added, looking at Alexander with great surprise. 'I see you've brought a guest?' he looked at his sister with an irate glare.

'Henry, Alexander,' said Clemmie airily. 'Alexander, my brother. The one with the teeth you were so keen to see. Henry, would you be a dear and show Alexander your teeth?'

Henry looked completely baffled, as did Stephanie, who was hovering awkwardly at the door. Christine, who was holding the tonic in mid-air, looked across at Alexander with some alarm.

Henry stammered, 'W-what the devil do you mean, show this man my teeth, Clemmie? I know Mother's losing her marbles, but don't tell me you are too?'

'Your *false* teeth, Henry. Granddad's collection of false teeth. You know, those grimy old things? Upstairs? Alexander is nuts about them. Tell him, Alexander. Tell him how excited you become when you talk about dentures.' Clemmie's tone was quite cruel and Christine suspected that Alexander had to count to ten several times before he replied. She noted how his square jaw clenched.

Christine finished pouring the tonic into the glass she was holding and whispered, 'Sounds like you'll be knocking this one back,' which made Alexander smile.

He rallied. 'Yes, Your Grace. Clemmie has told me all about your collection of antique dentures and odontology, and offered to bring me here so I could take a look at it. I realize I am asking a great favor of you, but I am something of a devotee of dentures, odd though that might seem.' Slipping his hand into his breast pocket, Alexander revealed the set of nineteenth-century dentures that he had brought with him.

Christine peered at them and said, 'I say, they're quite something.'

'Waterloo Teeth,' he explained, smiling broadly.

Christine continued to examine the piece in his hand. 'Really? I've never seen them "in the flesh" before. Do you mind?' She held out her hand.

'Not at all. I'm pleased to meet someone who isn't repulsed by the sight of antique false teeth.' He placed them carefully in her palm.

193

Feeling her way around the plate and the teeth themselves, Christine said, 'These are remarkably stable, for such an old item.'

'That was the second selling point for them in their day,' replied Alexander with enthusiasm, 'the first being their affordability. It's a sad fact that the terrible toll taken by the battlefield produced the best possible opportunity for those without great means to be able to eat something other than boiled food. Imagine losing all your teeth in your twenties, and never again being able to crunch into a vegetable, or bite into, or even chew, a piece of meat? It must have been dreadful.'

Christine looked into the grey green eyes which glowed with passion and replied, 'I'd never thought of that before. You're right, it must have made for a very boring and miserable life. No wonder so many people ate gruel, or soups. Even bread must have been an effort. Ha! I wonder if that's when people started cutting off the crusts?'

'It's certainly likely,' continued Alexander, 'imagine having the money for good food, but no ability to eat it. The middle classes finally had the opportunity that the wealthier members of society possessed – the chance to buy dentures that could change their lives, without bankrupting their family. Waterloo Teeth? Almost a revolution,' he finished with a smile.

'They are truly hideous and disgusting,' said Clemmie flatly. 'Good God, have they been in your pocket all this time?'

'I thought I'd bring them along,' replied Alexander, sounding as patient as possible.

Henry looked at his watch, then disdainfully at his sister, then at her guest, then at Christine. He took his time.

He sighed as he pronounced, 'The public will be gone in about fifteen minutes, which will make it easier to get to the east wing. Until then let's enjoy a drink, come on in, Stephanie, do join us, please. Let's do that and I'll take you over myself, Alexander.'

'Thank you, Your Grace,' said Alexander.

'It'll be Henry while you're under my roof. I assume Clemmie has invited you for the night?'

'Yes, darling,' called his sister. 'Will you tell someone in the kitchen we'll be here for dinner and make sure some rooms are made up for us? Or could your little helper, Steffy, do that for us?'

Christine noticed that Alexander relaxed a little as Clemmie referred to 'rooms' in the plural, and also felt the anger with which Henry jumped in with, 'I'll do it, Clemmie. Stephanie will help herself to a drink, and will pour one for me, while I call for Edward. We don't need to have rooms made up for you. You know very well that your apartment is always ready, Clemmie. I'll make sure that someone airs out a place for Alexander.' He looked Alexander up and down. 'Have you come able to dress? Or will it have to be a lounge suit for dinner?'

Alexander nodded. 'I can accommodate black tie.'

'Good,' said Henry and nodded happily, 'because my mother and her weekend guest will also be dining with us, and she likes to keep

195

standards as high as possible. I like black tie and don't often get the chance to wear it anymore. I'll confirm with Edward and Mother. I say, why don't you join us too, Stephanie? You've never dined with us before. I think it would be rather fun. We'd all make quite the party.'

'An odd number at table, Henry? How very nonconformist of you,' snarled Clemmie. 'I wonder how long you've been waiting for a chance to get Steffy and Mummy with their trotters in the same trough?'

Christine wondered if Clementine had been a poisonous little girl, because she certainly had venom to spare as an adult.

Stephanie Timbers rose to the challenge like a trooper. 'I'd be honored and delighted, Henry, thank you' she replied quietly. She looked at her watch. 'I'll need to drive back to the village to change, it won't take me too long, but maybe I won't have that drink after all.'

'Right – what's that you have poured there, Stephanie? A G and T? Excellent, I'll have that one, and you can have something soft. I'll ask Edward to arrange a room for you tonight too, then you can have a glass or two with us all at the dinner table.'

Stephanie looked a little panicked. 'Oh, no, please don't do that. I can quite easily get a car back to my house after dinner and up again in the morning. I'll ring Davies the taxi to book one.'

Henry's voice sounded unusually assertive to Christine's ear as he said, 'If you insist upon going home after dinner, Stephanie, I'll get Ian Cottesloe to take you. He'll be driving Mother and her guest back to the Dower House in any case. So he can run you back to the village. How about that?' It was clear to everyone in the room that Henry wanted Stephanie to join the group for dinner, but didn't want to put her in an embarrassing situation.

Stephanie Timbers acceded to Henry's suggestion with humility and grace. Christine couldn't help but wonder how the dowager herself would deal with the dining arrangements, but she realized it wasn't her problem. Indeed, it could turn out to be an interesting evening.

'I say, Clemmie, aren't you getting hot sitting in that sunshine?' said Henry much more jovially than Christine had heard him before. 'Come and join us over here, why don't you? Please, everyone make yourselves comfortable.'

Clemmie unwound herself from her chair and trudged across the room. She slid into another seat, closer to the drinks table, where she lit a cigarette and began to blow smoke circles toward the ceiling. 'Don't tell Mother I'm here, Henry. Let it be a surprise?'

'It might give her a shock, rather than surprise,' replied her brother.

'Oh, hardy-har-har, Henry,' snapped Clemmie.

Christine exchanged a glance with Alexander that was surprisingly empathetic, then, as they both flushed, they attended to their drinks.

The silence in the sitting room was deafening, but neither Christine nor Alexander felt able to broach a topic of conversation. It was clear that

Stephanie and Henry were equally stumped, and Clemmie was in her own little world. Eventually Alexander set down his glass, having rather rushed his drink, making it clear to his host that he was ready to move as soon as Henry saw fit to take him on the expedition to see the antique dentures.

Stephanie took her cue and announced, 'If it's all right with everyone, I'll head off to change for the evening.'

Henry sprang to his feet. 'But of course. We'll see you later. I'll ask Ian to collect you and bring you here before he drives Mother over, that way your car will be at your house for the morning.'

Having removed any possible concerns on the part of Stephanie, Henry waved her farewell, checked his watch once more and announced, 'Right then. Let's go. Are you going to join us, Christine? Clemmie?'

Christine smiled and stood, while Clemmie threw her brother a glance that quite clearly told him she didn't want anything to do with the whole thing.

'When will you stop acting like a teenager, Clemmie?' said Henry as he exited the sitting room, leading Christine and Alexander on their way.

'As soon as you stop treating me like one,' called his sister after the threesome.

TWENTY-TWO

Henry guided Christine and Alexander to the main entryway, then across to the wing opposite the one they'd just left. It appeared to Christine that the only security measure preventing the public from doing exactly as they were was another of the hall's red velvet ropes.

'We don't use this wing much anymore,' explained Henry as he wound them through a couple of doors and corridors, all of which contained items of furniture and decoration hidden beneath ghostly dust sheets. 'As you can see . . .' He waved his arm toward shuttered windows and gloomy rooms that had once gleamed with the light from chandeliers, which hung, bagged up like monstrous chrysalises, from the dark ceilings.

Having led them up a staircase, clicking switches as they went, Henry finally stopped in front of an unassuming door. 'Here we are,' he announced. He opened the door which groaned on its hinges, then stepped aside to allow Christine to enter, which she did with some reluctance.

The room was not large and had an unpleasant odor. Christine sniffed, as did Alexander.

Henry pushed them a little as he shuffled in and felt about the wall for something that would bring the room some much needed illumination. Eventually, a couple of rows of rather ancient fluorescent tubes burst into sputtering, humming life.

'Oh, good, they still work,' was Henry's surprised comment.

The room had a high-coffered wooden ceiling and was filled with cabinets made of dark wood and glass. It reminded Christine of the Victorian schoolrooms where she'd spent so many years. A patina of age coated everything and the smell in the room developed to that of burned dust as the lighting heated up.

Henry's nose wrinkled. 'I say, I'm terribly sorry. I think that something has . . . well, died in here at some time. Probably a small rodent, or maybe a bird?' He didn't sound too sure of himself.

'I think you're right. But probably a very long time ago,' replied Alexander. He was almost salivating at the sight which met his eyes. He was imagining the wonders in the cabinets.

He looked to his host and said, politely, 'Would you mind if I began to wander?'

Henry laughed. 'Please, make yourself at home. I must confess that I haven't been in here for many, many years. I recall that my grandfather would bring me here and try to engender in me the same enthusiasm he felt for these objects, but, although I remember thinking that they were at once repulsive and funny, I never really became as involved in the collection as he was. My father had no time for this whole thing, so I think it's rather fitting that I should be opening up the room for someone like yourself, with a real passion for this type of thing. The last time we opened it up was for the youth from the village to visit. Some years ago now. Maybe a dozen. I recall that the boys were especially entertained. What about you, Christine? Does this appeal to you?'

Christine was always happy to consider new interests, but she had to admit that she didn't think that ancient dentures would be finding its way onto her list of 'must do' hobbies. 'I'll follow and learn,' she answered, which clearly pleased Alexander.

Christine noted that Alexander Bright moved like a man possessed. He began by flitting from cabinet to cabinet, reading the yellowing type-written labels, clearly getting the overall idea of what the room held. Then he made straight for a small cabinet which sat upon a dusty mahogany table.

'Look, you really do have them,' he said with a beam on his face. 'A set of Winston Churchill's dentures.'

Christine looked inside the cabinet as Alexander wiped off the worst of the dust with a silk pocket handkerchief.

'Is that plate made of gold?' asked Christine.

'Yes,' replied Alexander with an almost quivering voice. 'The plates were cast in gold, from molds taken by his dentist, Wilfred Fish, though the dentures were made by the dental technician, Derek Cudlipp.'

'Fish was my grandfather's dentist,' said Henry. 'He told me when I was a boy. Ha! I didn't remember that at all until you mentioned his name. Imagine that! I believe that's why we have them. My grandfather recommended him to Churchill. They knew each other, of course.'

'Fascinating,' replied Alexander eagerly. 'These are wonderful. Just wonderful. Look, you can see from the porcelain facings that he actually used these. See the wear, where they met his natural bottom teeth?'

Christine could feel the heat of Alexander's body as she drew close enough to the small cabinet to see the evidence to which he referred. She noted he smelled of a subtle and rare cologne which she recognized as being only available from one very exclusive shop on Savile Row. A friend of her brother also favored it.

'I see,' she breathed. 'They are quite beautiful.'

Alexander stood bolt upright. 'Without these dentures, made to fit in a very precise manner, Winston Churchill would have lost his distinctive voice. Did you know he suffered from a speech impediment that meant he couldn't pronounce his "s" or "sh" sounds properly? Something he eventually learned to use to his advantage during his triumphs of oration.' Alexander spoke with the enthusiasm of a zealot, which took Christine aback somewhat. She wondered why this man with his even features, excellent physique, and enigmatic skin tone felt such a connection to a British hero with a speech impediment.

'He used to flick them out of his mouth and use them as a comical projectile,' added Alexander laughing, then he moved to another cabinet, upon which a large sign read: 'Waterloo Teeth.'

Pulling the set from his pocket with one hand, Alexander wiped dust from this cabinet too, though there was a good deal less on this one.

'What a collection,' he said in amazement. He stood and looked in awe, nodding his head, then moved around the cabinet, peering more closely. He looked puzzled, then called to Henry. 'Henry, when did you say you last saw this collection?'

'Not for years,' replied Henry. 'Why?'

'I wonder, would you mind if I opened the door of this cabinet?' asked Alexander. 'There's a little key in the glass door, which I believe might do the trick.'

'Feel free,' replied Henry in a rather cavalier manner.

Alexander opened the door carefully and reached in his hand. Using the fine silk handkerchief he touched one set of teeth, then another. Eventually he lifted one set off its mounting, just a little, then placed it back again.

He stood back from the cabinet and scratched his head.

'What is it?' asked Christine. It was quite clear to her that Alexander was grappling with confusion.

'It doesn't make sense,' he replied. 'I . . . I don't understand.'

'Don't understand what?' asked Henry, finally joining the couple at the open cabinet.

Alexander held the set of teeth he'd brought with him in front of Henry and Christine. 'You see the way these teeth are mounted in the bone? They are still pretty rigid, but they are, in all honesty, just a little loose, because they have to be fitted into the bone receptacle. It's an inevitable part of the process of creating the dentures.'

His audience duly examined the specimen, and nodded.

'Now look at these,' he pointed to the contents of the cabinet. 'At first glance they appear to possess the same property. But, upon closer examination, you can see that the teeth are not individual teeth set with metal pins into a bone "gum line", but are, in fact, teeth carved from the same mass as the gum.'

'Does that mean they aren't Waterloo Teeth, as the label suggests?' asked Henry, baffled. 'I don't think that my grandfather was one to be duped by replicas. Unless he knew that was what he was purchasing all along, and just spun me a yarn or two when I was a boy.'

'I just lifted a set and it felt very lightweight,' replied Alexander. 'Would you mind if I brought one set right out of the cabinet?'

'As you please,' replied Henry. 'My interest is piqued.'

Alexander used the silk handkerchief to remove a set of dentures from the cabinet and looked at them very closely.

'Look, these teeth are modeled. They have been painted to look like teeth, but they aren't, and the gum section has been painted to look like bone, but it's not. The texture is all correct, almost as though they have been made using a mold of the originals.' He pressed his thumb against the 'bone' section. 'This substance yields under pressure, like some sort of plasticized material. And I suspect that all the other sets are the same.'

'What was grandfather playing at?' mused Henry.

'I don't think your grandfather had anything to do with this,' replied Alexander. 'Every one of these sets of dentures is a copy, a fake. And I think they are relatively recent.' He held the dentures directly under his nose. 'Very recent. I can still smell the chemicals coming from the material and, if I'm not very much mistaken, there's a faint aroma of paint. I'm sorry to say this, Henry, but I think you've suffered a very significant theft. And by significant, I mean in both terms of the importance of the collection that was once in this cabinet, and its value.'

'Which would be what?' asked Henry casually.

Alexander studied the cabinet and its contents. 'If everything in here was what these labels suggest, and was original and in good condition, of course, two collectors vying for it could easily run it up to a million, or more.'

'Do you mean a million *pounds*?' asked Henry aghast.

'Yes,' replied Alexander calmly. 'Or more.'

'Oh dear Lord,' exclaimed Henry. 'I'd better phone the police right away. I say, would you mind taking a look at the rest of the collection Alexander? I'm sure you can find your own way back to the other wing. I'm off to the nearest phone.'

'Here, use my mobile,' offered Christine.

Henry grabbed it from her hand, trembling.

TWENTY-THREE

When Althea, Dowager Duchess of Chellingworth, and her guest, retired army nurse Mavis MacDonald, alighted from the ancient, if elegant, vehicle in which Ian Cottesloe had transported them from the Dower House to Chellingworth Hall, it was already dark. The sunny afternoon had clouded over, robbing the sky of what had promised to be a pretty, if brief, sunset.

'I don't mind admitting that I'm feeling pretty peckish,' commented Althea as they mounted the stone steps, with Ian offering each of them an arm.

Mavis looked behind Ian's back at the dowager. 'Aye, me too,' she replied with a wink. 'I hope the cook here is as good as your Mary,' she added.

'Different scale of job here, dear,' replied the duchess. 'My Mary's good, but Davies the cook is very good indeed.'

'Davies the cook?' queried Mavis.

'There's Davies the housekeeper and Davies the cook here at the hall and, I dare say, a few other Davieses I don't know. We add their occupation to their name around here. It's the only way to keep all the Davieses, Joneses, Hopkinses, Robertses and Reeses straight.'

Mavis nodded. 'Aye, it's much the same with the Mac- and McSomethings in Scotland. Though you might be surprised to find out how many

206

people are named Smith or Brown back home. I was in school with three Dougie Smiths, which was more than a wee bit confusing for the teachers.'

Arriving at the front doors, Ian handed responsibility for his charges to Edward, who led them to the library, where drinks were being served by a very upright young man wearing a suit that Mavis noted was somewhat too large for him. But, before Mavis was able to be handed a drink, or even asked what she might want, there were the introductions to be dealt with.

Immediately they entered the library, Mavis sensed a significant change in Althea's mood. She even caught a quiet, 'Well, well. Good for you, Henry,' as Althea moved past her to greet a woman of quite alarming aspect, who was clearly the Lady Clementine. Mavis was shocked at Althea's daughter's appearance – not because of the purple hair, or even the purple chiffon garment she had swathed about her tiny body, but because of the unnatural pallor of her skin. Mavis's nursing instinct kicked in and it was all she could do to stop herself from telling Clementine to lie down while she drew blood for a whole raft of tests. Instead, she waited patiently while Althea introduced her daughter, while Clemmie introduced Alexander, then Henry introduced Christine and Stephanie Timbers.

Christine and Mavis handled being introduced to each other as though they were strangers much better than Henry managed the entire matter. After what seemed like an entire ballet of noddings and hand-shakings, drinks were finally brought to the now seated group. Small talk ensued, then, eventually, Henry began to regale the group with the tale of the terrible loss he had discovered that afternoon. His recounting of the events caused him to frequently call upon Alexander and Christine to support his points and his astonishment, which they dutifully did with grace and attentiveness.

Mavis listened patiently, while she and Christine kept their eyes averted from each other.

'The police will be here in the morning,' Henry concluded. 'I've already told them that I expect them to send someone who knows about these things, and Alexander has been most helpful in being able to refer the matter to a special department within Scotland Yard that has experts in rare antiques.'

Althea settled her shoulders, and sipped her sherry. 'I cannot remember a time when you regarded your grandfather's collection as anything but a fairground item,' she observed acidly. 'Could your horror at this theft be seen to be a realization of the collection's value on the open market?'

'It's the principle, Mother,' replied Henry.

'He's already checked the insurance, Mother,' said Clemmie. 'The collection is covered, but not for as much as it might be worth.'

'I understand that these items are rare, but why are they so valuable?' asked Althea of her son.

'I think our resident expert might be able to address that,' replied Henry, nodding in Alexander's direction.

'Indeed?' replied Althea, looking at Alexander

with barely veiled suspicion. 'How fortunate to have an expert at the hall the very day you discover you have been burgled, Henry. Exceptional planning on your part.'

'Your Grace,' responded Alexander, pointedly ignoring the dowager's insinuations, 'the market for such specialized antiquities is always unpredictable, but, if there are two or more collectors who wish to acquire such items, that usually pushes up the price. The more people vying for the items, so long as they have the means, the more the price rises. Simple supply and demand.'

'So am I to assume that such items are in small supply?' asked the dowager.

Alexander nodded. 'Due to their unusual, and some might think, less than attractive nature, not many antique dentures have survived. It's not the sort of item that most people would keep, for display purposes, after they have fulfilled their function within a family. Most will have found their way out of the home either because they have become broken and useless, which many early dentures did, or because they were viewed as unpleasant by those left behind after the death of a loved one. I happen to know there are several obsessively keen collectors in the world looking for such items at the moment. I will, obviously, be happy to lend any knowledge that the police might find useful, and I have already sent an email to my contact at Scotland Yard, who will doubtless be familiar with the names I have listed.'

'Are they international art thieves?' asked Clemmie with the gleefulness of a teen, which, for a woman in her early fifties, drew a withering glance from her mother.

'Not exactly,' replied Alexander evenly. 'One is a dentist in Moscow, a very wealthy one. Another is an oil magnate in Texas, who collects a wide range of medical, as well as dental, objects. The third is a gentleman not known to me personally, but whom, I understand, holds a significant position in the government of an African nation. I do not know if any of them are sufficiently driven, or reckless, enough to do it, but theft to order, in the world of art and antiquities, is not unheard of.'

'And you think one of them sent someone here to steal our teeth?' asked Clemmie with a laugh. 'Wait till I tell them this up in London,' she giggled.

'What I don't understand,' said Henry, ignoring his sister, 'is why they went to the trouble to make fakes to replace the real ones. Unless you'd come to visit, Alexander, we wouldn't have been any the wiser. Maybe not for years.'

'Don't be silly, Henry,' chided his mother. 'The insurance people come every year to count the teaspoons. They'd have noticed.'

Henry shook his head. 'I know that, Mother, but when they go through that part of the hall they don't poke about too much. Everything's closed up. We never move things, and no one goes in there to damage them. As I recall, last time they walked into the collection room, wandered around for a few moments and just counted things in cabinets. The person responsible for checking the east wing appeared to be a twelve year old.'

Mavis wanted to say something, but didn't dare. Luckily for her, the dowager said it on her behalf.

'So the thieves had a jolly good idea that fakes might be enough to keep the theft quiet for some considerable time to come,' she said thoughtfully.

'Which means they might have knowledge about the way in which your collections are examined each year,' said Christine quietly. 'Which, in turn, raises questions about the insurance company, and their valuers.'

Mavis nodded. 'I'm sure the police will look into that angle, my dear,' she said, drawing a peculiar look from Alexander. 'They will arrive in the morning, you said, Your Grace?' she addressed her host.

Henry nodded. 'Yes. I'm afraid we'll all have to make statements,' he said, sounding worried. 'Of course, you weren't here at the time we discovered the loss, Stephanie, but you know the place so well, you might be able to throw some light on matters?'

Stephanie had been sitting very upright, sipping her drink and keeping her own counsel, but now Henry had drawn her into the conversation, she was forced to speak. She did so quietly, and without looking directly at Henry. 'Of course I'll be glad to help, if I can. But I've never been to that part of the building.'

Henry smiled gratefully at the woman, who still didn't make eye contact with him, then added, 'This whole thing about being questioned by the police? It might make things a little tricky.'

He looked first at Christine, then at Mavis, with concern etched on his face.

Mavis felt she had to make something very clear. 'I don't see why it should be at all difficult, Your Grace,' she said forcefully. 'Christine and Alexander happen to be your guests this weekend, and I happen to be your mother's. Stephanie works here on a daily basis. I am sure we will all be interviewed in private, so we can each tell our story of how we come to be here, or what we might know, or not know, that way. Privately. Not tricky at all.'

'Yes, Henry, stop panicking,' added his mother pointedly.

The doors to the sitting room opened and Edward announced dinner. Henry took his mother's arm, and, rather markedly, Stephanie's. Alexander accompanied Clemmie, which allowed Mavis and Christine to hang back for a moment – something they had both hoped would happen.

Taking each other's arm, with a flourish, Mavis whispered, 'Think the two things are related? The disappearing dentures and the bloodied bobble hat?'

Christine hissed, 'That sounds so strange, but, yes, I do. Though I don't know why. Something's gone from here, something's been left behind there. No signs of a break-in in either place.'

'Think the sister, Clemmie, might have something to do with it?'

'I haven't warmed to her, but why?'

'Money.'

'But why would she want money?' asked Christine.

Mavis looked at her young colleague with disbelief. 'Everyone wants money, dear. Even if they're a lady with a selection of big houses to live in. For free. I don't know where she gets her cash – her spending money – from, but I bet she'd like more of it. That gaunt look she has? I've seen it before; it suggests to me she could have some unhealthy habits. She might know some people who could make those fakes, if she's as tight with the arty crowd as she mentioned over drinks.'

'Henry was fortunate that Alexander wanted to see the collection,' said Christine.

'I wonder if that's the case,' replied Mavis thoughtfully. 'Bit of an odd one, that Alexander. I cannot put my finger on it, but there's something there. Reminds me of someone, but I can't think who. Very annoying. What do you make of him?'

Christine hesitated. 'I don't know what to make of him. He's enigmatic.'

Mavis slowed as she walked, and cocked her head to look up at her companion. A strange little smile played on her face as she said, 'Now isn't that an interesting thing for you to say about him?'

'Heard from Annie at all?' asked Christine quickly, as they approached the dining room.

Mavis shook her head. 'Only the report she copied to us last night. Nothing today. Maybe she's off with her long lost East End friends again? She really came up trumps finding out about that pub in London where they use the hats, didn't she?'

'Typical of Annie,' breathed Christine, 'always lands on her feet. Like a cat, that woman.'

'Aye,' said Mavis with feeling, as Alexander came to escort them to the table, where chatter and fine dining ensued.

TWENTY-FOUR

Annie Parker peeled her eyes half open, and immediately regretted the final few drinks she'd had in the pub downstairs last thing on Saturday night with Jacko James. Each limb of her body felt as though it weighed a ton, so she lay quite still in her terribly uncomfortable bed. The room was no more than a wash of dim light about her, probably thanks to the old fashioned, thick curtains she recalled fighting with, so she closed her dry, aching eyes again, and tried to grasp at the fringes of her last memories before she'd fallen asleep.

Unable to settle after writing and sending her report about her exciting discovery at the Saxby home to her colleagues, she'd decided to stay awake to find out why Tristan Thomas had mentioned to Jacko that he'd see him behind the pub at midnight. Luckily for Annie her room overlooked the side and back of the pub, so all she had to do was open her window and make sure she could hear what was going on.

Around ten past twelve she'd heard a muffled conversation between two men. She hadn't dared poke her head out to confirm that it was, indeed, Tristan and Jacko, but she didn't need to really, because Jacko's cockney accent and Tristan's Welsh one were quite distinctive. Unfortunately, all she'd been able to catch was a variety of words which, when taken either as a whole, or alone, made no sense.

Nonetheless, Annie dutifully noted each word: Hoops. Too late. Cops. Tidy. Idiot. Safe. No. Yes. She. Him. Never. No. Tuesday. She didn't feel very hopeful that the list would ever make sense, but she'd written it down in her notebook in any case.

Having heard the back door to the pub being locked beneath her window, Annie was startled by a loud bang and a crash not long afterwards. This was immediately followed by the sound of Delyth James screaming down the stairs. 'You all right down there, Jacko?'

Annie opened her bedroom door, to hear Jacko hissing, 'Shhh,' up the stairs. He noticed the crack of light behind Annie and added, 'Sorry to wake you. Had a bit of an accident.'

Annie took her chance and stepped out of her room. 'No worries, doll. I couldn't sleep anyway. Too quiet. No traffic. Who'd have thunk I'd miss it, eh?'

Jacko smiled and his wife withdrew into their room, nodding at the fully-clothed Annie, as she clasped her nightie about her throat.

'Since you're up and about, and obviously still wide awake, do you fancy a sneaky one? A drink, I mean, of course,' called Jacko, chuckling.

Annie made her way down the creaking

staircase. 'Is the Pope a Catholic? You won't have to ask me twice,' she quipped. 'I'll go with a G and T, please, doll. I can have a bit of a lie-in in the morning – it's Sunday tomorrow, after all.' She looked at her watch and added. 'OK then, it's Sunday already, just about, but you know what I mean.'

Settling onto a bar stool, Annie decided that she'd try to find out what she could about Jacko's son, Mickey, since she'd realized, at Wayne's house, that if he was playing for a football team in the East End of London that wore bobble hats like the one the dowager had found, he was her lead suspect in the case of the disappearing corpse.

Annie was good at chatter, and she knew it. Largely she knew it because most people told her so after she'd run off on a stream of consciousness for about five minutes. In her previous life, as a receptionist at a firm of Lloyd's brokers in the City of London, it had been viewed as a quirk. Now she found she could use the technique to lull people into a false sense of security that they were passing time with a dimwitted chatterbox. It made them open up a treat.

Halfway through her second drink, Jacko let it drop that he'd seen his son not too long ago, and Annie suspected that the timing might tie in with the incident at the Dower House. She also managed to establish that, yes, Tristan Thomas did indeed put some money into the Coach and Horses football team and, when Annie mentioned seeing the photographs of the teams at Wayne's house, Jacko confirmed that Mickey still played for the team at the Hoop and Stick in Mile End. Happy that she had such confirmation – because she knew that confirmation was what good investigators always sought – she allowed Jacko to ramble on about Delyth and her dad for a while, then he offered her a brandy before bed.

The last thing Annie recalled with any clarity was taking the brandy from Jacko and chinking glasses with him. Then nothing.

Now it was morning, or, at least, she thought it must be, and she tried to arch her aching back. As she did so, Annie realized she was in more pain than she'd imagined and it wasn't just the result of a hangover.

Did I fall over? She couldn't recall doing so.

How did I get into bed? She couldn't remember that either.

She sat up and rubbed her still-closed eyes with little fists, like a child. Good grief her room smelled bad.

Gordon Bennett! I'm not in me room at all. The bed was uncomfortable because it wasn't a bed, but a mattress on the floor and a very lumpy one at that. The room wasn't dark because the curtains were thick, it was dark because the only light was coming from one pathetic light bulb, encased in a grimy, round plastic cover, hanging on a wire behind her in the corner of the brick box that surrounded her.

Annie's stomach panicked and the rest of her wasn't far behind. Peering about in the dim light, she allowed herself a couple of minutes to try to get her heart to stop thumping and to allow her eyes to acclimatize themselves to the gloom.

217

The little room smelled of stale beer, dampness and general yuck. It didn't smell of beer in the way a room does if people have been drinking in it, it smelled of beer in the way a place does if it's been sloshed about all over the place. For years. Putting two and two together, Annie suspected that she was in the cellar of a pub. She couldn't see any kegs about the place, but she was pretty certain of it. *I'm in a pub cellar, or a pub store room.* Immediately she was certain she must still be at the Coach and Horses. Where else? *But why am I hidden away in a cellar?*

Putting aside the bigger questions for a moment, Annie allowed herself to consider her physical wellbeing and comfort for a moment or two. She felt herself all over, but couldn't find any specific form of injury. *Good, I'm still in one piece.*

There was no obvious source of heating in the room. She was cold. She pushed herself upright and looked all around the rough walls. She realized that the switch for the light must be beyond the heavy wooden door which was, of course, locked.

A bucket in one corner provided her the only place to relieve herself. Even though she found the idea disgusting, she had little choice but to use it. There was a row of bottles of pop and a pile of chocolate bars. She panicked again that someone expected her to be in the room for long enough to need to use such 'amenities'.

Annie pounded on the door and shouted. She kept it up for at least ten minutes, or so she thought, then she took a break. Her throat was sore already.

Retreating to the comparative comfort of the mattress, she sat herself down and gave the matter some thought. She reasoned that Jacko James had somehow twigged that she'd overheard him talking to Tristan Thomas. *Maybe he heard me closing my window?*

After Annie had quizzed him about his son and the way that he played for the football team in London, Jacko must have decided she knew too much and had somehow drugged her – *probably that final brandy?* – and hidden her away in the cellar, or an outer store at the pub.

Annie further reasoned that, because the Coach and Horses pub was in the village, even if the little brick-built room she was in was at the back of the building, she might be heard by someone, so she got up again and renewed her efforts at making as much noise as possible. *The village is so quiet, someone must hear me.*

Annie had checked and knew she had no handbag, no phone, no watch, no shoes and, possibly worst of all, no cigarettes. Otherwise, she was still in the clothes she'd put on when she'd dressed at the pub in Talgarth on Saturday morning to take her bus journey to Anwen-by-Wye. She had no idea what time of day it was, or even if it was day or night. Realizing she was very, very hungry she began to wonder if it might not be Sunday morning at all, but much later in the day, or even heading for Monday. *I have no concept of how long I've been unconscious.*

She swore at the door, then at Jacko James, then at everyone and anyone else she could think of. Then she did it all again, even more loudly. Eventually, Annie retreated to the mattress once more, and sat down.

She finally allowed herself to give in to the wave of terror that was about to drown her and she cried like a baby, sobbing and sniffling, feeling completely and utterly alone, and trying to fight her fears about what was to become of her.

After a while she began to get annoyed with herself for being so weak, so she dried her eyes and nose on her grubby top and, Annie being Annie, she began to try to work out what it was exactly that had worried Jacko James so much that he'd felt the need to drug and kidnap her.

TWENTY-FIVE

Monday morning began very differently for each of the women of the WISE Enquiries Agency.

Although she wasn't aware of it, it was the morning when Annie Parker awoke in a brick box, bloodied her knuckles beating on a door, almost lost her voice calling for help, then cried like an infant.

Carol got her husband ready to take the Tube train into Liverpool Street station. Having kissed him goodbye, she waved to his back, then settled herself at the dining table and powered up her laptop, ready to do battle with the world of data and translate it into information.

The Honorable Christine Wilson-Smythe lay beneath a fine duck duvet thinking about Alexander Bright. He'd been witty and entertaining at dinner and she wished there were more men like him in her social circle. Finally rising, she gave some consideration to how to dress to be interviewed by the police. Then, rather surprisingly, she got a phone call from Mavis MacDonald.

Mavis MacDonald was woken by her mobile at seven thirty that morning, when she was informed, very gently, that her mother had suffered a second stroke at her nursing home in Dumfries. She phoned Christine, who offered to drive Mavis to Scotland to see her mother, but Mavis declined, insisting that Christine needed to remain at Chellingworth Hall to retain some control over the case. The dowager very kindly volunteered Ian Cottesloe to drive Mavis to Scotland, which the ex-nurse also declined calmly. She finally acceded to Althea's insistence that he be allowed to at least drive her to the railway station at Hereford, where Mavis had discovered there was a train departing around eleven a.m. which, with changes at Crewe and Carlisle, would get her to her mother by that afternoon. A concerned Althea hugged her new-found friend as she departed. Mavis assured her she'd keep in touch and that Christine, Annie and Carol were more than adequate to the task of following the leads about the bobble hat that would, surely, lead to discovering who the poor dead boy had been.

TWENTY-SIX

Annie had eaten a few of the chocolate bars and drunk a bottle of the pop with which she shared her cell, but she felt sick and even hungrier. At least she could feel her energy and spirit return a little, but she still had no idea why she'd been locked up. She was absolutely desperate for a cigarette, too, which blackened her mood even further, if that were possible.

She'd worked out that none of her colleagues would be likely to realize she was in trouble for hours. She'd sent her report to Carol, as required, at the end of Saturday. They didn't have a real system or protocol for keeping in touch, and she wondered if that wasn't something they should talk about for the future. As time dragged on, she imagined Christine wafting around a grand country estate like something out of a 1920s fantasy, while Mavis drank endless cups of tea with a withered dowager. Carol she imagined talking to her little bump. None of this helped her feel any better.

She at least held out hope that her colleagues would worry if she didn't report in at some point. They would expect to hear something from her on Sunday. Not for the first time Annie wondered what day it was.

She'd continued to make bursts of effort through the day, or night, or whatever it was, shouting

222

and banging her fists against the door, but to no avail. What worried her most was that she hadn't heard any sounds at all from outside her place of incarceration. She'd expected something. A vehicle passing. The sound of humanity in some form. But she'd heard nothing.

She couldn't imagine why on earth that would be the case. Yes, Anwen-by-Wye was a small village, but it was full of people. She hadn't even heard a church bell peal, or the honk of one annoyed motorist's horn. It was as though the world beyond the brick walls which surrounded her had ceased to exist.

She counted the chocolate bars and cans of pop again, consumed one more of each, and wondered how long she could live off the remaining store. Then she began to feel dizzy, so she lay on the mattress, hoping that sleep, and answers, would come. Sadly, all that met her on her pillow was a worried, sweaty slumber, in which she was haunted by visions of her mother, Eustelle, crying at her daughter's grave, which was a giant brick box.

TWENTY-SEVEN

After her sad and worrying telephone conversation with Mavis, Christine could do nothing but await the arrival of the police at Chellingworth Hall. Following coffee in her room, she thought she'd better check on any feedback she'd received from Carol, or any reports she'd been copied in by Annie.

She was a bit miffed to find that Annie hadn't been in touch at all on Sunday, and was disappointed by how little Carol had been able to discover about the link between Anwen-by-Wye and the East End pub, where they wore black and blue bobble hats, and Mickey James. Christine didn't know the East End terribly well, and she made a mental note to get a full briefing from Annie.

Thinking of her colleague, she checked the time. She reckoned that Annie would be up and about by this time on a Monday morning, especially since she was on a case, so she phoned her mobile number. It went straight to voicemail. Again, Christine's immediate reaction was to be annoyed. Yes, Annie had found their big breakthrough clue on Saturday evening, but she could have tried to do a better job of keeping in touch since then, even if she had chosen to go romping about the countryside with some long-lost old friend!

Christine gave the matter some thought, then decided that it would be just fine to phone Annie at the pub. She could be an anonymous friend to whom Annie had given the name of the pub. She pulled up the number in Carol's records and dialed. A woman with a Welsh accent and a grumpy tone answered.

'Hullo. Coach and Horses.'

'Hello there – could I by any chance speak to a guest of yours, Annie Parker, please?' asked Christine, using her best Irish accent. Having spent her earliest years on the family's estate in

224

Ireland, it was her second most natural accent – right behind her more usual clipped and cultured English tones.

'No. She's gone.' The woman sounded angry.

'Did she say when she'd be back?'

'I mean *gone* gone. Left. You know, gone for good. And good riddance.'

Christine was confused. Had Annie maybe gone to stay with her old friends from London? Had she done something to annoy this woman? 'She told me she'd be there until today. Did she leave this morning? Already?' Christine sounded as confused as she was.

'Yesterday. I got up and she'd gone. All her stuff. She never even paid for any of her board. Very unfair, I call it. When you talk to her, you tell her she won't be welcome here again. I don't care if she is friends with Wayne-flamin'-Saxby. He might think he's Lord Al-flamin'-Mighty around here, with all and sundry at his beck and call, but I don't think it's right to take bread off someone's table by telling them you'll be paying for two nights, staying one, then going off without paying a penny. Theft, it is. Plain and simple. Tell her to shove that in her pipe and smoke it.'

The woman Christine deduced to be Delyth James hung up.

Where was Annie?

Christine phoned Carol, who answered immediately, 'Yes, is that you, Christine?'

'Yes. I can't find Annie,' said Christine, feeling it best to get to the point. 'Have you heard from her at all?'

Carol's voice communicated concern when she

replied, 'Not a dickie bird since Saturday night's report. I know she's not the world's best at keeping in touch, but I must admit I was a bit surprised to not have heard from her myself.'

'Oh, crikey,' said Christine. 'Well, it's just you and me then, Carol. We've got to track her down somehow. The woman at the pub said Annie stayed one night, then left, and of course Mavis can't help, because she's off to see her mother, because of her stroke.'

'What stroke?' asked Carol, sounding even more concerned. 'I thought I was our communication conduit. I thought I was supposed to be kept in the picture by everyone, then I let you all know what's going on. How can I do that if no one tells me anything?' Christine could tell that Carol felt slighted, but that was the least of her worries.

Christine knew she had to take control, and do it smartly. 'OK,' she began, 'I dare say Mavis might get in touch with you when she's got a chance, but, until further notice, she's off this case. She's getting herself sorted out to get to her mother's bedside in Dumfries. I've got access to all her reports and we had a quick catch-up this morning when she phoned to tell me what was happening. I'm afraid it doesn't sound as though her mum's going to make it, though Mavis is being Mavis, and all "nursey" about it, so she won't say. Her eldest son and his wife are already at the old folks' home where they are looking after her mother. Anyway, I thought I'd check in with Annie and the landlady at the pub told me she left there yesterday morning.'

Christine thought she could hear the tension in Carol's voice when she said, 'What's she up to, Christine?'

'Have you got a number for that Saxby house she visited?'

'I haven't but I can find one, I'm sure. I've got all the names of the people there. I'll get onto it and get back to you. Have the police arrived at Chellingworth Hall yet? Mavis told me in her report from last night that they'd been called there. Something to do with missing false teeth, I gather.'

'Yes, it's true,' replied Christine, 'but let's not worry about that for now. Can you get onto the Saxby house phone number and maybe try to reach Annie there? I'll be here handling this end of things. And, look, whatever else happens, let's not lose touch with each other. I might get stuck talking to the police for ages, but it would be good to know you're looking for Annie.'

'Will do,' replied Carol. 'I've got to go, my other line is going, and it might be the people who make the bobble hats. Even if Annie saw a photo of a football team wearing similar ones, I need to check the facts. I'll let you know when I get the Saxby number and I'll report back to you on what they say when I phone them. And I'll text Mavis to wish her all the best. And I'll text Annie too, just in case. Got to go, bye.'

Christine looked at her phone, accusing it of being useless. She felt as though it was now her sole responsibility to try to piece things together.

A knock at her door told her it was time to meet the police, which she did in the study in the west wing. Two very pleasant, conscientious officers from the Dyfed-Powys police were in attendance, and they took all the details of her actions the previous day. Her response to the questions about why she was at Chellingworth Hall was, as agreed with Henry and Althea, merely that she was a friend of the family. Her father's title of viscount helped, and she was dismissed rapidly. She managed to glean that the general police position was that the teeth could have been taken months earlier and no one would have been any the wiser. She left without having to mention the dead body or the bobble hat at all, and the police certainly didn't raise the topics, which allowed her to leave the interview with a certain sense of relief.

Knowing that Mavis had left already and that Annie was missing, but possibly still in the area, Christine had decided that she would stay until lunchtime, hoping for Carol to come through with a phone number for at least one of the Saxbys, or a message to say that she'd spoken to one of them, then, failing all else, Christine would drive back to London. Though she couldn't imagine doing that without knowing where Annie was.

She was very distracted throughout lunch, something that did not go unnoticed by Alexander. Clemmie didn't join them for the meal, and Christine was surprised to discover that Alexander didn't seem to care that she wasn't with them. Puzzled about their relationship, and worried to death about Annie and Mavis, she decided to distract herself.

'So, tell me, Alexander, how did you and

Clemmie meet? You didn't tell us much last night.'

'Quite right, you didn't,' said Henry, peeling the skeleton from the small trout that lay on his plate.

'We met at an art gallery,' said Alexander.

'Ha! That makes sense,' said Henry, pushing the bones to one side of his plate. 'Clemmie seems to live in those places. I hope it was one of the better ones, with real art in it, not one of those dreadful modern places she espouses.'

Christine and Alexander exchanged a glance which betrayed gentle amusement at their host. 'I'm afraid it was a terribly modern one,' replied Alexander. 'Over in the East End of London, which is where all the really avant-garde stuff is being developed these days.'

Henry looked up from his fish and said, 'Codswallop. Usually a load of old rubbish. What was it? Horse hair and old bits of string?'

Alexander smiled broadly. 'As a matter of fact it was a collection of installations featuring barbed wire and reclaimed wood. They were, shall we say, "challenging" pieces, though there were some very interesting models of the face of the artist who created them on the walls, made with the use of 3D printers by someone else.'

Henry looked triumphant. 'What did I tell you? Just a lot of people who can't be bothered to learn how to paint, *saying* they are artists. And Clemmie encourages them. So, what's your excuse? Listening to you go on about those teeth I'd have thought you to be a man possessed of better taste.'

Henry was attending to his fish, so Alexander looked directly at Christine as he replied. 'I knew of your collection, discovered where I might encounter your sister, and set about securing myself an invitation.'

Christine's eyes widened. This man was brazen. He'd connived an invitation to an exhibit, which was now discovered to have been burgled, and he was being quite open about the whole thing. Christine wondered if this was a clever bluff on the part of the darkly suspicious man.

Henry looked up from his plate. 'What's that? You made a beeline for Clemmie just to come and see my collection? Weren't thinking about trying to buy it from me, or steal it from me, were you?' said the duke, now fully alert.

Alexander looked from Christine to Henry. 'I would have offered you a good price for it,' he replied calmly, 'and I still would, for the Churchill piece. Why? Would you be interested in selling?'

Henry wiped his mouth. Christine was fascinated as she watched Alexander operate.

'I can't see that it wouldn't hurt to discuss a figure,' replied Henry cannily. 'Of course, I might not be able to do anything until the insurance people, and the police, say I can. But it would make sense for the Churchill piece, at least, to be in the possession of someone to whom it means more than it does to me.'

'Then maybe we should have a quiet chat after lunch,' said Alexander. Returning his attention to Christine he added, 'So that's *my* true motive for being here out in the open. Now what about you?' He didn't bat an eye.

'I say,' said Henry.

Christine weighed her options. She'd been a champion chess player at her school, which had the best chess team in the south of England, so it didn't take her long to make her decision. No members of staff were present, the police had left the premises, and she felt, for some reason she couldn't properly name, that she could trust Alexander. And not just because of his warm voice and piercing eyes.

'With your permission, Henry?' she asked her client.

Henry looked alarmed. 'Are you quite sure?'

Christine nodded.

'Very well then,' acceded the duke. 'Tell him everything. I could do with being brought up to speed myself.'

Christine spent the next twenty minutes pouring out the whole story to Alexander, who interrupted only to ask pertinent questions, which Christine answered.

When she had finished, Alexander said, 'I'm very sorry to hear about your colleague's mother. I wish her either a speedy recovery, or a swift and painless passing. Mavis MacDonald struck me as a woman who has seen a great deal of suffering in her time, and has borne it with self-less patience and fortitude.'

Christine was taken aback, but thanked him. She'd never thought of Mavis in that way, but, upon reflection, suspected that Alexander's assessment was apt.

Alexander continued, 'The critical other matters are, what has happened to the body of the young man the dowager saw in the Dower House and, of course, who was he, and who killed him? And the current location of your other colleague, Annie, of course.'

Christine nodded again. 'I'll admit I am very concerned about Annie and Carol hasn't got back to me with a number for the Saxby family yet.'

'That's something with which I might be able to help,' said Alexander.

'How?' asked Christine and Henry in chorus.

'I know someone who knows him,' replied Alexander coolly.

'Do you know someone who knows everyone?' asked Henry, flummoxed.

Alexander smiled. 'Not quite, but I do have a good number of acquaintances, who, themselves, are very well connected. In this instance Wayne Saxby is someone I know of because I, too, am involved in the world of London property. Not in the same way that he is tied up with large redevelopment projects, but on a smaller, more domestic scale. I believe I could make a few calls and come up with a number. I suspect your Carol might face something of a problem; Wayne Saxby likes to remain as private as possible.'

'Why is that?' asked Christine, pretty sure she wouldn't like the answer.

Alexander considered his response. 'If what I have heard about him is to be believed, he has some rather questionable friends. He is known to be a man who prefers that deals work out exactly as he chooses. Sometimes his questionable friends are able to make that happen for him.'

Christine shuddered. 'I wonder if Annie knows that.'

'If she doesn't, let's just hope she doesn't find out in an unpleasant way,' replied Alexander. 'I tell you what, why don't I make my calls, you try to contact Carol, fill her in on what I'm up to, and we'll get some coffee. I'm sure Henry could arrange that?'

Henry nodded, coffee was ordered and phone calls were made.

TWENTY-EIGHT

With coffee and notes at their sides, Alexander and Christine sat opposite each other, with Henry in attendance.

'Clemmie said she would join us, but I hope she doesn't,' said Henry blackly.

'If she does, I believe that we shouldn't discuss this in front of her,' said Christine.

'Oh, come along now, she's my sister. She can't possibly be involved,' said Henry unconvincingly.

'Links to the East End of London, links to artists, access to both the hall and the Dower House?' said Christine. 'I'm sorry, Henry, you asked me to enquire into these matters, and I am putting two and two together and coming up with the possible involvement of Clemmie.'

'But why?' whined Henry.

'Money,' chorused Christine and Alexander, each smiling at the other's perspicacity.

Christine nodded for Alexander to proceed, which he did, with some delicacy. 'Despite her background, her ability to live in palatial homes, and her title, your sister lives an expensive life-style, Your Grace.'

'Oh for heaven's sake, Alexander, it's *Henry*. I've told you before. Call me Henry. If you're accusing my sister of being a thief, at least you can address me by my given name. I am not feeling terribly gracious at this moment.'

'And I am guessing that's because you think we have a point. Am I right?' said Christine pointedly.

Henry nodded. 'Clemmie has an allowance, but she runs up some dreadful debts. I've bailed her out a few times, but Mother says I must stop, that she must learn to live within her means. But it reflects so badly on the name, you see. I can't have it. It's one of the reasons that I'm always so hard up when it comes to spending money on this place. I'm pinching pennies on restoration, and she's out supporting artists who are only starving because they have no talent.' Henry deflated as he spoke. Christine's heart went out to him. He really did seem to feel the weight of responsibility upon his shoulders.

Even Alexander looked apprehensive as he continued. 'Has Clemmie got into any trouble of this sort before, Henry? Has she, maybe, taken items from here without your permission?'

Henry looked horrified. 'I . . . I wouldn't know. I mean, if something large were to go missing I'd notice, of course, but there is so much that I do not see, especially in the east wing. As Mother pointed out, the insurance people do visit each year, so they would raise a hullaballoo about something not being right, and that's never happened. Well, except for the spoons, and that was next to nothing.'

'Spoons?' asked Alexander.

Henry waved away the question. 'It was a misunderstanding. One of the lists said we owned two fifteenth-century silver spoons, but they were, in fact, two seventeenth-century silver spoons. It was all cleared up. It was something and nothing.'

'Hardly,' said Christine. 'Fifteenth-century silver spoons are exceedingly rare, whereas seventeenth-century ones are much less so. There would be a huge variation between the value of two such sets.'

'They are merely spoons,' replied Henry dully.

'I have to agree with Christine,' said Alexander. 'I own a business, Coggins and Sons, which trades in antiques, and I happen to know that there could be a difference in value of many thousands of pounds.'

Henry stewed as he sipped his coffee.

'I don't suppose you know Tristan Thomas, the antiques dealer here in the village, do you, Alexander?' asked Christine.

'I don't, but I am due to receive a phone call from an acquaintance of mine who might,' replied Alexander, smiling.

'You're like another Carol,' replied Christine. 'Speaking of Carol, I managed a brief chat with her, and she confirmed that, even with her wonderful abilities, she hasn't been able to get a number for any member of the Saxby clan, nor for the house. You were clearly correct in your assumption that Wayne Saxby likes to keep his private life private. She did discover, however, that Mickey James is known to be often in the company of a young man who works at the Mile End hospital. He's in his early twenties, is Asian, possibly Bangladeshi because he's from the Brick Lane area originally, and plays on the Hoop and Stick pub football team with Mickey. Althea pegged the dead body as having dark, coffee-colored skin. It might be a fit, but Carol hasn't been able to pin down who the young man is, or whether he's even missing. So it might be nothing.'

Alexander reached into his pocket as Christine was talking and pulled out his vibrating phone. 'I'll take this,' he said and did so. Listening, he nodded, then hung up. He pushed a few buttons then held his screen toward Christine. 'Here's Wayne Saxby's home phone number. Will you phone him, or shall I?'

'I'll do it,' said Christine.

'What will you say if he asks how you got his number?'

'I'll wing it,' smiled Christine, punching the numbers into her phone. 'It's ringing,' she whispered. 'Hello, yes, could I speak to Mr Saxby, please? Really? Would this be his mother, Olive, by any chance? Oh, good. Look, I'm a friend of Annie Parker. Yes. Yes. I know. Well, I wondered if she was with you? No? She left yesterday. Yes. No, I rather hoped you did. Yes, we spoke and she mentioned that. No. Yes. I certainly will. Thank you, Mrs Saxby. Bye. Yes, I will. Bye.'

'Not there?' said Henry.

Christine shook her head.

'That was the mother?' asked Alexander.

Christine nodded.

'Do you think she was telling the truth?'

'I think so. She sounded pretty genuine, or else she's a very good actress. Does your source suggest that she's involved in any of her son's funny business?'

Alexander shook his head. 'Do you want to get in touch with the police? Or would you like to join me in a visit to the Coach and Horses to see if there are any clues there as to her whereabouts?'

Christine was on her feet in an instant. 'Coach and Horses. If we take our luggage and our own vehicles we can meet there, see what's what, and decide what our next move should be.'

'You can't leave Clemmie here with no way to get back to town,' wailed Henry. 'And what about Mother's bobble hat and my teeth?'

Alexander sounded impatient as he replied, 'Henry, I am sure you have sufficient vehicles here for Clemmie to drive herself back to London, or she could take the train. And it might be that all these issues are connected. So we will, indeed, be trying to find out if there are links between each of these elements. But, for now, a missing person must take priority over a missing corpse and some dentures, however wonderful they might be. But, speaking of dentures' – he scribbled something on a piece of paper and handed it to Henry – 'this is what I'd be prepared to pay for the Winston Churchill piece. You can think about it and I'll be in touch. My pal from Scotland Yard will be trying to get hold of you later today and I know he'll want to come here to get the lie of the land. Brace yourself for some harsh words about your utter lack of adequate security in the east wing, Henry, but be open and honest with him, and just let him poke about as much as he likes. He's got a well-deserved reputation for being able to follow the most obscure of shipment routes. Don't forget, Henry, your collection might have been stolen, but it might not yet have reached its intended, or final, destination. If it isn't yet resting in the bowels of someone's very private collection, there might still be hope.'

Alexander looked across the room at Christine, who was already at the door. 'Let's get a move on. I'll meet you at the stable block and we can leave at the same time.'

'Right,' said Christine. 'I'll be in touch, Henry,' she called, as she dashed up the stairs to her room.

Henry Twyst was transfixed by the number he saw on the piece of paper Alexander had handed to him. A smile crept across his face as he mouthed the figure quietly.

TWENTY-NINE

When Mavis MacDonald entered her mother's small room at the nursing home in Dumfries, it was immediately clear to her experienced eyes that she'd arrived just in time to say her farewells. She'd been hugging her son upon her arrival at the home at four thirty, and by a quarter past five, it was all over. Her mother had never regained consciousness after suffering the stroke in the early hours of the morning, but Mavis was quite convinced that she had known her daughter was with her at the end, which comforted her somewhat.

Having been the matron of an establishment that provided housing for retired servicemen, Mavis was well acquainted with the process that followed the death of an elderly person who had been under the care of a resident physician. She, the doctor in charge and the matron of the home had a very professional conversation, after which she left with her son, having arranged to stay with him for a few days and to return to the home first thing in the morning. It was expected that the funeral directors' staff would arrive within a few hours to remove her mother's remains to the funeral home, and Mavis was relieved, if not happy, that she and her mother had taken the time to discuss her wishes for her final arrangements when she had still possessed the wits, and the ability to speak, to be able to make her desires known.

Mavis was ambivalent about her mother's death. She had loved her, and would miss her, of course, but she would have hated to see her exist, rather than live. She finally understood the truth in the words she herself had spoken on so many occasions as a part of her duties. 'It was a blessing.'

She helped her son, Duncan, explain to her grandchildren what had happened to their great granny, though they seemed more excited to have her in the house than to be bothered by the idea of a death in the family.

Mavis succumbed to the convenient temptation of haggis and chips from the chip shop on the corner of the street where Duncan lived, and regretted it within half an hour of having eaten the plateful. Walking around her son's kitchen with a hot cup of tea, rubbing her tummy, she realized she owed it to her colleagues to let them know what had happened and that she would be staying in Scotland for a few days.

She couldn't face talking to them; listening to their words of consolation would upset her. She decided to send a text to each of them, explaining what had happened and her plans. She told them she'd let them know as soon as she had a date for the cremation and, finally, wished them all well. As she crawled into the small bed in the miniscule spare bedroom in her son's neat and pretty bungalow, she felt her age. And also knew that she was, finally, an orphan. When she eventually managed to find sleep, the loss of her mother filled her dreams and her pillow was wet with tears within the hour.

THIRTY

Carol was sitting at her dining table, petting Bunty and her little bump when she got the text from Mavis. She pondered her friend's loss even as she countenanced the new arrival in her life, and how she'd have to begin to plan for the future. Frustrated at not having been able to find a phone number for the people she was sure Annie must now be staying with, she'd been pleased to hear that Christine was making progress, thanks to the intervention of the enigmatic Alexander Bright. But she was terribly worried about Annie.

Realizing that there was only so much she could do from her Paddington flat, by way of a diversion she began to investigate the mysterious stranger who had turned up at Chellingworth Hall and with whom Christine seemed quite taken.

She was surprised at what she discovered about Mr Bright.

One of Carol's fortes was to be able to discover information about people by searching seemingly unrelated sources, and putting the pieces together. What she'd discovered was that Alexander Bright was the pretty anonymous head of a great number of companies, and the very open owner of several more. Her interest had been piqued by his desire for privacy, so she'd set about finding out more. Unusually for Carol she'd hit a big, fat, dead

241

end. There had been no electronic trace of Alexander Bright until he hit the age of about thirty-four, when he seemed to emerge as a moneyed investor in property, from, literally, nowhere. But, other than tracing three British-born Alexander Brights, and discounting two of them, she was left with a scant record of a son born to a Marion Bright of Brixton. She noted that her address was close to where the riots of 1985 had begun. Since one of Alexander Bright's businesses was named Marion, Carol was pretty sure she'd found the right person. What she couldn't fathom was how someone could be, essentially, invisible to all record keeping between the ages of six and thirty-four. She didn't like it. But she wasn't sure what it meant, or whether she should alert Christine.

With such a hole in Alexander Bright's life proving to be almost frustrating beyond words, Carol recalled something Annie had asked her to look into. Searching back through Annie's last report, she found the name of the infant school teacher who'd died in a fire and set about finding out all she could.

Once again Carol's fingers tapped and her brain whirred. Even as she was doing it she was aware of how very much she enjoyed her job. This was so much more interesting than what she'd done for that reinsurance company. This was real; she was digging into real people's real lives, not trying to come up with some complex program that manipulated data about theoretically nonexistent, if massive, amounts of money.

She was elated when she found the beginning

of the trail and she kept at it, until she had what she thought was the whole story, then she set about condensing the critical information from the various sources, citing them as she typed, and ended up with another neat, comprehensive report. Feeling the satisfaction of a job well done, she had, sadly, increased her own anxiety about her missing friend.

THIRTY-ONE

When she arrived at the Coach and Horses pub in Anwen-by-Wye, it was immediately clear to Christine that a Monday afternoon was a quiet time in the village and for the public house itself. Only Alexander's car was parked in the court-yard, which she'd reached by driving under the old coaching arch of the pub. Walking out onto the street again, to get a good look at the place, Christine noted its great age, the Victorian updates and the fact that it had a considerable number of outbuildings. The hanging baskets at the front door had seen better days, but, Christine told herself, it was almost the end of September and summer annuals were going to be getting chilly at night.

The interior of the pub offered low ceilings, beams, an inglenook fireplace that wasn't in use yet, but looked as though it could be if needed, and a long bar with a brass rail and a grumpy looking, blousy woman standing behind it.

Her arms were folded and her mouth puckered in anger. Alexander stood in front of her next to a barstool, his hands on his hips. Christine sensed a showdown.

Ignored by the woman she assumed to be Delyth James, Christine found herself to be the object of some particular curiosity for two aged men who were nursing half-pints of beer in dim corners.

'I don't care what you say, I don't know who you are and I'm not tellin' you nothin',' said the woman behind the bar to Alexander.

Alexander replied in tones too low for Christine to catch.

'Not flamin' likely,' said the woman, her Welsh accent stronger than the one Christine had heard on the telephone earlier in the day.

Again Alexander spoke.

'I told you he's not here. And it's none of your business. And if you go poking about, I'll phone the police, I will.'

Alexander said something, then turned, catching sight of Christine. 'We're searching the place,' he said in what was almost a growl. 'Let her phone the police if she wants,' he added so that Delyth James could hear him. 'Come with me, Christine. At least this woman's told me that the rooms are upstairs.'

Alexander darted up the staircase that ascended from the end of the bar. Christine followed, but he was quick on his feet and she could hear him throwing open doors ahead of her. Below her she heard Delyth shout, 'That's it. You've got no right to do that. I'm phoning the police, I am. Now!'

Christine hesitated. She knew the woman was correct, that she and Alexander could face charges if they invaded this woman's privacy, searching her home without her permission. And that could jeopardize her investigators' license. But Annie was missing, and it was either this approach, or bringing the police into the whole thing, which she felt might make matters worse. Always an independent soul, she knew in her heart that she wanted to get to the bottom of everything under her own steam. Or at least with the help of Alexander.

Entering what was clearly the James's own bedroom, she saw Alexander pulling open a built-in wardrobe, but all it held was clothing.

Next they entered a small, dingy room with heavy, floral curtains. Alexander pulled open the few drawers in the flimsy chest and dressing table, then almost succeeded in hauling the aged wardrobe on top of himself as he wrenched the doors open. Save for some dismal wire hangers swinging on a rail, it was empty.

Christine checked the bedding – it hadn't been used, but she sniffed the pillows and the covers nonetheless. 'Annie hasn't slept in this bed,' she announced, 'but I can smell her perfume on the covers. She always wears the same one, Yardley's Lily of the Valley. Body lotion, talc, eau de toilette – the lot. There's no mistaking it. She's at least spent some time sitting here.'

Throwing herself to her knees, Christine peered under the bed. 'Look!' she said triumphantly, 'this is her notebook.' Frantically flicking through its pages, she made her way to the window to let more light fall on the penciled notes Annie had made on the last page.

Christine read aloud, 'She's scribbled, "Hoops. Too late. Cops. Tidy. Idiot. Safe. No. Yes. She. Him. Never. No. Tuesday." I've no idea what any of that means and there's nothing here to give any of it any context in any case.'

'Something she partially overheard?' asked Alexander.

Christine continued scanning the pages, hoping to find something more illuminating, as she muttered, 'Possibly. Rats! Why didn't she write more?'

Exasperated, she looked up to see Delyth James standing in the door, holding a telephone handset.

'See? Not here, is she,' she spat. 'Gone, and all her stuff too. Stayed Saturday night, then off without a by-your-leave. Terrible.'

'She didn't sleep in that bed,' said Christine. 'You can tell that the sheets haven't been disturbed at all.'

Delyth James looked taken aback, then curious. 'She must have straightened the bedspread before she left. I . . . um . . . I haven't got around to stripping it and making it up again yet. No one else due here till next weekend, see.' She sounded a little less vehement and took the two steps needed to reach the bedside. Pulling back the covers, she pulled a little at the sheets, then lifted the bottom corner of the bedspread to reveal neatly tucked corners. Shrugging, she said, rather grudgingly, 'Well, I'll give you that. I know my own hospital corners when I see them, and that bed hasn't been disturbed at all. You know, not by someone sleeping in it. I won't say it hasn't been sat on, mind you, but, no, not slept in.'

Seemingly confused by her discovery, Delyth softened, then looked blankly at Christine and said, 'So where did she sleep that night then? I saw her up here, I did, must have been about midnight. Still dressed, but in her room. Jacko was crashing about in the bar, and her and me both came to the top of the stairs to see what was happening. That's a bit peculiar, isn't it?'

'Might she have joined your husband for a late-night snifter?' asked Christine, knowing full well that any offer of a nightcap would be happily accepted by Annie.

Delyth pouted. 'Well, as it happens, yes, he told me he offered her one, you know, just to be hospitable, like. I went back to bed and let my tablets work. Terrible bad head I'd had that day. Couldn't shake it at all. By the way,' she added, waggling the telephone in front of them, 'Jacko, my husband, wants to know exactly who you people are.'

Christine decided to take a different approach with the woman and appeal to her better nature, if she had one. 'I'm Chrissy,' she said, knowing that, if word of her visit to the pub reached Annie in any way, the use of the diminutive might tip her off that she wasn't being ignored. 'I'm a friend of Annie Parker, and it's really not like her to disappear at all, and certainly not without paying her bill, or without letting anyone know where she's going. If it helps, I'm quite happy to pay what she owed you, so if you just tell me what it is, I can give you cash, now. How about that?'

Delyth James seemed to soften even more when Christine handed over the amount she quoted. She visibly brightened when she realized that Christine had added quite a large sum 'to allow for her inconvenience'.

Now sitting on the edge of 'Annie's' bed, Delyth mused, 'She seemed tidy enough that Annie, your friend. You know, for one of them.' She cocked her head as she spoke.

Christine felt her shoulders hunch. She hated it when people judged Annie, or anyone else for that matter, by the color of their skin. She wondered how the woman's comment had made Alexander feel, given his obvious mixed-race background.

She knew she had to respond, because she felt that to ignore racist comments was to be complicit. 'That's not a very nice thing to say.' It was about as impolite as she felt able to be, under the circumstances.

Delyth looked horrified. 'Oh, don't get me wrong, I didn't mean 'cos she's black. Well, she's not even that black, really, is she? Bit darker than you, like—' she smiled at Alexander – 'and she's got a lot of those funny black freckles they have. But she's not shiny black, is she? No, no. I'm not a racist, me. I meant because she's English. Of course, I know Jacko's English, and I married him, so I s'pose I of all people should know that they aren't all a complete waste of space. Some of them are very nice, really. So, like I said, she was quite jolly, considering.'

Accepting that, from her perspective, Delyth James clearly didn't believe that denigrating the entire population of England was racist, Christine decided to let her comment pass.

'But, you know, what was I to think?' continued Delyth, unfazed. 'It's not nice to do what she did. I wonder why she went? And where do you think she can have gone? Jacko said she came here on the bus. There aren't no buses at that time of night. Stop at six o'clock, they do, then the first one's at eight in the morning. But that would have been Sunday morning, yesterday, and the first one then isn't till ten.' She looked even more puzzled. 'There was another woman looking for her, by the way. On the phone this morning. Irish woman she was. Another friend of yours too, maybe? Sounded a bit *twp* to me, mind. But, there you are. You can't say that Annie Parker isn't popular, I suppose.'

'*Twp?*' queried Christine, realizing that she was the 'Irish woman' in question.

Delyth looked around and whispered, 'You know, a bit soft in the head. Dim. But, there, that's the Irish for you. All that Guinness they drink, I suppose.'

Doing her best to ignore Delyth James's rather critical analysis of almost everyone she mentioned, Christine judged that the woman was truly at a loss as to what had happened to Annie, but didn't want to take her into her confidence too far.

Christine shook her head and tried to squeeze out a few tears. Alexander took what he saw as his cue, and put his arm around her shoulders in a most reassuring manner. Looking down at the seated Delyth with her saddest eyes, Christine said, 'Is there any way I might be able to speak to your husband myself? He might know something about her whereabouts, especially if they had a late-night drink together on Saturday. She might have said something?'

Delyth James shook her head sadly and passed Christine a paper serviette she pulled out of her pocket. 'When you two came up here I phoned him, not the police. He was very angry, but he said he doesn't know where she is, see? He said she just came back up to her room after they had a quick drink and that he didn't even know she'd gone. Out of here himself in the early hours of Sunday, he was. He helped Tris move some stuff to London. Didn't know where he'd gone when I got up, I didn't, then he phoned to say he was with Tris.'

'Tris?' said Christine.

Delyth smiled. 'Tristan Thomas. Owns an antique shop on the common. Jacko helps him out when he can. It's all the barrels, see. Good at lifting stuff, is Jacko, but there's nothing of Tris – more meat on a butcher's pencil. Doesn't even look like he could lift a pint, but he manages that all right, he does. It's his van, but Jacko does the lifting and they share the driving.'

Christine said, in as pleasant a voice as possible, 'They must be good friends, for your husband to leave home so early on a Sunday morning to help him out.'

Delyth stood up from the bed and replied, 'Not exactly friends, but, you know, it's a small village and we've been here a long time. You get to

250

know people.' She looked up. 'Have to, in this line. Like them or not, they've got to think you love 'em to bits or they'll go somewhere else to drink.'

In that instant, the Honorable Christine Wilson-Smythe was terribly grateful that she'd been born to a viscount and would never, hopefully, feel the resignation to a less-than-happy life that this woman obviously did. Her Mensa-sharp mind compartmentalized her emotion and snapped her back to the reality of her situation. She'd established that Jacko James had driven to London in a van on Sunday morning and that Tristan Thomas, the toothy local antiques dealer, was with him. *Might Annie have been an unwilling passenger?* was her next thought.

With all three of them standing in the tiny room, it seemed the right moment to Christine for her to suggest they all moved back downstairs to the bar. She didn't think there was anything else to be found in the bedroom, but her mind was racing. How could she convince Delyth James to allow her and Alexander to hunt through all the pub's outbuildings? Annie might have been spirited away in the night, or she might have just been dumped nearby.

'I wonder, Delyth, do you think Annie might have wandered off, maybe a bit drunk, in the night?' said Christine quietly as they all descended the stairs.

Reaching the bar, Delyth replied thoughtfully, 'Well, I suppose she might have. Do you want to have a look round the back? We've got lots of old buildings out there – the old stables for a start and some other places that Jacko uses to store all sorts of rubbish. Always telling him he should clear stuff out, but he never does. Thinks he's going to need everything again, he does. Make do and mend is all well and good, but when it's broken, good and proper, you might as well get rid of it. Anyway, I've got to be here, in the bar – not that it's busy, but one of these two might take it into their heads to have another, I suppose. But you go ahead, I don't mind. I don't think anything's locked back there – nothing to steal.'

Christine and Alexander thanked Delyth and were already walking out of the front door when Delyth called, 'But if that's what happened, then has she been there all yesterday, and last night too? And where did her bag go?' They ignored her, and kept walking.

It took about half an hour, but, by then, Christine and Alexander were both convinced that Annie Parker was nowhere on the premises of the Coach and Horses pub in Anwen-by-Wye, and there was no evidence, anywhere, that she had ever been held in any of the stables, the cellars – which were clean, brightly lit, whitewashed and well stocked with barrels – or any of the other ramshackle structures around the place that, as Delyth had told them, were all bursting with clutter.

Christine was frantic when she whispered to Alexander, 'I'm guessing she was in that van that Tristan Thomas provided and Jacko James drove from here on Sunday morning. But, if Jacko and Tristan, for whatever reason, thought they needed to scoop Annie up, why would they then risk taking her to London – if, in fact, that's where they've gone. We only have a conversation between Jacko and Delyth to suggest that and, while I think she's telling the truth, there's no reason to believe he would. Why wouldn't he just keep her hidden here, somewhere?'

Alexander brushed down his clothes and gazed at Christine with what she thought was a deeply enigmatic expression.

'We've just seen for ourselves that there isn't anywhere he could keep her here. Maybe, if she was unconscious, she could have been bundled into a tiny corner of one of those buildings, but there's so much scrap and rubbishy stuff here, there's hardly room to squeeze in another bin-bag full, let alone keep a live person hidden.'

'Don't say it, Alexander,' warned Christine, shaking. 'Don't you dare suggest that Annie's not alive.'

'I'm sorry, I didn't mean to suggest that at all. Look, I say we have another go at Delyth and, this time, let's try to find out where Jacko might have gone in London, if that's where he is. You know, sound her out a bit more? And, when we've finished with her, let's get back to your Carol and see what she can tell us. OK?'

Christine nodded her agreement.

Alexander added, 'If I take the lead, will you follow?'

Christine knew he meant with regard to the conversation with Delyth, but it felt as though he might have intended his question to have more depth. She barely hesitated before nodding again.

'I'm not that good at playing Follow-my-Leader, unless I'm the leader, but I'll try,' she said with a smile.

Entering the pub once more, Christine and Alexander headed for the bar, where Delyth was busy dusting bottles of spirits. Alexander cleared his throat, causing Delyth to spin around, then he looked down at Christine and said warmly, 'Thanks for that, there's no sign of Annie. And I'm sorry we got off on such a poor footing, Mrs James. I overreacted. But if my lovely girlfriend is worried, I must act to help her. I'm sure your husband would do the same for you.'

'Oh, yes,' replied Delyth, smiling. 'Always helping people out, is our Jacko. You know, like Tristan, and always doing his best for me and Michael, that's our son, and a lot of the young-sters in these parts. He does so much for people and never says nothing about it. Out till all hours he is, in the van and everything, helping people. Ah, love him. He's a good man.'

'I'm sure he is,' replied Alexander. 'And your son too, no doubt. Is he here by any chance? Might he know something?'

Delyth smiled. 'Oh, no, he's not here these days. Lives in London now, he does. In fact, Jacko's going to drop in on him while he's there, that's why he stayed over last night. Likes to do that.' She looked at her watch. 'I bet they'll have had a nice pub lunch together, somewhere. Poor dab, Jacko misses his boy a lot, he does. Not that I don't, but there's nothing here for him, you see. Michael, I mean. So many more chances for him to make a go of it in London. Not that he's found a job yet, but he will, I'm sure of it. Mind you, he comes back to see his mam now and again. Like his dad in that respect – hard on the outside, big softy on the inside.'

'We all are, Mrs James,' replied Alexander with a grin, squeezing Christine's shoulder in a boy-friendly way. 'Aren't we, Chrissy?'

Christine played along. 'Well, you certainly are, Alex. Does your son have to share a place in London?' she asked as chattily as she could. 'Whereabouts is he, exactly? I live in west London and I know it's a very expensive place for one to live alone.'

Delyth leaned on the bar, clearly happy to be chatting about her beloved son, rather than a missing guest. 'Oh, you're not wrong there. But he's lucky. Jacko's still got family in the East End, somewhere around Bethnal Green, not that I know it that well, and Michael stays with them. So Jacko gets to see lots of family when he visits there and they've got room for him too, when he wants. Which I know he enjoys. He works so hard here, it's only fair he gets a bit of a break now and again. Though I wasn't expecting him to go anywhere yesterday, I must say. But there, Tris must have got wind of a good deal and off they went to get it. It happens like that, some-times. Funny old world, antiques. Drive all over the country, they do, though mainly to London and, you know, places like Dover and so forth. All international now, it is.'

As Delyth mentioned international ports, Christine's stomach clenched. It hadn't occurred to her that Annie might have been spirited out of the country.

Alexander began to make as though to steer Christine away from the bar by her shoulders. 'Well, I think we'd better get going ourselves, Mrs James. I expect your friend Annie will turn up somewhere, darling. Maybe she's gone to visit her friends the Saxbys again. Remember she mentioned them to you?'

'Oh, no, she won't be there,' said Delyth just before the couple turned to go. 'When the postman came in this morning he said he'd seen them and they'd asked him to hang on to their post for a while. Off to Spain tonight, or somewhere, he said. Or was it America? I can't remember. Always going off somewhere they are. Lucky devils. And Olive always sends a postcard, bless her. She knows how much I like to get cards from people when they go away. Look, there's the last one she sent.' She waved her arm toward a collection of postcards pinned to the wall behind the bar. 'Mind you, what they went to Houston for is beyond me. She said it was a bit boring. They couldn't even find anything pretty for the photo on the card. See? It's just all buildings and motorways, by the looks of it.'

Christine and Alexander followed the woman's gaze and saw a collection of brightly colored shots from beaches, tourist attractions and landscapes around the world. One was, indeed, from Houston, and the landlady was correct, the photograph made it look like a very unappealing place comprising skyscrapers and spaghetti-like roads.

'I hope they have a lovely time,' said Alexander,

now pushing Christine toward the door. 'Thanks for your help.'

'Why are you pushing me?' snapped Christine as they exited the pub. 'Stop it.'

Alexander removed his arm and apologized. 'We need to go to London, now,' he said firmly.

'Yes, I understand that, Alexander. I am quite capable of putting two and two together, you know. Annie's not here. I am not stupid, I'm worried. Very. About Annie. I know I should be more concerned about the dead body that Althea saw, but, for now, Annie's my priority.' Christine heard her tone and knew it was harsher than she'd meant it to be, but she was so used to men thinking that it was impossible for her to be rich, well-born, beautiful *and* intelligent, that it was her default setting. 'I wonder why Olive Saxby didn't mention that she was leaving the area when I spoke to her this morning,' she mused.

Alexander marched toward his car, with Christine following. Once there he opened the door and then replied, 'It might have been perfectly innocent, in that it's not something one would normally tell a complete stranger on the telephone, or she might be part of an incredibly complex, nefarious plot of some sort. I don't know. But what I do know is that I am getting back to town as fast as I can, now. I suggest you do the same. Drive safely. I've got your mobile number. I'll be in touch.'

Christine sounded sulky as she replied, 'Yes. I suppose there's not much point hanging about here. Though I do wonder if I should talk to the police about Annie being missing.' With Mavis dealing with the possible loss of her mother and Carol in London, Christine felt quite alone.

'Don't tell them,' said Alexander forcefully. 'Not yet, anyway. Get yourself back to your place in London, then phone me. I might have some news.'

Christine brightened, but was puzzled. 'Really?'

Alexander nodded. 'I hope so.' He curled his tall frame into the low, sleek car. As it purred out of the parking area, Christine acknowledged that she was sad to see him go. Climbing into her own vehicle, she plugged in her tablet to charge as she drove, and buckled up. She allowed herself a moment to regard her reflection in the rearview mirror. She looked as worried as she felt. But determined, too. She wondered why, as an independent young woman, she'd allowed herself to come to feel as though she was relying upon a man so quickly. Then, cross with herself, she pulled out onto the road and began to head for London.

THIRTY-TWO

When Annie Parker awoke, she knew she was still lying on the mattress in the pub cellar, or whatever it was, but, this time, everything was pitch black. She panicked. Then she tensed. She knew with certainty that someone was standing close by. She flailed her arms as someone grabbed her and stuck something across her mouth. She

258

struggled, but she could only make loud humming noises through her nose. A graveled voice whispered very close to her ear, 'If you want to live, you'll stop struggling and do exactly as I say. Now!'

She continued to push against her assailant, but he quickly bound her hands with something which, although tight, didn't cut into her flesh. Then he bound her feet. Next he wrapped a cloth around her eyes. All she'd had a chance to glimpse in the darkness was the fact that the man was large, evidently strong, was wearing a dark hoodie and had something obscuring his face. A balaclava, she was sure of it.

Annie was surprised when the big, strong man picked her up like a sack of potatoes and slung her over his shoulder. Completely disoriented, she decided that the best thing to do was allow her body to become as limp as possible, and make herself a dead weight. When that achieved nothing, she wriggled and writhed, though she knew that the most likely outcome was that the man would drop her, and then she'd be on the floor as helpless as a caterpillar.

Eventually, having felt herself being carried up some stairs, Annie saw no change in the level of light through her hood. It might have been day or night, for all she knew. Then she felt the rush of cold air hit the exposed parts of her arms and legs. *I'm outside.* She inhaled the fresh air through her nostrils as hard as she could, though not much of it reached her through the thick cloth that wrapped her head. In the distance she heard a siren. *Really? A siren in Anwen-by-Wye?*

Then she heard something that any Londoner would recognize instantly – a Tube train passed by, not far away. Annie was immediately reminded of the scene from one of her favorite films, *The Ipcress File*, when Michael Caine escapes from what he believes to be a place of captivity somewhere in an Eastern Bloc country to see the most welcome sight he can imagine on the street – an illuminated London Transport sign, telling him he's on his home turf.

Annie's heart swelled with joy. *I haven't been in Wales all this time, I've been in London. I'm home!* The realization hit Annie just as she felt herself being lowered onto a hard, cold, metallic surface. She knew she was being placed in the back of a van or lorry of some sort. She felt the shudder of the man jumping into the back of the vehicle. He pulled her to a corner, where he surrounded her with what felt like blankets of some sort.

'You're going to feel me inject you with something,' said the disembodied voice.

Annie recoiled and began to squirm and groan again. *Don't move me. I'm in London; don't take me back to Wales.*

'Stop it, or this'll hurt,' he shouted.

She knew he meant business. He grabbed her arm and she felt pressure, then a stinging sensation. Annie's insides clenched and she screamed as best she could through her nose. *Oh, Gordon Bennett, please let it not kill me.*

'I need you to sleep,' said the man bleakly. 'And you'll be grateful you did,' he added.

Annie's head swam. She vaguely felt the hood

being removed from her head and caught a glimpse of daylight, then she was aware of pressure as the man pulled the tape from her mouth, but it didn't hurt a bit.

She was sitting on the bank of her beloved Thames, which was now no more than a bubbling stream, dangling her feet in the cool water while waiting for Eustelle to bring her a raspberry ripple ice cream. It was a sunny day and her teddy was beside her. She was happy.

THIRTY-THREE

'Mother, the art policeman will be visiting you shortly. I do not think this is the best time for you to venture out with McFli.' Henry sounded cross as he addressed the dowager on the telephone.

'I have been held captive in my own home for months, Henry,' retorted his mother firmly. 'Since our last open day on Sunday, I had to spend yesterday up at the hall with you, being poked and prodded by real policemen, so this is only the second day I have had a chance to venture beyond the walls without bumping into all sorts of people. Now that the torrential rain has subsided, I shall be walking with McFli. It cannot be beyond the abilities of a policeman to find one elderly lady and a dog on the estate, even if this one is an art expert, not a proper copper.' Althea pushed the button to disconnect from her

261

son's voice and sighed at McFli, who sat at her feet looking excited.

'Yes, we will. Momentarily,' she said to her dog, then pushed herself to a standing position and made for the door. McFli scrambled behind her making squeaking, wheezing noises. Althea could see that he was smiling as broadly as she at the prospect of being able to wander freely across the landscape. She pulled on her walking jacket, grabbed the gnarled old stick she always took on her expeditions, and tied a scarf about her head. Her stout shoes were equal to anything the final, muddy days of September could throw at her, she decided. The heavens had opened around eight o'clock the previous evening, and she'd imagined that many people were considering whether it was time to build an ark, so heavily had the rain been falling for more than twelve hours. Opening the front door, McFli shot out ahead of her, turning in circles with delight as his mistress caught up with him. Althea smiled at his puppy-like antics, which belied his age.

Walking through the gate set into the walled garden of the Dower House that Tuesday morning felt, to Althea Twyst, as though she were escaping a prison. She set forth, in the cool, wan sunlight, to enjoy the glories of nature. She was looking forward to roaming about for at least a few hours. Adequate seating set about the place was one of the only perks of having opened the estate to the public, so she knew she could take rests when she needed. Neither she nor McFli were as spry as they had once been, though he continued to look as though he was possessed of boundless energy as he frolicked away from her toward the lower copse.

She'd been walking for no more than ten minutes when McFli romped back to her with a trophy in his mouth. Dropping it at her feet he yapped with excitement. Seeing something blue in the grass, Althea knew he hadn't brought her a half-eaten rat, which he was wont to do on occasion.

'Thank you, McFli,' she praised, then bent slowly to examine her gift. It was part of a ripped, blue, rubber glove. Althea picked it up, much to McFli's delight. It was a puzzling item for him to have found and her immediate response was to be glad that he hadn't swallowed it.

'We've placed enough waste bins for people to put their rubbish in, haven't we, McFli?' said the dowager. 'Now where did you find this?'

Once again McFli shot into the copse and Althea set off after him. His yapping led her to him. He had the rest of the blue glove in his mouth, but she was horrified to note that it contained a hand, a brown hand, which was still attached to an arm, which poked up from the wet ground in the hollow.

'Come along now, McFli, put it down. Down!' she ordered, and the happy little creature let the hand drop onto the ground. With his ears down, he trotted to Althea's side. She praised him heartily, then turned and slapped her thigh. 'Come along home,' she said, and began to make her way back toward the Dower House to alert someone to what they had discovered.

It took about an hour, all in all, for the police

vehicles to arrive. The first on the scene had been the art policeman, who'd turned out to be quite a dish, thought the dowager. He'd followed her directions to the copse, then he'd made things happen.

Once again confined to her home, Althea was now being attended to by her frantic son who, once he discovered that a body had been located, was overcome with guilt at ever having doubted his mother.

By dinner time on Tuesday, Althea and Henry Twyst had been informed that the cadaver she and McFli had discovered was that of a young man, and that he had probably been dead for more than ten days. It appeared that he had been buried in the copse under a good covering of soil, but that the rain of the previous night had run down the hill at such a rate that a small stream had developed and washed away enough of the earth mounded on top of him to expose a hand, which McFli had scented. The pleasant policeman with an interest in art had been replaced by a somewhat abrupt detective whose accent made it clear he originally hailed from Birmingham, though he was now some sort of high-up in the Dyfed-Powys police force.

He'd put Henry through the ringer. At least, that was what Henry had told his mother. She'd thought him quite pleasant, if brusque. Already up-to-date with the discovery of the bloodied bobble hat and the dowager's claims of having seen a dead body in her home, the senior policeman had taken time to explain that she didn't need to look at photographs of the dead man because it would be too upsetting, so he only showed her photographs of the man's clothing, because he said that the condition of the body was poor.

Althea's response of, 'Yes, that looks like what the body was wearing when it lay on my hearthrug. I expect the poor devil is black with putrefaction if he's been in the damp soil for a fortnight,' took the police officer aback and utterly shocked Henry.

The interview with Mary Wilson, the cook, delayed dinner, but she provided sandwiches for all the police on the estate, which the detective ate while he interviewed Jennifer Newbury and Ian Cottesloe. Upon taking his leave of the Twysts – Henry had decided to stay with his mother overnight in case she felt any ill effects after her shock – the detective was tight-lipped. He'd taken the contact details of the WISE Enquiries Agency from Henry and said he would be following up with them.

'Of course, we should tell the women that the police will be contacting them about the dead man, Henry,' said Althea to her son as they finished dinner. 'Why on earth would we not inform a group of professionals you hired to investigate an incident that the incident has seen such tragic developments?'

'I don't think the police would care for our doing that, Mother,' replied Henry.

'Tommyrot!'

'What I cannot fathom,' mused Henry, 'is why the criminals would try to hide the body here, on the estate. Why would they do that? Why wouldn't they take it away with them to . . . dispose of . . . somewhere?'

'Henry, look at where we are,' replied his mother. 'These people could not have arrived at the Dower House in a motor vehicle – it would have been far too conspicuous. They must have walked. We are sitting in the middle of a six-thousand-acre estate. Finding themselves with a dead body to conceal, what were they to do? Carry it away with them? Much better to let the poor man roll down the hill to the copse and cover him over with soil down there. If it hadn't been for the rain last night, their plan might have worked.'

'It's terrible,' said Henry blackly.

'That a man died, or that the people who killed him had the temerity to dump his body on our land?' Althea tutted at her son. 'I shall telephone Mavis right away. She needs to know what's going on. I'd like to find out how her mother's recovery is progressing, in any case. I rather think Mavis feared the worst. If death is the worst thing that can happen to us. I can see myself wanting to be turned off, or unhooked, or whatever it is one does, rather than existing as a vegetable in a stinking bed for months on end.'

'How can you say such a thing, Mother?' bleated Henry. 'I would never do that to you.'

Althea sighed and stared at her son. 'I'm afraid you might not, but you need to know that would be my wish, should I come to it. But maybe I had better enquire with our solicitors about what I can do to ensure that choice is my own, not yours to make.'

266

'Mother, why are you speaking this way? Is there something you're not telling me?' Henry looked truly alarmed.

Althea reached out to touch her son's arm, which he graciously allowed to remain within her grasp, after initially flinching.

'Henry, I am getting old. I know it. But I am still in good general health and my mind, as the terrible events of today have painfully illustrated, is as sharp as it has ever been. But, recently, I have been listening to some books that have made me think anew about planning for my twilight years, and I believe I need to take more responsibility for my final plans.'

'Listening to books? What do you mean?'

'Henry, I realize that you're still in the twentieth century when it comes to utilizing technology. Fortunately I am not. Yes, it is true that I do not care to have a telephone in my pocket all the time, or even in a room where I am sitting, but that is purely because I do not care for interruptions. But books that one can listen to as one walks to the village, or potters in the garden? What a wonderful invention. I can pop them in my pocket and listen to them on tiny little things which fit inside my ears.'

'Really?' said Henry. 'Is that comfortable?'

'Quite, my dear,' replied Althea. 'I have gained an enormous amount of pleasure listening to some wonderful voices reading poems I haven't heard for many decades. It's been quite a surprise to me to discover that pieces I learned by rote as a child still come back to me, and I am able to speak the words aloud as though I had seen them on the page just a short while ago.'

Henry gave the matter some thought. 'Have you been walking to the village reciting poetry that you've been listening to at the time?' asked Henry abruptly.

Althea looked puzzled by his attitude. 'I believe I have been, yes. Why?'

Henry shook his head. 'Oh nothing, nothing at all. It's just that I think some people have seen, and heard, you doing it and might have thought that you were . . . well, you know, chatting to yourself.'

'You mean as though I'm going batty?'

Henry nodded.

Althea smiled. 'Well, I'm not, dear. Though why chatting to oneself should be viewed that way is beyond me. Sometimes the most sensible person with whom one can carry on a conversation is oneself. Or one's dog.' She smiled down at McFli, who'd been given several very special treats for having made such a big discovery.

Henry sat back while Jennifer Newbury cleared the dinner things and placed a pot of coffee on a tray at the end of the table.

'We'll serve ourselves,' said Henry, sounding rather distracted.

After he'd done just that he said to his mother, 'There was an incident in the village that concerned some mushrooms, Mother. Do you recall? You had a bit of a turn. You, apparently, felt it necessary to throw all the mushrooms from the little stall outside the general store across the street. Do you remember why you did that?'

Althea looked puzzled. 'Really? Is that what I did?'

Henry adopted a gentler tone. 'I'm afraid you did, Mother. Several people saw you, and there was quite a commotion. Don't you remember that Ian had to come to collect you and bring you home? You said that the mushrooms were inedible, so you threw them away.'

'Oh, Henry, you sometimes only hear what you want to hear. I remember now how I tried to tell you what had happened, but you were terribly cross with me. Do you have any idea what it feels like to have your own child chastise you? Well, no, of course, you wouldn't. Well, let me tell you, it is a very unpleasant experience. The reason I threw those mushrooms, not into the street, but into the rubbish bin, was because I had been inside the shop moments earlier when I overheard the new woman who runs the place telling someone on the phone that she was hoping they'd all be sold by the end of the day because they were well past their sell-by date, so she'd ripped off all the packaging to make it look as though they were local and good to eat. Mushrooms become dangerous when they are old, Henry. I acted out of a desire to prevent anyone from becoming ill.'

'They can't have been too bad if people were still prepared to buy them,' sulked Henry.

'I think you're rather missing the point. The point is that I didn't have what you described as a "turn", I had a very good reason for doing what I did. I would have paid the woman for the wretched things if only she hadn't created such a fuss.'

A silent truce held for a few moments, then Althea rang the little bell that sat at her elbow. Jennifer appeared at the door.

'Yes, ma'am?'

'Telephone, please, Jennifer. Henry will dial for me, thank you.'

A few moments later Henry listened as Althea consoled Mavis at the loss of her mother, then pass on the news about the discovery of the body. He only heard half the conversation, so his mother relayed Mavis's side of things after he had hung up for her.

'The cremation will take place next Monday. Mavis will stay with her son until Tuesday. It sounds as though it will just be the three of them, plus the matron from the mother's nursing home, at the service, which I think is terribly sad. Maybe we should go too? Yes, maybe I shall. Who do you think will come to my funeral, Henry? Would it be a good turn-out, do you think?'

'I will not discuss such matters with you,' replied Henry abruptly.

'Well, I'd better warn you now that I want the "Liberty Bell" played as they carry my coffin up the aisle,' said Althea.

'I'm sure that whatever music you want can be arranged,' replied Henry more gently. 'I don't think I know that piece. Does it mean something special to you Mother?'

'Yes, it's the theme music from the Monty Python TV series. I want that exact version, and I want it timed precisely so that the farting, squelching sound is made as my coffin is placed upon the stand at the altar.'

'Mother, you cannot do that. You are a duchess.' Henry was scandalized.

'I am a person with a sense of humor, Henry, never forget that. You, sadly, do not possess one at all, it seems, which I believe is one of the reasons you are, usually, so unappealing to women. They do not care for stuffed shirts. So you'd better get on with wooing that Stephanie girl who is continuously making goo-goo eyes at you. She doesn't seem to mind that you are the person you are. In fact, I'd go so far as to say she rather likes you, warts and sense of humor bypass and all, dear.'

'Stephanie Timbers couldn't possibly care for me in that way, Mother,' said Henry sadly. 'Besides, whatever she and I might think of each other, I know you wouldn't approve of her as a possible duchess.'

Althea Twyst shook her head. 'Henry, my dear boy, sometimes you are such an idiot I can hardly believe that your father and I created you. You know very well what I was when your father met me. I've told you often enough. I was a dancer and a pretty poor one, at that. You cannot believe me to be so much of a snob that I'd think Stephanie Timbers unsuitable for you? Good grief, Henry, what must you think of me? I won't say I'm not sorry that she's not named Tracey, or Kylie, or Apple Sunshine, or something like that. Some names don't lend themselves to titles as well as others, that's true. But, for heaven's sake, just be a man and say something to the poor girl. She's intelligent, she understands country life, could make a real go

271

of this place, and she's still young enough to pop out a couple of children. As the sad death of your brother illustrated, the need for both an heir and a spare is critical for those of us with a line to continue. It was quite clear to me at dinner the other evening that you and she click. If you don't do something about it, I shall, so get going.'

'Oh, Mother!'

'Yes, Henry, I shall say something myself, if you don't. Get on with it. I believe she's your last hope of keeping the title alive.'

THIRTY-FOUR

Mavis had truly believed that Monday had been the worst day of her life; the dreadful, desperate rush to reach her mother's bedside and the ultimate inability to communicate with the woman who had brought her into the world, before she herself left it. Mavis couldn't imagine how it could get any worse. But it did.

Tuesday brought her the stark realization that she had tasks ahead of her that would force her to become 'the relative to be managed', rather than simply a grieving daughter.

Mavis MacDonald absolutely understood the balance of sympathy and professionalism that the matron of the Castle Douglas home was using to manage her. Throughout her nursing career, and especially as the matron of an establishment where her charges were all expected to die, she'd done it herself often enough.

She arrived at the large, rambling house set back from the Castle Douglas road out of Dumfries at eight thirty on the dot on Tuesday morning, and applied herself to paperwork and clearing out her mother's belongings. She knew very well that rooms in such a nice place were always in demand, and it was the matron's responsibility to allow as little time as possible to elapse between residents.

By the time she stopped for a late lunch comprising some fruit and a couple of sandwiches she'd made for herself in her son's tiny kitchen that morning, Mavis was happy with her allocation of small mementos to her mother's friends, the bagging up of items to be taken to the charity shop, and those items she felt she wanted to keep, for the time being. She'd spent time meeting the people who had known her mother during the last few years of her life, and had enjoyed hearing their stories about her. She'd laughed more than she'd cried, and she was sure that was a good thing. Her son was collecting her later in the day, so she decided to sit in the grounds, on a seat her mother had favored before her first stroke, and take some time for herself.

'I'm glad I found you,' said Matron McGregor as she sat beside Mavis on the wooden bench. 'We took these from your mum when she was taken ill, just in case. I don't know what you want to do with them. Sometimes people like to give them to the undertaker, to allow for a more lifelike appearance for their loved ones, but I don't know what you want.'

She handed Mavis a set of dentures, encased in a plastic bag.

Mavis regarded them dubiously. Looking at the matron she said, 'I know from my experience at the Battersea Barracks that they'll be of no use to anyone else.'

'Och, no,' replied the matron with a smile. 'All made to measure. They'd not fit anyone else. It's a shame, too. Randy only made them a year or so ago. Your mum liked Randy. Always joking about together, they were, like wee kiddies. Did you find the sets he gave her to paint?'

Mavis had mentally wandered back to the days when her mother egged her on to do naughty things, with devilment, giggling like a wee girl herself. 'Sorry? The what?'

'Randy, he's our man for teeth. Believe it or not he does all the old folks' homes round these parts from his van. Got these brand new machines that take photographs of the patient's mouth, then they make the molds from that. Print the molds they do, if you please, with 3D printers. Aye, it's amazing what they can do these days. And so good for the older ones, of course. They always hated having to put all that goop in their mouths and bite down for an age. Not that I can blame them. But now? Randy just waves a wand with a very bright light thing in their mouth, then prints up an exact copy of everything. He works on it back at his laboratory to make the dentures themselves, then brings them back. Your mum thought it was great fun, so he gave her the molds for her to work on in her art sessions. The molds with teeth in them, not the ones where they just had gums. You see, it's not like in the old days now, the dentists don't have to keep the molds forever, they just print a new one.'

Mavis gave the matter some thought. 'I didn't think to go into the art room,' she said sadly. 'Mum hadnae been up to anything like that for so long, it didn't occur to me.'

'Och, come with me. Of course, her pieces are some of our favorites, but you're welcome to them if you'd like. I'll show you. They're all still on display on the windowsills. Her great-grandsons might like a set each. They are the sort of thing that boys would enjoy, vividly painted, jolly old dentures.'

When her son collected her, Mavis didn't have much to load into his car. She was surprised at how little of her mother's life was worth keeping. But two sets of comical dentures made of printed material, were in her pocket. Her grandsons fell upon them with great glee when they got home from school, and she was glad to know they would have something to remind them of their great-grandmother that would make them laugh, not cry.

By the time she received the phone call from Althea, she was very tired. She'd made the mistake of putting her feet up after an early cup of tea and had dropped off to sleep. Not something she ever did. Mavis knew she sounded sleepy when she answered the phone, but, as soon as the dowager mentioned that a body had been dug up on the estate, she was suddenly wide awake. Her faith in Althea was proved correct. She felt relieved. An odd sensation on such a fraught day.

She thanked the dowager for her solicitousness, accepted her kind suggestion that she attend the funeral, and sat quite still for a moment, wondering who the poor dead man might be. Althea had told her that Henry would be telephoning Carol with the news too, so Mavis felt quite happy to settle to a nice meal of spaghetti bolognese with her two grandsons, and tried to put the matter out of her thoughts, but she found that, when she wasn't thinking about the dead man at Chellingworth, she was thinking about her dead mother. She didn't know which was more depressing.

THIRTY-FIVE

Christine's Tuesday began badly. She'd hardly slept, she was so worried about Annie. At least, that's what she told herself. The truth was that she couldn't help but keep thinking about Alexander Bright, and she was cross with herself about it. Eventually she fell into a very deep sleep, so she didn't wake until almost ten a.m., then ran around in a panic trying to get out of her flat and up to the office.

Her plan for the day wasn't so much a plan as a vague idea of what she'd do when she got to the office and had a chance to talk things through with Carol. But, while she was sitting in traffic on the way to Battersea Bridge, she got a call from Alexander, who suggested that they should meet for lunch at the Hoop and Stick pub in Mile End. Christine jumped at the chance for a couple of reasons, and told herself that visiting the pub where Wayne Saxby sponsored the football team that wore the black and blue bobble hats was a very good idea indeed. She wondered why she hadn't thought of it herself, then told herself that she was tired and it would have come to her when she'd talked to Carol.

It wasn't going to be easy to get to the East End from where she was; she had to decide whether to cross the river and drive along the Embankment north of the Thames, or stay south and cross at Tower Bridge. She suspected it would take just as long either way, so she decided to cross the river right away, and hug it for as long as she could. She'd lived in so many places in her relatively short life – Ireland, the south of England, Switzerland, Oxford and then the years she'd been a nanny in the USA and Canada – but London had found its way into her heart and the Thames had become terribly significant to her. She felt it to be the most important part of London and she found herself drawn to it.

It took her twice as long to reach her destination as she had hoped, but that gave her a chance to have a quick word with Carol who was at the office. She informed Christine that, yes, the Hoop and Stick pub was one of the places that had ordered the black and blue bobble hats. Christine phoned Alexander when she'd parked on Carlton

Square, a couple of streets away from the pub itself. He told her he was already inside, that he was about to buy her lunch, and that she should steel herself. Christine entered the pub not knowing what to expect. A bare wooden floor, an eclectic collection of wooden furnishings, a dart board and a bar bedecked with a long row of all sorts of small-brewery beers quickly told Christine that she was in an old building that had been largely gutted and redecorated to appeal to a younger clientele.

Alexander was sitting at a corner table, studying a menu, and leapt up to greet her, which he did with a kiss on the cheek. By far the two best-dressed people in the place, the other patrons were mainly wearing a uniform of jeans and shirts – even the women – or, in a couple of cases, scrubs under jackets. Sanitary issues aside, Christine wondered why people wouldn't want to get out of their work clothes before coming to the pub, but reasoned they might be on their lunch breaks, which some of them clearly were, because they were eating and drinking what looked to be soft drinks.

Sitting next to Alexander, Christine felt abnormally flushed. He handed her a menu and directed her attention to a blackboard behind the bar, where there appeared a list of food items, some crossed through.

'I think we should order some food,' whispered Alexander, 'but also keep an eye on the blokes at the far end of the bar. See the one with the teeth? Do you think he could be your Tristan Thomas, the antiques dealer from Wales?'

Christine held up her menu, as though to get a better light on it from the window, and was able to turn to see the man to whom Alexander had referred.

Turning back again, she said, 'Well, he certainly seems to have enough teeth to be the man Annie described in her report, and I think I can catch a Welsh accent from that corner. I tell you what, I'll go and have a proper listen.' She was out of her seat before Alexander could pull her back.

Standing at the bar, close to the four men who were eating and drinking together, Christine caught an unmistakable Welsh accent from the oldest, skinny man with too many teeth, a broad cockney from the man with gray hair and an expensive shirt, another broad cockney from the very young man with short, dark hair and a habit of hunching his shoulders as he spoke, and a more tempered London accent from another older man, who bore a resemblance to the youngster of the group, which extended even to the hunching habit.

'Is all the apple crumble really gone?' asked Christine of the grizzled barman who finally attended to her.

'Sorry, love. Very popular it is. Goes quick. Drinks?'

Christine looked over at Alexander, who seemed to be drinking orange juice. 'Just a fizzy water, please. Ice and lemon, thanks. I'll give the food some more thought. Do we order here at the bar?'

The barman nodded his response to her question then handed her a glass of fizzing water. She paid for her drink and returned to Alexander.

With her menu held between them, as though discussing its offerings, she said, 'My money is on that lot being Jacko James, and his son Mickey, Tristan Thomas and Wayne Saxby. I have no idea what any of them look like, but the toothy one is most definitely Welsh, the two blokes without gray hair look to be a father and son, and the other chap seems to have money and an attitude. Do you know what Wayne Saxby looks like?'

Alexander held up his phone. 'Like this. Is it him? All I've seen is the back of his head.'

Christine looked at the man in the dark suit and striped shirt who'd been photographed for his website standing in front of a gleaming skyscraper, looking masterful.

'A bit older, and flabbier around the jawline, but, yes, it's him,' she replied. 'Have they all been here since you arrived?'

'Saxby got here about ten minutes before you. When you were at the bar, could you see if they've nearly finished eating? I can't tell from here.'

Christine shook her head. 'They all seem to have full plates of fish, chips and mushy peas in front of them. I think they might be here for a while. I didn't have any breakfast and I can't face fish and chips, but I am hungry and I could murder a cottage pie.'

Alexander grinned. 'No murder necessary. I'll sort it for you. Back in a mo.' He darted to the bar.

Retaking his seat Christine leaned in and said, 'You told me you might have some news about Annie. I'm worried sick about her, but the only thing I can think to do is phone the police. Have you found out anything? I just spoke to Carol and she's at the end of her tether, and that's not good for her. She wants us to get the police involved and I can't say I disagree. I didn't push because of what you said, but now—'

Alexander shifted in his seat, then he, too, leaned forward and took Christine's hands in his. Christine was aware that his hands were warm and soft. He was very close and his voice very low. 'I know we've only just met, and that you don't know me very well. But I need you to trust me. Do you think you can do that?' He was pleading.

Christine looked into his light eyes, which seemed to her to be filled with hope and earnestness.

'You're right, I don't know you at all, and I want to trust you, but I'm not sure I do. Why?'

He looked at his watch. 'Just go with the flow for the next twelve hours or so, that's all I ask.'

Christine looked at Alexander with fresh eyes. Yes, he was very attractive, but there was something else about him. There was an air of danger, of a life lived on the edge. She wondered about his past, about which she knew nothing, and about how he had made the money which he so clearly possessed. She couldn't quite imagine him being involved in anything like petty criminality, but she did begin to wonder if he might be some sort of Mr Big. The brains behind big heists, or something along those lines.

Her imaginings were interrupted by the arrival of two plates bearing very appealing cottage pies.

Christine dug into hers with gusto and was pleased to discover it was very tasty. She polished it off with a speed born of hunger, finished her glass of water, then looked around for the loo.

'Won't be a mo,' she said as she left her seat and headed off following arrows into a corridor. On her way back to her seat Christine noticed that she'd raced past a double row of photographs of football teams. No longer distracted, she stopped and studied them. They went back several years and she managed to find the more recent ones. They were remarkable because the entire team was kitted out in black tracksuits and everyone was wearing a black and blue bobble hat. She gathered from some other photos, of play in action, that these were the team's colors.

A young man in scrubs approached as she was peering at one of the photos, where she'd spotted the young man she believed to be Mickey James. She caught his eye. 'Are these photos of the pub football team?' she asked innocently.

'Yeah,' replied the young man casually.

'Any good, are they?'

He stopped at the photograph Christine was examining and pointed at the person standing next to Mickey James. 'He is. Ajit. Ajit Patwary,' he said. 'The rest? Pretty average. But Ajit? Brilliant. Scored every goal for the team last season. Don't know what they'll do without him.'

Christine peered at the dark face of the young man in question. 'He's left the team?' she asked.

'I s'pose so. He's left his job at the hospital, for sure. Well, he hasn't shown up for a couple of weeks, so they've fired him. Good as, anyway.

He was always talking about going off to the States. Maybe he went, I don't know. But he left them in the lurch over the road in the hospital, and he's left them in the lurch here at the pub. Golden right foot. Brilliant. Shame.'

Before he had a chance to disappear into the gents, Christine asked, 'And the chap next to him – isn't he in the pub today? I thought I recognized him.'

The helpful young man squinted. 'Yeah, Mickey James, in with his dad he is. He's good too, but not like Ajit.'

Polite though he was, it was clear to Christine that he was happy to leave her and head for the loo.

Alexander was looking impatient when Christine returned. 'Saxby left,' he snapped, 'but I couldn't follow him because you weren't here. Where did you get to? You were gone for ages.'

'I was making enquiries,' said Christine with a winning smile. 'And I have discovered that the young one over there is, indeed, Mickey James, and that, furthermore, there is a young man in the team by the name of Ajit Patwary. He's the star player of this pub's football team, and therefore the proud owner of a black and blue bobble hat, and he, apparently, walked away from his job at the Mile End hospital a couple of weeks ago and hasn't surfaced since.'

Alexander looked deeply concerned. 'Do you think we've found a name for Althea's disappearing corpse?'

Christine nodded. 'We might have done, but, if we have, where is his body? And why would someone who works in a hospital in Mile End be rummaging about at the Dower House on the Chellingworth Estate?'

'And who might have killed him, and why?' added Alexander.

'Of course.'

'So, what's next, Sherlock?' quipped Alexander. 'Try to find out more about this Ajit Patwary?'

Christine nodded. 'Yes, and I know just the girl for the job. I'm going back to my car and I'm going to phone Carol. She's really good at this sort of stuff. What about you?'

'I have some business that I must attend to back at my place. I have to do it there.' He looked at his watch again. 'Listen, if you do some digging about the footballer, I'll do some of my own into Saxby. How about I meet you at the Dickens Pub at St Katherine's Dock at six p.m.? It's easy for you to park at the Tower Hotel and stroll over and, being selfish about it, it's very close for me. OK?'

'So I'm on an extended pub crawl today?' joked Christine with a smile. 'More pub grub for dinner? You're trying to fatten me up.'

'No pub grub for dinner. I know a place that does wonderful sushi not far from the pub, and I promise to take you there, if you meet me. Date?'

Christine nodded. 'Date,' she replied, a frisson of excitement shooting up her neck.

'But you've got to promise me you'll stay out of trouble and won't do any sort of "enquiring" until then,' added Alexander, 'other than by talking to your Carol, or using the internet and so forth. No actual, physical snooping, OK? If there's a killer in the mix, and I believe there is, we could be dealing with people who are ruthless enough to hurt you, or, God forbid, even kill you, if they know what we're up to. These four have seen us now. They might look as though they haven't noticed us, but either of us turning up where they are again might remind them that we were here today. They cannot have failed to notice you, for a start.'

'What do you mean?' asked Christine, sounding hurt. 'I was very careful to be unobtrusive when I was at the bar. I'm pretty good at undercover work.'

Alexander smiled. 'Well then, you must wear some very good disguises, because when you're just like this, just yourself, trust me when I tell you that every man with a pulse notices you. You are a very attractive young woman, Christine Wilson-Smythe.'

He stood and Christine followed suit, feeling a little giddy. They left together, parted company, and Christine allowed herself a few minutes when she got back to her vehicle to calm down. She phoned Carol, but all she got was voicemail, so she left a message about the missing footballer. She tried Annie's phone one more time, feeling helpless even as she did so, then tearful when she heard her missing friend's voice. Finally, she contemplated phoning Mavis, but knew that wasn't fair. In fact, it was just plain selfish. She'd simply have to try to do for herself what she'd been about to ask Carol to do, but for that she needed the internet. Knowing how much time she had, and acknowledging the fact that she'd like the chance to change before she met Alexander again, she decided that the best thing she could do was head back to Battersea, and use her home computer.

THIRTY-SIX

By the time Christine had reached her flat, showered – for the second time that day – and changed her clothes, Carol was on the phone with information about Ajit Patwary. Carol explained hurriedly to Christine that she had discovered that the young man had gained qualifications which allowed him to become a dental technician at the Mile End hospital, where he'd worked for three years. He'd often appeared in the local newspaper, hailed as a hero of the Hoop and Stick pub football team. He was a relatively local lad, having lived his whole life in Tower Hamlets, but there wasn't much else to tell.

With the matter of the star footballer out of the way, Carol keenly returned to the issue of Annie's whereabouts. Christine tried her best to calm her colleague, but Carol was insistent that they got in touch with the police.

Christine finally tried to close down their conversation with: 'Look, Carol, I know you haven't met him, and I cannot honestly tell you why I feel this way, but I am inclined to give Alexander Bright the benefit of the doubt. So I say we wait until the morning to report Annie as officially missing.'

Carol countered with: 'For the record, I think you're dead wrong, and I also believe we might be putting Annie's life at risk. If you'd read the newspaper stories about that Wayne Saxby that I have, you wouldn't be so ready to wait.'

Christine, all but ready to hang up on Carol, faltered. 'What stories? What do you mean?'

'Remember in her last report, on Saturday night, Annie asked me to look into the death of an old school teacher of hers?'

Christine wracked her Mensan brain. 'Vaguely,' she replied honestly.

'Well I've been doing my usual stuff and I've found out quite a lot. In fact, I've had a pretty good couple of days of rooting through all sorts of old newspaper stories and so forth, and it looks to me as though quite a few convenient fires have allowed Wayne Saxby to buy up properties over the years at extremely favorable rates.'

Christine was horrified. 'Are you saying that this chap Saxby has killed to be able to get his hands on sites he wants to develop?' Her mind was racing. Alexander had said he was in property development too. Were these normal tactics in that type of business? She was angry that she'd allowed herself to be taken in by his charms.

'I'm not saying he did and I know the police have investigated but don't have anything to nab him on,' replied Carol.

'How do you know that?'

'I've been having another chat with Bill Edmunds, the one who's after Annie's number.'

Christine guessed where the conversation was going. 'Have you said anything to him about us not knowing where Annie's got to?' Christine was cross with Carol, not something she often felt. Carol was the agency's rock, its static, reliable center, around which the others swirled.

'No, I didn't,' replied Carol huffily. 'I *specifically* didn't. Though I wanted to. But I did manage to winkle some nuggets out of him about Wayne Saxby. I told him we were looking into a case I couldn't speak about, but I might have hinted that Saxby's second wife was considering engaging us to keep an eye on him. Just in case he's been playing away from home, you know? Bill seemed pleased at the idea that a woman might be about to hurt him in a way the police can't.'

Christine's anger dissolved. 'I should have known better. You're very clever, Carol, good job. So what did Bill Edmunds tell you, exactly?'

'To be honest, not much of any substance, just that a pattern had been officially spotted, and unofficially looked into, but that Wayne Saxby's pretty quick on his feet and, although they are keeping an eye on what he buys, and how he comes by it, most of the questionable transactions were some years ago, back in his early days of operating, before he became as big as he has been this past ten years or so. So there's nothing doing there, though they, like I, have suspicions.'

'I don't like the sound of that,' said Christine.

'My point exactly,' replied Carol. 'If there's some sort of link between Annie's disappearance and this Wayne Saxby, she could be in great danger.'

'I saw him this afternoon,' said Christine glumly.

'You didn't tell me that in your message,' snapped Carol. 'Where? When? Doing what?'

Christine sighed. She inwardly admitted she hadn't been very forthcoming in her communication with Carol, and determined to put that right. 'He was in the Hoop and Stick pub, where they wear the black and blue bobble hats, having fish and chips with Jacko and Mickey James and Tristan Thomas.'

'Oh, no,' was all Carol could manage. Then: 'This isn't looking good, is it? Then there's the missing dental technician who plays football at the same pub, too. Can this really be just a series of coincidences?'

Christine was standing in front of the mirror in her hallway as she listened to the alarm mount in Carol's voice on the telephone. She'd done a good job of making herself look attractive. She'd been excited about meeting Alexander Bright for a 'date', but now? Now she saw herself as a cheap, easy touch, who was allowing a man she didn't know at all well to talk her out of alerting the proper authorities to the possible abduction of a good friend and colleague. What was she thinking?

'I tell you what though,' said Carol finally, 'at least Saxby's a lot more dodgy than that Alexander Bright. He, at least, does a lot of good with his property holdings.'

'What have you found out about Alexander?' snapped Christine, her pulse quickening.

'He's rich, clever, rents out property to those in need, at lower than average rates, and has an excellent reputation as a landlord sought out by those who try hard, but have little. All his business dealings seem completely above board.'

Christine felt a tingle of delight.

'But,' added Carol – Christine held her breath – 'he just sort of appears, fully formed, from nowhere. I cannot find a reliable background for him. Well, I've found one for someone of the same age and name, but I'm having a hard time believing it's the same person.'

'Why's that?' asked Christine, trying not to let her voice tremble and telling herself off for being such an idiot at the same time.

'Very bleak background. Came from almost less than nothing, via the streets of Brixton, it seems. Then that one disappears and this one emerges with a bundle of money and mountain of good deeds. I'm going to do some more digging on him, but I got a bit caught up with the Saxby stuff.'

Christine didn't know what to think, but a quick glance at her watch told her that, if she didn't get a move on, any chance to grill Alexander Bright about his possibly murky youth would be lost, because she'd be late for their date and then she'd be on the defensive.

'Leave it with me, the Annie thing, please Carol? Just until the morning. Look, I must go, I've got to meet Alexander and I'm already late, so I'll hang up the landline and you can phone me on my mobile if you need me again, OK? Bye for now.' Christine spoke with a tone that signaled finality and all she heard was Carol shouting, 'Why are you meeting—' before she hung up the handset and sprinted for her car.

As she cursed the early evening traffic on Waterloo Bridge, and inched her way beyond the Thames, she answered an incoming call, dreading it would be Carol again.

'Where are you?' asked Mavis's disembodied voice abruptly as Christine connected the hands-free system.

'Hello Mavis, how are you? I'm in the car,' replied Christine, surprised to hear from her grieving friend.

'Yes, I can tell that,' snapped Mavis impatiently. 'I mean whereabouts are you and where are you going?'

'Heading to St Katherine's Dock to meet Alexander for a drink,' said Christine, not wanting to worry Mavis at such a terrible time. She wasn't lying, she told herself, she was merely being economical with the truth.

'And where's Annie? Has anyone heard from her yet?' was Mavis's next and much more challenging question.

Christine sighed as she negotiated her way around the Aldwych. 'I'm not quite sure,' was all she was prepared to say.

'Ach, you have no idea where she is, do you? You're worried to death about her but you don't want to get me into a state too. Am I right?'

'Yes,' sighed Christine, 'but we do have some leads. I'm . . . I'm sure she's safe,' she added enigmatically.

'I don't know how you can say that,' snapped

Mavis. 'And, by the way, I cannae reach Carol either, her line is constantly engaged, and I keep leaving messages, but she's no come back to me yet, so I'll tell you too. I have some very important information, so listen up.'

'I have very little else to do but listen. It'll stop me swearing at the traffic in any case,' replied Christine with great honesty.

'First of all, Althea phoned me earlier on to tell me she found a body on the Chellingworth Estate this morning. It seems that the Dyfed-Powys police have been at it all day there, and she phoned me again, just now, to say they finally had a name for the poor boy. Now hang on, I've written it down so I get it right. I spelled it out for Carol on the message I just left for her. He was Ajit—'

Christine jumped in with: 'Ajit Patwary, right?'

'How on earth do you know that?' exclaimed Mavis. 'I put down the telephone to Althea not five minutes ago. Has Carol spoken to you already?' The poor woman sounded very confused.

'No, that's not it, Mavis. I was at a pub in the East End of London today, where I saw a photograph of a young man whose name I discovered to be Ajit Patwary. He was the star of the team and, apparently, a good friend of Jacko James's son, Mickey. Carol did her thing and discovered he was a dental technician at the Mile End hospital, but I know he hasn't been at work for a couple of weeks. I already had my suspicions that he was the person Althea had seen in her dining room, but this, of course, confirms it.'

The women agreed that there was a certain, sad

satisfaction to be gained from knowing that the identity of the poor dead man, Ajit, had now been discerned, and they both felt an amount of investigative pride when they realized that Christine was able to place the dead man at the Hoop and Stick pub, and as an owner of a black and blue bobble hat.

'I'm sure Carol will have got your message by now, Mavis, and I suspect she'll get hold of the Dyfed-Powys police to pass on the information she's gathered about the connections between Ajit and the James family and therefore the Chellingworth Estate.' Christine took a moment to sigh with relief as she finally got onto Great Tower Street and realized she'd make her 'date' time after all. 'Well, that's that, then. The reason Henry called us in is all sorted, so now I can concentrate on locating Annie.'

'Aye, that you must, and I don't disagree that should be your priority. But there's still the matter of the fake false teeth that we need to consider,' said Mavis with what sounded, on the speaker-phone, to be a straight face.

'Yes, we do, but I don't see the connection at all – not between the dead body and the dentures, nor Annie and the dentures, or the dead footballer.' She honked at a cyclist.

'Aye, but there again, I think I can help you with that a wee bit. You're thinking of the dead boy as a footballer, but I'm thinking of him as a dental technician. I found out a lot about false teeth today, as it happens,' added Mavis.

Christine was very surprised, but didn't interrupt her friend's flow. Having explained all about the way the dental technician at her mother's nursing home worked, Mavis added, 'So, like I said, we have a dead *dental technician* at the Chellingworth Estate. I admit I don't know everything about it, but it seems to me that there is a chance that the fake dentures at Chellingworth Hall might have been made with a 3D printer, then painted up to look authentic. I'm sure Carol can find out all about it. I have no idea how the technicalities of this printing thing work, but she'll be all over it in a wee while, I'm sure of that. But I havenae been able to get through to her. But don't you worry about it, you try to find Annie, and I'll keep phoning and sending texts and emails to Carol until I can get ahold of her. She must be busy.'

Christine smiled. It was clear that Mavis's accent had thickened in the short time she'd been back in Scotland. She mimicked her colleague with great accuracy when she replied, 'I cannae say. The poor wee thing's been busy with so many bits and bobs all day.'

'Och, listen to yoo,' replied Mavis happily. 'Mocking your elders will always get y'intae trouble,' she said, 'no matter how good you are with your fancy accents. It's no fair to go making fun o' me like tha'.' She played along and Christine was heartened to know that her friend was not so overcome with grief that she didn't have a smile left in her.

'Seriously, Mavis, I know we're joining the dots. In fact, I think it's time I stopped being an enquiry agent and became a police informant.'

'What's up?'

'Look, Mavis, I don't want you to worry, because there's nothing you can be, or should be, doing about any of this. So, rather than tell you all about it, I think it's best if I get off the phone with you and get hold of Alexander as fast as I can. I think I need to change our meeting place to the gallery he told me about when I was lunching with him and Henry at Chellingworth Hall on Monday. It's the gallery where he met Clemmie. He mentioned that he saw portraits of artists there, created by a guy who used a 3D printer. And I'm going to propose that you do, indeed, continue with your best efforts to connect with Carol, and make sure she passes all this information directly to the detective in Dyfed-Powys who's leading the murder enquiry. I really believe that all the information we've gathered could give them some very good leads, and it's our professional responsibility to pass on that information.'

'Aye,' said Mavis, 'I'll do that. Now go on with you and find out what you can about the printing stuff and if it's all connected to our poor wee Annie.'

THIRTY-SEVEN

Having made some hurried, revised arrangements with Alexander, Christine finally arrived at the address of the art gallery in Hoxton Square he had given her on the telephone. She managed to find a place to park her vehicle, then ran to the stark building, which was hosting an evening exhibit. Alexander was at the door to greet her – *how did he always manage to get everywhere first?* – and escorted her into the large, open space which was thronged with people, all trying to out-enthuse each other about the works on display.

'The chap at the door told me who to look out for,' said Alexander loudly. The chatter from the attendees was bouncing off the high ceiling and making it difficult to hear. Christine nodded and clung to his arm as they navigated their way between knots of people congregated around great big mounds of what seemed, to Christine at least, to be grubby, misshapen, plastic rubbish.

Tapping a short, bald man, who was dressed entirely in black, on the shoulder, Alexander bent to his ear. The man nodded, then motioned that the pair should follow him. They exited the building through a glass door that led to a small balcony. Christine was relieved to get away from the noise, the bright lights and the smell. She suspected that the aroma of the pieces was supposed to be a part of their artistic integrity but, to her mind, it was just the reek of a dustbin.

'What can I do for you, Mr Bright?' asked the man politely.

'I understand it was you who created the 3D sculptures of the face of an artist who had an exhibit here last weekend, is that correct?'

The man nodded. 'Indeed it is. I am retained by the gallery to create such pieces for each artist who exhibits here, though this week's creative genius declined my offer. His loss. What of it?

Did you want to make a purchase of one of those pieces? Or maybe you'd like to commission a portrait?' His light tenor was pleasant enough, but Christine felt it held a hint of mockery.

Alexander shook his head. 'Sorry, no sale. My tastes run to more traditional works. But I think you might be able to help us out. I noticed that, while several of the masks were made of plain-colored material, one had been painted to look very lifelike. Who did that work for you? Or did you do it yourself?'

The man smiled and extended his hand. 'Luke Hall, portraitist, at your service. I find few people want what I used to offer, which was a traditional, fine arts approach to portraiture, so I branched out. Making those masks with the 3D printers requires technical skills, not artistry. It's the finishing that makes them special and I cannot resist the temptation to do my thing with at least one piece. I trust you liked it?'

Alexander nodded. 'It was excellent work. Have you ever done anything else like it? I mean, you know, make another printed piece look as though it's real?'

Christine noticed that the artist's expression became more guarded. 'I have done a few other things, yes. Why do you ask?'

Alexander sighed. 'It's a long story. Tell me, would some of those items have been a collection of dentures? Waterloo Teeth, to be exact.'

The artist beamed. 'They were disgusting – but such fun to do. I did those, oh, it must have been back in June, I think. Have you seen them on display somewhere? I hope the owner liked them.'

Christine was confused. 'You made the models months ago?' she asked urgently.

'Ah, no,' replied the artist, looking indulgent. 'I didn't *make* those models. They were brought to me as pre-printed items, already finished models, by the owner of the originals. A Mr Saxby, I believe. I don't know who had created them, but they certainly had a great deal of skill when it came to the finer finishing, and carving, of the teeth themselves. Very intricate work. All I did was the paint job. The chap had photos so I could color match.'

'June,' mused Alexander.

'Yes, I'm pretty sure it was June because we had two exhibits each installed for a fortnight here that month, so I had a bit of extra time.' Luke Hall looked both convinced and convincing.

'And nothing else?' asked Alexander.

The artist gave the matter some thought. 'As I said, I do special commissions, and I did have a young man, whose name I cannot recall – rather a rough sort, I thought – come in one day with a bit of a challenge. He had what I thought was a piece of carved ivory, but it turned out to be a 3D printed piece. It was a copy of an old letter opener, heavily worked and beautifully engraved. I'm sure the original would be wonderful. He wanted it to be painted up to look like the real thing, because the real one was beginning to crack. I said I could and I did a little something on it right there and then, so he'd get the idea. But that was it. He didn't come back, though he did telephone me again just a couple of weeks ago to find out if I had space in my schedule for a bit of work. But he hasn't booked me, or brought anything in. It can be like that, sometimes. People have what they think is a bright idea, then it goes away and nothing comes of it for me.'

'Can you explain how 3D printing works?' asked Christine.

The artist looked annoyed. 'I really should be inside, trying to sell what I do, you know, not out here nattering to you two.'

'I'd like to commission a portrait of this young lady,' said Alexander. 'The cost is immaterial, but I'd like you to explain the process, from start, to finish, if you please.'

The artist laughingly repeated his earlier actions. 'Luke Hall, portraitist, at your service,' he said with a grin. 'You're a very determined man, Mr Bright, who is about to spend a couple of thousand pounds on a unique piece of art which will capture your companion's beauty forever. Congratulations.' He bowed at the waist and winked. 'A gentleman's agreement. Now, to explain the process. Well, it's terribly simple, and that's the beauty of the 3D printing thing, really. What you need is to create a 3D image of the object you want to print using a software program that utilizes computer aided design. Now I'm not an expert in that side of things, but there are geeks-for-hire who are. Basically, what you do is take photographic scans of the object. If it were to be your face, you would be sitting, quite still, as a scanner was used to capture every detail of your face. You would need to be well lit. Sometimes the lights can become a little hot for the sitter, so I am afraid it can become a little uncomfortable, but it helps the scanner to get every detail, you see. The digital record is then fed into a printer, which quite literally moves back and forth, spraying very fine layers of your chosen material onto a surface, gradually building the 3D representation of whatever you scanned. I'm sure you noticed that a couple of the masks I had on display were of the whole head of the artist, like a traditionally carved bust, whereas some were more abstract, stretched and manipulated representations of just the face. The computer allows you to play with the digital record if you wish, then print what you want. In your case' – he regarded Christine with some care – 'I would suggest a classic pose. A three-hundred-and-sixty-degree bust, from the neck up. It should be lovely. You have excellent bones.' He beamed.

'You said that there is a choice of materials?' urged Alexander.

'Oh, indeed,' enthused the artist, 'and it's getting better all the time. The way this technology is taking off is quite something. Most of this 3D printing comes to us from industrial applications, originally. They've been using it for years to create cheap prototypes, models of components, and the like, so the material was never meant to be used for much more than display purposes. Plastic-looking stuff. But, because all you're really doing is spraying out material in a pre-determined pattern, you can now spray ceramics, or even metals. It seems as though consumer interest has been piqued, and there is now a push for people to 3D print foodstuffs, purely as a lark, of course – they print out some-thing that looks like an ice-cream cone but it's made up of a spray of mushed-up bacon, or things like that. It sounds utterly disgusting to me, but people will eat almost anything these days, it seems. The breakthrough will come when they can print with multiple materials all at once. Then they'll be able to print circuit boards. That's if they aren't doing it already. What would I know? I'm just an artist.' Again he flashed a full grin at Christine, who was finding the small, bald, bespec-tacled man to be quite alarming, if informative.

'To be clear,' said Christine, leaning in, 'all you need to do is scan an object with a special camera, then print it out with a special printer. Is that correct?'

'Essentially, yes,' replied Luke Hall. 'Though the scanning can take quite some time, the printing usually takes much longer. And the printing machines can be quite large. Yes, the scanners can be small, but the printers, well, they don't need to be large enough to accommodate the item being printed, because they can float above the material and spray downwards, so some are just a few inches cubed. But I have seen some that are much larger. I don't get very involved with the scanning, or the printing, just the management of the image before it's printed, then the finishing of the printed item.'

'And what does that involve?' asked Alexander. 'Does one simply paint the surface and that's it?'

'No,' replied Luke with great animation, his hands and eyes darting with delight, 'and that's where the work of the artist comes in. In this case, *moi*!' He bowed. Christine smiled politely. 'I told you that the teeth, the sets of dentures I received, had already been finished by a skilled person. They were already filed and rounded, or a little jagged, where they needed to be. Good work, I must say. Probably done by someone who knew teeth. Well, dentures, in any case. That's what I do with my portraits. The printers are good, but I still have the chance and the ability to refine the surface, maybe amend the features just a little. I remove imperfections, of course, and then, finally, I color. That is the art of it.'

'It all sounds fascinating, doesn't it, dear?' said Alexander, taking Christine's arm.

'Indeed it does,' replied Christine, determined to not be steered away from a conversation which, for her at least, was not yet finished. 'I wonder, Luke, do you happen to know Lady Clementine Twyst?'

The artist clapped his hands to his face. 'Clemmie? Oh, yes, everyone hereabouts knows Clemmie. Do you?'

Christine threw her most coquettish smile toward the man. 'Oh, yes, indeed I do. I just wondered if she had any connection with the man who you said owned the originals of the dentures. A Mr Saxby, was that it?' Christine hoped she'd sounded vague enough to allow the question to seem casual.

Luke Hall gave his answer some thought. 'I don't believe she does,' he replied slowly. 'Clemmie would be one to mention something like that. If you know her at all well you'll be aware of her love affair with all things alcoholic,

302

and she's got a very loose tongue when she's had one, or four, too many. The chap who brought them in wasn't at all her type. Not the same sort of crowd. Clemmie runs with the art wannabes, not the owners of collections. Though I realize that's an ironic statement given that her family owns some significant collections itself, I dare say. I know little about the Twyst family estate but, if the ones I do know are anything to go by, she grew up eating her breakfast beneath portraits I would happily sit and study for months, just because of the way the artist had painted the hair, or the folds in a velvet gown. But I mustn't grumble. I am fortunate; I have found my niche. And I am good at what I do.'

'You are indeed. So, when can you do it?' asked Alexander.

'Next week some time?' replied the artist, studying Christine's face.

'I'll take your card and Christine and I will attend the scanning phase together,' said Alexander calmly.

'You're not serious?' gasped Christine as they left the smiling artist. 'I thought you were leading him up the garden path so he'd tell us how it all works.'

'That wouldn't be being honest, would it?'

Christine scampered to keep up with Alexander as he strode through the crowds toward the exit. Spinning on his heel to look at her, taking Christine by surprise, he shouted above the melee, 'I want a portrait of you exactly as you are now. I want always to be able to see you as you were when I first met you.'

303

'Men!' said Christine, as Alexander grinned, turned and left.

Outside the gallery, on the wet-again pavement, Alexander stood stock still, looking thoughtful. 'I don't think Clemmie's responsible for this. Like the man said, she drinks and probably more than drinks. She would have mentioned the dentures. Probably boasted about how she'd wangled some sort of heist, seeing it as a game. And she and Saxby are not likely to be mixing in any sort of circles. She's interested in the strange little creatures who talk about making art, rather than doing it. We just saw them in there. They are caught up with idea of creating art. They are like people who are only interested in kneading and squeezing a tube of oil paint. Some are squeezing just a little, some a bit harder. But all they do is talk about the process, and the feelings it gives them. About what they will create, one day.'

'And most will never take the top off the tube to let it come out to create anything at all,' mused Christine.

Alexander laughed ruefully. 'Quite. If oil paint is even something any of them would ever countenance using.'

Christine hovered, picking the sides of her fingernails, then she said, 'My money's on Mickey James and his father Jacko, an electrician, being the people who disarmed whatever excuse for an alarm system they have at Chellingworth Hall, and breaking in to scan the Waterloo Teeth, months ago. Alternatively, they just walked in with the public and simply unhooked a bit of velvet rope, and got to the collection that way. They'd need to know about it, and where it was kept, of course. I'll give that some thought.' She did, with Alexander not taking his eyes off her for a moment.

He smiled warmly when Christine's face lit up and she exclaimed, 'Got it! Anyway, I believe they took the now-dead dental technician Ajit Patwary with them to do the technical bits of the scanning, knowing he could also do the finishing work on the molds when they were eventually printed. Who knows, maybe he even printed them out on his hospital equipment after hours. I believe that Mickey found out from his footballer friend about the techniques being used in dentistry and, having seen the dentures in the hall when he was a boy, which, if you recall, Henry told us was something the kids in the village had done – which would include Mickey, possibly accompanied by his father – he came up with the idea.'

Alexander added, 'Jacko's wife, Delyth, said that the Saxbys have visited Huston, Texas, in the past. That's where one of the big collectors of orthodontological rarities I know of lives. Maybe Saxby set up a purchase? He might still have the originals, or else he might have shipped them off with his wife and mother while he stays in London.'

Christine looked thoughtful and not totally satisfied. She threw up her hands as she said, 'But none of that explains why Ajit Patwary ended up dead in the Dower House two weeks ago, if they scanned, then stole and replaced, the Waterloo Teeth at the hall months ago.'

The couple stared at each other for a frustrating moment then, in chorus, said, 'The dowager's netsuke collection!'

Christine sounded excited as she said, 'Yes! She and Mavis talked about it at dinner. I bet the Jameses got greedy. They could have definitely used their electrical skills to break into the Dower House to scan the ivory collection. Jacko James was there earlier in the day for a meeting about the harvest supper with Stephanie and the cook, so he could have drugged the stew to give them a clear run at it.'

Christine paused and clapped her hands in glee, realizing as she did it that it must have made her look a bit of a twit. 'Of course. The smell! Althea told Mavis she smelled something in her dining room – a hot smell, like ironing, but not ironing. Well, when we went to Henry's dental display room and he turned on those grubby old overhead lights, I smelled the dust heating up and almost burning in the air. That might have been the smell that Althea got a whiff of: the lingering smell of dust on bright, very hot light bulbs, the sort they would have used to be able to scan the netsuke collection. If, as Luke Hall said, I will get hot under the lights they use for scanning, that might explain the smell. So, the Jameses, and Ajit, went to the Dower House, broke in, used their equipment to scan the collection – maybe Ajit was there as a sort of technical advisor – and then . . . then . . . I don't know, something must have happened and the poor boy Ajit was killed. If he had a head wound, as Althea said, then maybe Mickey, Jacko, or whomever else they had

306

working with them on that occasion, maybe even Tristan Thomas – who I bet was the dealer who was going to move the original netsuke when they had been replaced – lost their temper for some reason, so maybe he was hit, and he fell. Or maybe . . .'

'I think that's something for the police to sort out, don't you?' said Alexander, looking at his watch. 'We – or should I say the women of the WISE Enquiries Agency – have a very credible, and creditable, set of circumstantial evidence, and you've all made some excellent connections between facts, the evidence that exists and the people involved. But I think now's the time for you to get in touch with the team investigating the death of Ajit Patwary, and tell them what you know, and what you think that means. Then it's up to them. Only the police should be involved when it comes to trying to apprehend this group of people. We know they are dangerous and they are possibly more desperate than we think.'

'Mavis is already due to have got in touch with Carol to ask her to bring the police up to date with things, but, you're right, this could be the clincher.' Christine hesitated. 'Do you think they might be able to find Annie too? The more we learn, the more likely I think it is that Annie must have happened upon some information that brought her to the attention of at least one member of the gang, and they decided to take her out of the picture. We really should be telling them about her now, shouldn't we?' asked Christine.

'Get hold of them on the phone, and let's take it from there, OK?' said Alexander.

'Right,' said Christine, 'let's do it. Do you want me to phone your contact in the art squad directly? Or do you somehow magically have the direct line to the police commissioner for the Dyfed-Powys force in your phone?'

Alexander handed his phone to Christine. 'Here's my art guy's number. Start with him. I think you should do it. This is your case, after all. You tell him what we've found out and he'll tell us what to do. He's good, and he's pretty high ranking. Good man.'

THIRTY-EIGHT

A couple of hours later, Christine watched with satisfaction as the police led a whole troupe of men out of the Hoop and Stick pub to waiting cars. Wayne Saxby, Jacko James, Mickey James and Tristan Thomas all looked angry and simultaneously deflated. The other pub patrons seemed delighted to be spectators of so much action on a Tuesday night.

Members of the Metropolitan Police had been asked to apprehend the men and take them into custody, while the police working the murder and art theft in Powys made their way to London to question the suspects.

A thorough search was made of the pub premises and a brick structure at the back of the pub was found to contain evidence that someone had been held for some time within its walls. Upon

308

hearing this news, Christine ran to the police cars, which were still parked in the street, and started screaming for attention.

A senior officer tried to quiet her, but she pressed him about Annie, and he, in turn, did what he could.

Wayne Saxby wasn't saying anything until his solicitor met him at the police station. Tristan Thomas broke down in uncontrollable tears and swore that he had nothing to do with the kidnapping. Scenting a lead, the helpful policeman – who bore more than a passing resemblance to a bulldog – pressed Mickey James to the point that his father told the policemen to stop harassing his son, because he knew nothing about Annie Parker.

Christine was beside herself and rushed to the car where Jacko James was now being pulled back out onto the street. There she heard him tell the policeman, 'I thought the nosey cow had worked out what was going on, banging on about the photos of the football teams she'd seen up at Wayne's house. I drugged her – nothing dangerous, mind you, just a few of me wife's sleeping tablets – and cleared all her stuff out of my pub. Then I brought her here in the back of a lorry, with Tristan Thomas as my passenger. I knew Wayne would know what to do. All we did was lock her up. She had food. Drink. We . . . we weren't going to do nothing to her. Honest.'

'Where is she?' said the policeman, with much more force, and patience, than Christine would have possessed.

'I don't know. Honest I don't. She was there,

where we'd left her, last night, then she weren't there this morning. Someone had busted open the door and she was gone.'

Christine pressed the policemen. 'He's lying. They've got her hidden somewhere. She could be dying. You've got to make him tell you.' She was crying, her nose was running, and she was all but begging him on her knees to take some sort of action.

The policeman looked at Christine with pity and handed her a tissue. 'I can only do what I can do, miss. This isn't a film, you know. I can't beat it out of him. We do have rules about that sort of thing.' He sounded irritatingly calm.

Alexander finally reached Christine's side. 'Where did you go? I couldn't find you.' He sounded anxious.

Christine sounded as terrified and frustrated as she felt as she shouted, 'He says Annie's gone, but he's lying. I'm frightened, Alexander. Where is she?'

Alexander shook his head. 'I've just been discussing the same matter with this officer's boss, over there, and I've sort of told him what I'm about to tell you,' he said, nodding toward the pub. 'Now, don't be angry when I explain all this to you, Christine. I know where Annie was around midnight last night – in a building around the back of this pub. And I know where she's been since about one this morning, and all day – fast asleep in a bedroom of a house I'm having remodeled in Brixton. In fact, I know that's where she was until about half an hour ago. But as for where she is now? Well, not even I know that.

310

The two men I trusted to look after her, and to be there with clean clothes, a telephone, food, drink and an explanation, when she awoke from her enforced sleep, have let me down rather badly. She's gone. Run off into the night. And they have no idea exactly when within the last hour she left, or where she went.'

Christine was dumfounded. 'What do you mean she's been in a house you're remodeling? How did she get *there*? What on earth is going on?' She smacked him on the arm out of pure frustration.

'I told you not to get angry,' said Alexander, looking concerned.

Christine was aghast. 'You also told me to trust you, but look where that got me. How did Annie Parker get from the Hoop and Stick pub in Mile End, to a house in Brixton, Alexander? Tell me. Now!'

Alexander noted Christine's clenched fists, scratched his head, and looked at his shoes. 'I made some phone calls while I was driving back to London yesterday and found out all about this place, and its connections to Saxby. I came here around midnight last night, and broke into the place they were holding her, bound and gagged her, drugged her – because she was thrashing about so much she might easily have hurt herself, or me – then delivered her to the safest place I could think of. One of the many houses I own in south London that I am in the process of having remodeled. She should have come out of it around nine o'clock this evening, but she didn't. The two blokes who were there to help her when she woke up, looked in on her an hour or so ago, and she was still out cold. They looked again when I phoned them to tell them that the police had arrested the people who were likely to harm her, the people from whose clutches I had rescued her, but she'd gone. I wish I knew more. The local police have been informed.'

Christine shoved Alexander as hard as she could, then ran from him, and burst into tears again. 'What have you done?' she wailed. 'Poor Annie!'

THIRTY-NINE

When Annie Parker woke, she was conscious of a figure standing above her. She didn't open her eyes, but lay very still.

A man's voice, just beside her, said, 'Still out of it. Let's check her in another hour. The boss said she'd be up and about by now. Dunno what's going on.' *London Irish accent.*

He left the room, creaking across ancient floorboards, and shut the door. Annie remained quite still, but listened as hard as she could. She heard footsteps on a wooden staircase, then the faint sound of recorded laughter on a television. *There's at least two of them.*

Listening to herself breathe allowed Annie to be grateful she was at least alive. Her head was on a pillow, she was on a bed, and she was covered with a sleeping bag. She wasn't

312

blindfolded, bound, or gagged. *To all intents and purposes I've been having a nice kip in a comfy bed.*

Unsure about where she was, Annie allowed her head to swivel, then she hoisted herself onto her elbows and gradually straightened herself into a sitting position. Her head was still spinning and she was thirsty, but she reckoned everything was working. *Oh, Gordon Bennett, me back!*

Pushing herself to a standing position, she took a moment to allow the room to stop moving. Her initial plan was to make her way to the window, to try to see where she was. Torn curtains were allowing some light to peep into the room, and she thought she could hear the odd car in the distance. Aware that she still had no shoes to put on, Annie was careful as she walked, in case there were splinters in the floorboards. She moved slowly, having heard how creaky the floor was. It seemed to take her forever to get there, but finally she was able to pull up the bottom of a curtain and look out. *Thank heavens. Life.*

Behind the house she was in, because that was certainly where she was, was another row of houses, each with its back facing her and, beyond that, she knew in her soul, was London. She had to get out. She wondered who 'the boss' was, and reckoned she knew. Though she hated to admit it, she'd worked out that, somehow, Jacko James and her old friend Wayne Saxby were up to something, though she didn't really know what. Whatever it was, though, Saxby would be the one in charge. She'd sensed a change in Wayne when she'd been looking at the photos of the football teams in his fancy house, and was certain that Jacko had drugged her. *I'll kill him when I get hold of him. Both of them. I'll kill them both. The nerve! But why did they move me out of that other place to this one?*

Allowing herself to take stock for a moment, she noted her bare feet, realized she hadn't eaten properly for possibly days, was painfully aware she was dehydrated, but it was the hope, and belief, that she was in her beloved London, and no longer locked in a brick box, that encouraged her to make an immediate plan to escape.

Moving as slowly as she could manage it, Annie made her way to the door, and began to pull it open. It creaked fit to wake the dead. Her only hope was that the television was turned up loudly enough in the room where it was being watched to cover any noise she might make. She tiptoed across the split-level landing and dared to step onto the topmost stair. Uncarpeted, with nails protruding on each side, she was grateful for the light from a streetlamp that filtered through the half-moon of glass above the front door. *That's my goal.*

Annie tried to breathe through her nose, so she'd make less noise. If anyone came out of the room at the bottom of the stairs, she was done for. The bannister became slick beneath her palm and she cursed her hot flashes. *Surely there can't be enough moisture left in me to make sweat?*

She counted the stairs, and each time she transferred her weight from one foot to the next, on the next step down, she cheered a little inside. With only two more stairs between her and the tiled hallway, she heard the television program end.

'Fancy a brew?' London Irish again. *Please say no.*

'Nah, can't be bothered.' *Thank you.*

'I'll do it, you stay there.' *Brace yourself, girl, he's coming out.*

Silence.

'Yeah, there's enough water in the kettle, I'll flick it on, and you can do the teabags when it boils.' *YAY!*

Fearing her time might be cut short, Annie finally padded across the cool tiles to the front porch. The door to the room with the television had been ajar, but no one had seen her. *Now what?*

Deep breaths. Deep breaths.

The lock mechanism staring her in the face was of the type with which Annie was familiar; a little oval knob set within a Yale box. She touched the cold metal and turned it. It didn't make a sound. *Don't let this old door stick!*

Feeling the cool night air on her face, Annie was overwhelmed with relief, and panic, in equal measure. *What if they feel this breeze coming in the house?*

With a jolt of adrenaline rushing through her system she pulled open the door and bolted. For some reason she automatically turned right at the bottom of the short garden path, and ran along the pavement. She couldn't feel her feet at all as they hit the rough pavers. As she ran, she tried to work out where she was. Residential street. Old houses. Not bad cars. Probably not too bad an area. Then she saw it. Across her entire line of sight was a plain stone wall, about thirty feet high. At the corner of the street she stopped, looking right, then left. The wall extended for at least a hundred yards. And she knew exactly where she was – behind the back wall of Brixton Prison. *What am I doing in Brixton?*

Annie had been in almost exactly the same spot not two months earlier, when she and an old friend had gone for dinner to the restaurant run by the trustees at the prison. The Clink. It had been a brilliant evening. Weird to eat inside a prison, but special. *The walls look bigger now.*

Immediately she knew where she was, she knew she'd come the wrong way! The quickest way to civilization was to get to Kings Avenue, but that was at the other end of the road she'd just run along. Did she dare run back in front of the house she'd just escaped from? Annie's brain was on more than full power. The girls in the office said she knew London well enough to do the Knowledge, the exams that black cab drivers had to pass to get their license. Which was quite ironic, given her feelings about driving. She knew it would take her more than twice as long to either get to Kings Avenue another way, or out onto Brixton Hill, so she took a few deep breaths and went for it. *Good job for big feet and long legs now, Annie Parker.*

When she got to the main road, she stopped. She could see people in cars, buses driving the night routes. Now all she needed was a cab and she'd be fine. But a cab, here, at night? There was a standing joke in London that it was tough to get a black cab to take you south of the river as the evening wore on, because all the cab drivers lived north. Annie decided to start to walk toward the South Circular Road, because it was the biggest thoroughfare in the area. *Where's a copper when you need one? And why did they take all the phone boxes away?*

Ten foot-throbbing minutes later, Annie saw a black cab coming toward her, with his light off. She didn't care. She leapt out into the road in front of him, waving her arms like a butterfly in need of Ritalin. 'STOP!' she screamed, and he did.

Sticking his head and a fist out of his window, the cabbie shouted, 'What the 'ell are you playing at, love. Nearly ran you over, I did. You could at least wear something white so a bloke would stand a chance of knowing you was there. Git off the road.'

Annie rolled herself along the hood of the cab until she reached his window.

'Listen, doll, you gotta help me. My name's Annie Parker and I've been kidnapped.'

'Yeah, right. And I'm the Queen of bleedin' Sheba,' replied the cabbie wearily.

'I need to get to the closest police station, quick,' gasped Annie. She reached for the handle of the passenger door and prayed it wasn't locked. A millisecond later, and it would have been, but, as it was, she managed to pull open the door and she threw herself onto the floor. 'I'm going to hide down here till we get there. I don't care which one you choose, just don't stop till you

317

get there. Please hurry?' She curled herself into a ball and began to sob.

'Care in the community, my foot,' said the cabbie, who turned on his meter, did a three-point turn and swung onto the South Circular. 'Best pull yourself together, love, and get your story straight. We'll be at Brixton nick in five minutes,' he called over his shoulder.

Annie was trembling, crying and laughing. 'Oh, good,' she said. 'I hope I bump into my mate the dishy Detective Sergeant Bill Edmunds. I'm sure I'm looking me best.'

The cabbie slammed the window on his passenger. He hoped that someone at the station would fork out for the fare.

FORTY

'Is there a Chrissy here? Chrissy, anyone?' A young officer was wandering the street outside the Hoop and Stick as the last of the police cars cleared out. Christine was sitting on the curb, her head in her hands. The police had asked that she present herself at Bethnal Green police station at ten the next morning. She'd worn herself out swearing at Alexander and he'd very sensibly retreated to a nearby wall to sit and swing his legs.

'Chrissy? Christine?' called the policeman.

'I'm Christine – here.' She stood and waved.

The young officer, who was wearing just

shirtsleeves – which puzzled her – said, 'Message just come through from Brixton station. They have a friend of yours there by the name of Annie Parker.'

'Is she all right?' Christine's voice quivered with emotion.

'A bit banged about and dehydrated, so they're sending her to St Thomas's hospital for a check-up. The police doctor has given her the once over. Nothing broken. No major trauma. Apparently she'll be fine, when she's had a smoke.' He smiled. 'Seems she was quite insistent about that.'

Christine laughed and hugged the very surprised policeman. 'Thank you. I'll meet her at the hospital.'

'She's OK then?' said a voice close to Christine.

Turning to face Alexander, she hissed, 'Yes, no thanks to you. I'm off. A friend needs me. Goodbye.' She turned on her heel and made her way to her car.

Alexander watched as she stomped off. He'd give her a while to cool down, then he'd try to reach out to her again. Now was not the time. He'd have to work hard to come out of this without the coppers beginning to get interested in him. He'd always kept out of trouble; always kept well away from the law, except to have a few carefully selected senior officers as acquaintances. Now he was on their radar, and all because he'd stepped in to try to keep a friend of Christine's safe. If there was any justice, he'd skate. But he reminded himself that he, of all people, knew how very unjust the world could be.

FORTY-ONE

Carol, Annie and Christine didn't meet up as a threesome until Thursday lunchtime at the office. Annie had been kept in a hospital bed, being 'observed' by various members of staff, and fussed over by her mother, who'd arrived at her bedside with a wide selection of delicious food-stuffs, all of which, apparently, required the liberal application of hot sauce. Christine had spent the majority of the time with either the police, or Annie. Carol had been taking care of business.

When they all finally stopped hugging, Carol told Annie to settle herself on the little office sofa and said, 'I promised Mavis I'd get you to phone her as soon as you got out, Annie. So why don't we try to reach her now? Let's all get her on a video chat.' Annie and Christine agreed, and soon it was as though all four women of the WISE Enquiries Agency were, once again, in the same room as each other.

'It's been a while since we all saw each other as a foursome,' said Mavis, smiling. 'You dinnae look too bad, Annie. Good girl.'

'Gordon Bennett, you've gone all Scottish on us, Mave,' chuckled Annie. 'You'd better be careful, doll, or they won't let you back into England.'

'How are you doing, Mavis?' asked Carol quietly.

'I've had a surprisingly good time with my boys and their boys,' said Mavis quite cheerily. 'Nice to have a bit of time with the wee ones, and I've been getting out for some good long walks. I'd forgotten how lovely it was here. The air is very fresh, you know.'

'And haggis for tea every night?' quipped Annie.

'No' every night,' replied Mavis.

'Carol's got some news,' said Christine.

'Everything's all right with the baby, I hope,' said Mavis, sounding concerned.

'Oh, yes, Bump is just fine, thanks. I just wanted to let you know that the police have informed us that they picked up Olive and Merle Saxby at Heathrow Airport with a bag containing all the stolen Waterloo Teeth. They'd been in London for a few days, and were about to head off to Texas with them. The police picked them up on Wednesday. So, when you speak to your chum, Althea, you can tell her they found the dentures.'

'I still can't believe Olive was mixed up in it all,' said Annie. 'I hope they find out she had no idea what was going on.'

'You can also tell Althea that Jacko had all the scans of Althea's netsuke collection ready to print up,' said Christine. 'Just like you said, Mavis, it was the chap with the experience in dental work who was the one doing all the polishing up and so forth. They've charged Mickey James with his murder. I expect it'll all come out in the trial – exactly what happened at the Dower House to set him off.'

'According to Bill Edmunds it doesn't take

321

much to set Mickey James off on a wobbly,' said Annie.

'Oo-er, did someone get a visit from a certain detective sergeant while she was in her hospital bed?' asked Carol with a wicked glint.

'Might have done,' replied Annie with a grin. Despite her coloring, it was possible for her to blush, and she did. It made her sweat.

'I'm glad to hear it,' said Mavis. 'So, what's next?'

'The duke has paid us,' announced Carol.

'That was quick,' replied Mavis.

Turning to Christine, Carol said, 'It seems he came into a very large cash sum, because Alexander Bright bought the Winston Churchill dentures from him. He's paid us, and put the rest toward new security systems for Chellingworth Hall and the Dower House, it seems.'

'Nice woman, Althea,' said Mavis wistfully.

'You liked her, didn't you?' observed Christine.

'Aye, and I don't say that about many folk,' said Mavis thoughtfully.

'Well,' continued Christine, 'I know you'll be seeing her again on Monday, when she arrives there for your mum's funeral, so maybe you'll tell her that, to her face. You should. She'd like it. And we'll all be there too. We wouldn't miss it. We won't have you alone. We know that the rest of your family will be there, but now you'll have all of us as well. We hope that will be acceptable.'

'Aye, it will be. And we'll all need to have A Serious Chat, after the service,' said Mavis gravely.

'What about?' asked Carol apprehensively.

'Well, here's some food for thought for you girls. I've had a day or so to think about it, and I have my own opinion about the matter. But we're a democracy, so here are the facts.'

Annie sat upright on the sofa, her eyes wide. The energy in the office had changed completely.

'Come on, Mave, what?' she shouted at the laptop screen.

The three woman in London watched as their colleague in Scotland hooked her hair behind her ears and straightened her small, defiant shoulders. Mavis spoke with simplicity. 'We have an offer on the table, girls. Althea and Henry Twyst have proposed that we make use of a recently renovated barn on their estate to house our new place of business. Our office. If we did that, I would give up my little place in Finsbury Park and take up residence at the Dower House. I think Althea and I would get along together there very nicely. We enjoy each other's company. There's an apartment in the barn, big enough for one, and I thought it would suit Christine very well. I dare say you could keep on the flat in Battersea, my dear, since it's your father's property and you don't pay any rent on it. Carol? There's a three-bedroomed house overlooking the village common in Anwen-by-Wye you could have. And for you, Annie? They have a tiny, thatched cottage, just a two-up, two-down, but certainly big enough for one, three doors along from one of the village pubs. *Not* the Coach and Horses. We could all live there, use the office there, and head out on our field work from there, without any of us

having to spend any money at all on office premises, or homes. It's well-positioned for us to gain
access to most arterial routes, as we all know.
Althea and Henry are so utterly delighted with
what we have done for them, that this is their
gift to us. On top of our fee. There. That's about
it. It's a lot to take in, and I dare say you'll have
some questions, which I'll probably not be able
to answer, but, for now, I think that's all you
need to know to be able to consider it as indi-
viduals. We can make a decision as a group when
you're here on Tuesday. You can ask Althea
anything you want to know at that time. Don't
tell me what you think now. I'm off to see my
boys and I'll leave you with it. I'll tell Althea
I've passed the offer on to you all when I speak
to her later today. Right-o – off you all go now
then. I'll say goodbye.'

They saw Mavis reach forward to hit the
keyboard on her computer, and she was gone.

The room fell flat.

'Leave London?' said Annie in a horrified tone.

'A three-bedroomed house in the Welsh countryside?' muttered Carol, her eyes ablaze.

'A barn conversion as an office and an apartment?' mused Christine, smiling.

Silence.

'Mavis is right,' said Christine eventually, 'we
all need to give it some thought before we talk
about it.'

'Too right,' said Annie quickly. 'Can't see it
being your choice to move out there, Chrissy,'
she sneered. 'Wouldn't see much of your
Alexander then, would you?'

'He's not *my* Alexander. Besides, why on earth would I *want* to see him again?' snapped Christine. 'He completely undermined me, and broke my trust.'

'He visited me in hospital and explained everything,' said Annie quietly. 'Told me all about how he needed to get me away from the lot at the Hoop and Stick, and keep me somewhere safe. He was right to knock me out, you know. I'd have tried to escape otherwise, and the other lot might have found me. Then who knows what might have happened to me. *I* forgave him,' said Annie thoughtfully. 'Maybe you could do the same? I mean, he's ever so good looking and not like the usual plonkers you go about with.' Christine glared at Annie. 'Sorry, doll, but they are. And he's got stacks of dosh, which never hurts. And, of course, he always seems to know someone, who knows someone you need.'

Christine fumed silently for a moment, then leapt out of her chair. 'I'll forgive him when hell freezes over,' she said angrily.

'Well, I tell you what, while me and Car go out for a special coffee, and talk about this idea of moving to the wilds of Welsh Wales, which I can already see she fancies the idea of, you can sit here and get a bit chilly, 'cos he's right by the door with the biggest bunch of yellow roses I've ever seen. Ta ta, Chrissy. See you later.' And, with that, Annie and Carol dashed past Alexander, pulling on their coats and rolling their eyes at each other like schoolgirls.

'Yellow. For friendship,' said Alexander timidly

holding out the flowers. Christine folded her arms and plopped herself back down into her seat.

As he approached, he laid the roses gently on her desk. 'Christine, I respect you too much to beat about the bush, so I'll come straight out with it. I know I have some questions to answer about this whole business, but, even before I get to those, there's some stuff about my past that I must tell you. I'll make it as brief as I can, and I realize that what I say might turn you against me forever. I have worked hard to redeem the actions of my past, but I fear it might not be enough. Indeed, whatever I do for the rest of my life, it might never be enough. But, if you will listen, I will tell you. Then you can decide if you would like to consider being my friend. And I emphasize the word *friend*.'

'I'll listen,' said Christine abruptly, not looking up into his eyes, 'but don't bother trying some old sob story on me. It won't wash. Just because my father has a title doesn't mean I'm an idiot.'

'You're the most sharp-minded woman I think I've ever met, and I'm not hoping for tears, but understanding,' replied Alexander.

'Go on then,' said Christine.

Alexander perched on the edge of the sofa. 'I need to tell you about someone called Issy,' he began. 'He was a boy who did some very bad things. He was a boy I used to be . . .'